THE ??? OF CASSIE CLEARWATER

JILL CLOUGH

SWALLOW BOOKS
OF THE ENGLISH LAKES

This edition published in 2024

Copyright © Jill Clough jillclough.live

Jill Clough asserts the moral right to be identified as the author of this work.

Text design: Paul Baillie-Lane and Debbie Aitchison

This book was authored by Jill Clough and not generated by any machine or artificial intelligence. This statement acts as a legally binding guarantee of authenticity and can be used to establish the true creator of this work should any doubt arise.

All rights reserved. No part of this publication may be reproduced, stored in a retrieval system, transmitted in any form or by any means, electronic, mechanical, photocopying, recording or otherwise, without the prior written permission of the author.

This is a work of fiction. Names, characters, businesses, places, events and incidents are either the products of the author's imagination or used in a fictitious manner. Any resemblance to actual persons, living or dead, or actual events is purely coincidental.

This book is sold subject to the condition that it shall not, by way of trade or otherwise, be lent, re-sold, hired out, or otherwise circulated without the author's prior consent in any form of binding or cover other than that in which it is published and without a similar condition including this condition being imposed upon the subsequent purchaser.

ISBN 978-0-9575740-6-9

Printed and bound in Great Britain by Clays Ltd, Elcograf S.p.A.

Dedication

To all good listeners, especially Samaritans, who give up their midnight hours, passing no judgement, and to Professor Linda Anderson, for her encouragement, feedback, and insight into the power of storytelling

Also by Jill Clough

Morph
Lakeland Book of the Year Award for Fiction 2019
Anna and the Snake Queen: *2020*
If Dreams Should Die: *2022*
Longlisted for Lakeland Book of the Year Award 2023

www.jillclough.live

SWALLOW BOOKS

OF THE ENGLISH LAKES

Author's Note

In my former life as a headteacher in secondary schools, I sometimes felt as if I were 'not waving but drowning' when I tried to get support for vulnerable students. Good intentions abound but resources seem to be scarce.

How do these students cope with the slow obliteration of identity that comes from so often being overlooked?

I'm not the protagonist in this novel but I've met her, or others like her, over the years and realised the story we tell ourselves about ourselves is our own - a resource we can develop even if no one is looking.

I've loved reading fiction for as long as I can remember, and the battered volume of Joseph Jacobs' English Fairy Tales is with me still. His stories and their illustrations haunt me, infiltrate my own writing. I've given them to Cassie

Prologue

> **We're waiting for your call.**
> Whatever you're going through, a Samaritan will face it with you.
> We're here 24 hours a day, 365 days a year. Call 116 123

Tuesday 14:14

C109: *Samaritans, hello.*
Caller: I rang and rang – why didn't you answer –
You're not one of those computer things?
It's all a mistake, I should never –
C109: *You sound very upset. Do you feel able to tell me why you have rung tonight?*
Take your time. I won't go away.
Caller: Nothing is ever going to work, nothing is ever going to be right.
C109: *I can hear that you're very distressed. Take a deep breath.*
Caller: Nobody listens to me. Why won't they listen? I've said – I've said – my baby –
why do they take my babies? I can't bear it.
C109: *What you say sounds very serious. You said, my baby, and then you said, my babies. Could you tell me a bit more?*
Caller: They took all my babies and they let me keep her and then they took her too and I can't bear it any more.
C109: *They took my babies. Can you tell me who took them?*

Caller: If I don't get her back I'm going to kill myself. I've still got my knife.
C109: *Your knife?*
Caller: I just want Cassie back, she's my baby. I could be a brilliant mum. Why won't they give me another chance with her? Why won't anyone listen?
C109: *I'm here, I'm listening. Take your time.*

Caller rings off.

Cassie

One: Tuesday 11:22

'Mr Etherington, I think you have Cassie Fenton in this class. Ah, yes. Cassie, would you mind coming with me, please?' The woman at the classroom door wore smarter clothes than the English teacher – blue and white checked trousers, a tight-fitting navy-blue waistcoat, and a white blouse with frills at the neck.

Cassie's scalp crawled. The boy next to her stuck his finger up his nose, pulled it out and waggled it at her. She ought to be used to bullying by now.

'Told you.' The whisper came from the desk behind. 'You're fucked.' Cassie's whole body clenched with the desire to swing round on her chair and give Taylor Lawson a slap on her fat nose.

Mr Etherington said, 'We've reached an interesting moment in the lesson, Dr Hume.'

'I'm sorry about that but I really need to see Cassie today. Can you get past, Cassie? It's a bit tight in here.'

Cassie's heart sank. This was the one lesson in the day that made her want to come to school. She looked at the paper on her desk with the opening words of her story.

> Once upon a time there was a small girl whose parents began to quarrel. She could not cry where they might see her. She could not cry if they could hear her.

Mr Etherington was the first teacher to say she was

good at writing.

'Take your stuff, Cassie,' said Mr Etherington, gesturing, sighing. As she squeezed past, the boy tried to wipe his nail on her hand but she shoved her backpack in front of her, skirted around the desks towards the door. Did she still smell like a victim? She had hoped this school would be different. The new foster-carers were different. What had she done? Dr Hume wasn't frowning but her eyes flickered round the classroom. She must have noticed something

for she tilted her head at Mr Etherington.

He lifted his eyebrows and turned. 'Chewing again, Taylor? Don't waste my time. You know our rules.' He stalked between the desks, reached Taylor and held out his hand. Taylor scowled through her mascara. Mr Etherington smiled. 'You want a round with Dr Hume too? Only one year before your exams. After you've given up your gum you can give me the plan of the story you're writing.'

Taylor spat gum into her hand before dropping it into Mr Etherington's. Everyone said, 'Yuck,' or 'Gross,' and she went red. Cassie expected her to give Mr Etherington the finger while he threw the gum into the bin but he had the teacher-knack of seeing behind him. He poured disinfectant gel into his palms and rubbed them, rolling his eyes. Someone laughed. Almost everyone liked him. It was stupid of Taylor.

What had Cassie done?

In the corridor outside, Dr Hume said, 'I'm sorry to pull you out. We'll talk when we get to my room.'

Cassie straightened her shoulders and tried to walk as if she hadn't done anything wrong. She could not think of anything she had done wrong.

The brown carpet in the corridor smelt new. Artwork from the exam years hung in pale wooden frames on the walls. There were no empty crisp packets, no bubble gum wrappers, no dropped bottle caps. Other schools had smeary marks on the doors and fringes of dust bunched in corners but not here. The walls were still pale blue. Everything in this school smelt clean. Some kids were vile, same as in other schools, but not so many. Maybe it was the way the teachers did things.

Why had Dr Hume dragged her out of class? Cassie hadn't taken a library book without signing for it, she hadn't refused to pick up somebody else's litter.

She had not poured water into Taylor Lawson's black leather bag, yet. If only …

She chewed her cheek. If the headteacher suspended her they'd have to put her in a room on her own till someone came to get her but they wouldn't leave her all day. Probably not.

Her heart kept mucking about. The strap of the backpack slithered in her fingers.

Dr Hume stopped in front of a door painted white and Cassie read the notice.

Dr Hume
Assistant Head Pastoral

Unlocking the door, she stood back, waving at Cassie to go inside. 'Do sit down. I'm sorry I had to get you out of class like that.

But I need to see you today. I'm away on a course for two days and this is important.'

The old chair had a high back, and broad arms. Cassie dug her nails into the wood, wishing her heartbeats would not echo in her ears. The seat was hard. The table was old, dark brown wood. New school, old furniture.

'Your foster-mother came to talk to me yesterday. She's worried about you.'

Cassie's lungs stopped working. Lucy talked about her behind her back?

'I can see this makes you uncomfortable. Normally with a girl your age you'd have been in the meeting, too, but I see why Mrs Robinson came on her own. You haven't been with her long.'

Dr Hume turned over sheets of printed white paper in the folder on the long table she used instead of a desk. She didn't sit behind it, with Cassie opposite, but at an angle, almost next to her. The checked material of her trousers was tight over her knees. Cassie glimpsed a heading, CASSIE FENTON. Dr Hume caught her eye and closed the folder. It was blue, cardboard.

Cassie's throat contracted and her hands stiffened into a tight knot under the table. There was broken skin over two knuckles. Yesterday she had punched the outside wall of the sports hall. She concentrated on freezing the muscles in her face.

'These reports are computerised, but I prefer giving real paper to people. You can write on it if you want, or take them home to read. You can take these, if you like. Don't look so scared, Cassie. There's nothing bad here — not about you, anyway. Social services are over-stretched. I don't have to tell you about that. You've had a rough time.'

You've had a rough time. You've had a rough time. Her fingers twitched to the rhythm of the words. She clenched them.

'Mrs Robinson says you've been bullied in previous schools and now here too. She thinks it's because you've been in a lot of foster-homes.'

There were pots of lavender on the end of Dr Hume's desk. There was lavender in the Robinsons' garden, pink, Lucy's favourite. This lavender was purple, and its sweet scent filled the air. Cassie stared at the nearest pot of lavender, trying not to blink. Her eyes prickled.

'Is she right?'

Cassie's neck was stiff.

'If ever you are bullied again, not just I, but all our staff will support you. Only you may have to tell us yourself. We know that, well, bullying is usually hidden.'

'People don't believe me.'

'I'm sorry – could you speak up, Cassie? I didn't catch that.' 'Never mind.'

'Did you say nobody believes you? Is that it? We take a very tough line on bullying. Girls are very clever at bullying where they can't be seen.'

Cassie's knees twitched. She wanted to duck under the table. 'Is there anything you'd like to tell me?'

Her eyes filmed over but she would not blink.

'You can knock on my door any time, you know. You can tell a teacher. We all understand your background.'

Cassie clenched her jaw, trying to stiffen so Dr Hume wouldn't notice. Why couldn't she be like other kids moving between schools? People were always waiting for her to mess up.

'Mr Etherington says you have quite a turn of phrase.'

She'd been talking to Cassie's teachers too. Cassie blinked, rubbed a hand over her face. It came away damp.

'He does?'

'He says you're a great reader. I wish I had more time for teaching. English is my subject. I love stories.' Dr Hume gestured at the huge bookcase behind her. 'Seen anything you recognise?' Cassie took a breath. 'Maybe – *The Old Man and the Sea?*' Cassie had seen it on Lucy's bookshelves. Lucy and Paul were the only foster-carers –

apart from the family she stayed with when she was small – who loved books and reading and gave her books of her own.

She could feel Dr Hume's gaze. Her face burned.

'You can borrow it if you want. If you're not sure. It's an amazing story about determination.'

Cassie nodded. What else was she supposed to do? Most teachers, in her experience, were too busy to notice her.

Dr Hume was still talking. 'You've been in so many foster-placements, you must have a lot of memories and feelings about them.'

Cassie's whole body went cold. 'I wondered, how would you feel about describing some of those foster-placements? Sometimes, finding the words helps us come to terms with what's happened. I know there are times I have to write things down, to know what I feel.'

Cassie's head jerked up and her eyes opened wide.

'I don't mean to make things more difficult. I mean, a private account, not something other people would read. Would that be a problem for you?'

'No.' Her heart jumped but it wasn't a bad feeling.

'You do like writing? Mr Etherington has got that right?' 'Suppose.'

Cassie looked up to find Dr Hume was smiling. Dr Hume didn't raise her eyebrows like people did when they wanted to show they thought Cassie was lying, or stupid.

And then she remembered. Lucy talked about her behind her back.

Lucy wanted the school to do something about bullying and Cassie ought to be grateful but didn't Lucy understand Taylor Lawson would never give up? She was born a bully. It was as much in her genes as having red hair or freckles, though Taylor had black hair and dead white skin.

Lucy had rung up the school and someone in reception

had put her on to Dr Hume because it was Dr Hume's job, and Dr Hume had dragged Cassie out of class so everyone could see something was wrong.

Only ... Dr Hume was ... ok. She understood how writing things down somehow changed the shape of them.

When Cassie wrote her stories instead of telling them in her head, the stories changed. She could start her story again at a different place, maybe.

'Cassie? Are you all right?'

Wriggling, Cassie said, 'I think Lucy has that book.'

Dr Hume pushed back her chair, stood up in a single move, and pulled the book into her hand. 'Take it home. It's very short.' Cassie realised the interview was over. She hovered in the corridor, eyes scanning the noticeboards, not focusing, automatically tucking *The Old Man and the Sea* into her bag. Why did Dr Hume call Lucy a foster-mother, not a foster-carer? Even these few weeks with Lucy and Paul, watching them with their twins, made her think differently about mothers. She would love to live with people who wanted to be stand-in-parents. Then maybe she wouldn't feel like a lodger who got in the way, or worse.

She chewed a nail. All the same, Lucy didn't have the right to talk to Dr Hume behind her back. Lucy was so going to be told.

Two: Tuesday 15:45

All the way home in the car, Cassie would not answer Lucy's questions. She sat hunched over her backpack, hugging it to herself, ignoring the quarrel on the back seat.

In any case, Lucy was hassled. 'Girls, be quiet. I must concentrate on driving. This road is getting so stuffed. It's going to be so much worse in half-term.'

Cassie ground her teeth. *Girls.* Why did their little girls have boys' names? What sort of parents made life difficult for their kids when they didn't need to?

They were approaching the village. Two campervans and a red car pulling a long caravan were having a face-off with one of the coaches trying to park beside Dalegarth Station. Another coach – huge and white, with red flashes along its sides – blocked the road. People dragged suitcases out of the storage space in the side of the coach, propped them in the middle of the road, argued with the coach driver, got out sunscreen and phones. Cassie tightened her grip on the backpack. If only she could throw open the door and run off – the argument on the back seat made her want to scream.

'I want a tent, can we have a tent in our garden?'

Lucy had to slow down, brake. The engine idled. 'Daddy's got to finish putting up the climbing frame.'

Someone in a blue peaked cap came out of the station and waved arms till the suitcases were heaved away. Cassie gritted her teeth.

When the car reached the cottage, she flung open the car door and hurled herself out, heading for the porch. Everything was locked. Paul wasn't home. She stamped into the garden and dropped on the grass under the half-built climbing frame. Grass smelt clean. A blade of grass slipped squeakily between her fingers. Grass was the smell of green.

I'm going live in a tent. In the summer. When it's cold I'll break into garden sheds and sleep in them. I'll use outside taps for fresh water and have a quick wash but not too much. Nobody will be able to find me and talk behind my back.

Her cheeks were wet.

The little girls rolled across the grass. Freddy was kicking. 'I hate you, I hate you.'

'You can't share my pens.'

'You can't play with my train set, I'm never never letting you play with my ambulance.'

'Girls, please.' Lucy balanced beakers, and a jug of what was probably her home-made lemonade, on a tray. Cassie's chest ached. Lucy's fingers were white from gripping the tray. She did not want to lose her temper. Cassie longed so badly to shout, her throat ached. *You interfered at school and now they'll think I complained.* She wiped her nose on the hem of her navy-blue skirt. In the last school, for summer, they could wear knee-length shorts, boys and girls, any colour they liked as long as it was plain. What school was it where she stayed long enough for summer uniform? Lucy had the summer uniform before Cassie arrived, the right size. Usually, she had to turn up in something the foster-carers guessed would pass.

How did Lucy know Cassie's size?

She likes you. Shit. Why did she talk to school behind my back?

Lucy said, 'Cassie, will you come into the kitchen?

Please?'

Cassie stood up and sniffed. She knew this script off by heart.

Maybe foster-carers were given it when they got their contract.

"Come here. We need to talk. You've been causing trouble again."

"Don't give me that look. There are other children in this house. We have rules."

"Get in here, Cassie Fenton. If you don't come when I tell you, there'll be trouble."

"I've tried being understanding, I've tried leaving you alone, but this can't go on."

"I'm fed up with your sulks."

"You ought to be grateful having a roof over your head."

"It's all very well saying you won't see your mother but what about us?"

Cassie folded her arms. The muscles were tight, a barrier keeping all the turmoil inside. 'Thought you wanted me to play with the twins.'

'Only if you want to.' Lucy set a glass down beside Cassie's legs and walked away. Her shoulders drooped and she swung the tray from two fingers.

The twins' hands were fierce, grabbing Cassie's wrists to pull her across the grass towards their game. 'Do your cross look, Cassie, you got a really good cross look.'

From the corner of her eye, Cassie saw Lucy's face at the kitchen window. She had promised herself she would do Lucy a favour and cut their nails, so they couldn't scratch one another so easily. They fought all the time, like kittens.

Lucy talked behind her back.

The twins could draw blood on one another whenever they felt like it.

Eventually she had to go indoors. She needed the toilet,

needed to change into shorts or something – not uniform anything that did not make her think of school. She had to go through the kitchen.

Lucy said, 'You can have supper with Paul and me, if you like. Now, tell me off.'

Cassie drew a deep breath. 'You went into school and you talked about me and I wasn't in the meeting and you didn't tell me, you didn't ask if it was okay.' Her heart galloped and now her bladder was full and she'd let Lucy know she was pissed off.

'I'm sorry. Obviously, I've upset you.' Lucy's hair hung loosely about her face, half-hiding the reddening of her cheeks.

'So why did you do it?' Cassie crossed her legs. 'Try and see it from our point of view – '

'Oh well, that's okay, I've got to understand you now.' The pee would just have to run down into her socks.

Lucy sat down at the table, and clasped her hands, staring at them. 'It's a two-way thing, you living with us. I'm used to going into school about the twins. I should have realised you ought to know. But it wouldn't have stopped me from going in, even if you didn't like it.' She looked up. Her eyes were darker than usual, the pupils larger. 'It isn't just that we're supposed to ensure you're safe, Cassie, it's that I am so angry, so angry about what you've had to put up with. If I could get my hands on those girls I'd wring their necks.'

Cassie seized the back of a chair, rocking it from side to side. She wished she could hiss like an angry cat. 'The teacher pulled me out in front of everybody. Other kids will go on and on. Whatever hap- pens they'll turn it into a fight.' Her heart still beat like a hammer against her ribs. Any moment now it would burst out, like a bloody fist and punch the world in the face. 'They'll say I'm a suck-arse, or some bitch'll say I hit her and I'll be in isolation for five days and do you know what that's like? They shut you in a tiny room like a box with nothing in it and nobody talks to you, nobody comes in. In one school I wasn't supposed even to turn my head. Not that anybody came to see if I was turning my head round.'

'Owls can rotate their heads round 360 degrees, I read somewhere.'

'What?' Cassie let go of the chair. It fell sideways. 'Owls?'

Lucy's eyes gleamed. She folded her arms, looking remarkably like Freddy when she wanted to make Tommy jump. 'It's called an isolation room?' She leaned forward, placing her elbows on the table. 'Sounds grim – cruel, uncivilised. Do they really isolate teenagers like that? Not in this school, surely.'

'Don't know.' Cassie fumbled for the chair, standing it up again, not catching Lucy's eye. She did not want Lucy to be kind when she needed to be furious.

'What did Dr Hume say? Did she say anything helpful at all?' Cassie chewed the end of her thumb. 'Suppose.'

'Why don't you get out of uniform and help me put the kids to bed? Paul will be home soon.'

'Did he know you were going behind my back?'

Lucy sighed. 'He said you'd be cross. Actually, he said you'd be spitting mad.'

'Did he?' She wanted to smile.

'He said we must consult you about practically everything, but does that mean even, "Do you want help crossing the road?"'

The idea of Paul and Lucy having an argument about her made Cassie feel odd. She could not find the right word for the feeling. 'I don't want to be asked all the time.'

'I don't want it to get so I don't know what to say to you, or I have to think twice.'

Cassie stared at her hands.

'Do you mind helping with the twins?' 'You're asking again.'

Lucy stood up, rounded the table, and stroked the back of Cassie's hand. Cassie snatched her hand back. Lucy bit her lip. 'Cassie, I truly could do with your help.'

'Don't see why.' Cassie had no intention of crying.

'Paul's got to start work on an assignment for his course. He's going to be busy. It's all a bit different from what he usually does. He'll have to concentrate. You're good with the twins. You know you are.' Lucy's eyes were almost pleading.

'Suppose.'

'They're getting fond of you. Do you need a pee?'

Cassie ran upstairs to her room, blew her nose, rubbed her face against a coat on the back of the door, took a deep breath and went into the bathroom. Then she walked slowly downstairs into the gar- den, to play the game. Tommy said she had to be Queen and they were princesses, hiding from the wicked witch who plotted to carry them off into the forest and leave them to die. Freddy said she had a better game. Goblins were hiding behind the bushes to kidnap them and a starship was landing and they would fly to the moon.

Cassie's role was to wave her stick and look important.

After supper, she drifted into the twins' room, drawn by the noise. They were quarrelling again and Lucy was sitting by the window with her head in her hands.

'My teacher said I could be in the relay team.' 'Did not, he said you day-dream.'

'I can be in the team if I conc'n – what's the word, Mummy?' 'Concentrate, probably. You do tend to day-dream, Tommy.' 'Told ya, you can't be in the team.'

'I can, I can.'

'We had horrible sausages.' 'My new reader is boring.'

'What's it about, your new reader?' Lucy tugged at her thick red hair.

'It's boring, it's baby, I can do bigger books.'

There was a shriek and Tommy had fallen off her chair. 'She pinched me, she pinched me, you said she mustn't pinch.'

'Did not, I did not, she took my book, I want it back.' 'Baby book, it's a book for babies.'

Freddy was trying to hide a small, brightly-coloured book by sitting on it. Cassie narrowed her eyes, jabbed a finger, and did her best scowl. Freddy poked out her tongue. Cassie poked out her tongue too. Freddy giggled, Tommy made a dive and snatched back her book, hugging it to herself.

'Wish you'd come to us sooner,' said Lucy, dragging her hands through her hair. 'You have the magic touch, Cassie.' Cassie's chest heaved. Lucy had deep blue eyes, very bright, and she kept taking Cassie by surprise, saying nice things. 'Tommy, did you tell Mr Spring you could read more interesting books?'

'He won't listen to me, he says I got to finish this one.' 'What is it?'

'I don't know. We don't have bears here. It's silly.' '*We're Going on a Bear Hunt*? But that's a lovely book.' Tommy scowled at Cassie. 'I want *Fluff the Farting Fish*.'

'It's the same writer, Tommy,' said Lucy. 'They're both great stories.'

Tommy carried on complaining. Cassie's eyelids drooped as images flickered through her mind. *Taylor Lawson, Taylor Lawson. You're fucked, Cassie Fenton. We all know about you. My aunt knows all about you. Mrs Robinson says you are being bullied. Fluff the Farting Fish?*

She drew her hands across her face, heaved a deep

breath, started.

'Once upon a time …' They did not want her to stop.

Stella

Three: Wednesday 10:36

Josie: Ah, good morning, Miss Fenton. Please sit down. Do you feel a bit calmer now?

Stella: Nothing wrong with me.

Josie: You created a bit of a rumpus in Reception.

Stella: Nobody listens. You social workers are supposed to listen.

Josie: I gather there were people with appointments ahead of you.

Stella: Yeah but mine's urgent.

Josie: Perhaps you could explain? You made a complaint that your baby has been taken away, but I checked our records and we have nothing on file recently about a baby being removed – that's if you gave your name correctly – it was a bit difficult with so much noise. I could hear you shouting from this office.

Stella: Fucking fuss.

Josie: You are Stella Fenton and you are thirty-five years old. Is that right?

Stella: You got it on your computer.

Josie: Well then. This baby – has your partner taken him? Her? How old is the child?

Stella: Why won't you fucking well listen? I'm going off my head –.

Josie: Please sit down –.

Stella: Can't sleep on the beach, I can't and the parks, they keep moving you on.

Josie: Sit down, please – sit down. I'm concerned about this child. Have you been to the police?

Stella: It was you lot took her and nobody tells me where she is and I want to see her, it's not fair, it's my right, she's mine.

Josie: Is your baby in foster-care, is that what you mean?

Stella: Why can't I see her?

Josie: I'll need to inquire. My colleague sent you to see me because he judged you were very distressed. To be honest – looking at you, I wonder when you last had a decent meal or a good night's sleep.

Stella: You saying I'm a mess? I know I smell bad, you'd smell if you hadn't anywhere to stay, nowhere to wash.

Josie: You're homeless? I can refer you to another agency to help with that.

Stella: I want my baby back. You're all the same, shoving me off.

Josie: I'm making allowances for you and you should understand that. When did you last have a proper meal, Miss Fenton? Not that it's an excuse for your aggressive attitude.

Stella: I told you – you think you're so superior? You got no idea –.

Josie: I suggest you stop being sorry for yourself and listen. You've obviously been in touch with social workers before.

Stella: Are you going to help?

Josie: Has a social worker been assigned to you?

Stella: They're useless.

Josie: I'll try not to be useless. Don't roll your eyes. I'll see if I can find you a temporary place in a hostel, a couple of nights.

Stella: Hostels don't let babies in. Have you got to answer that phone? They'll shove me out. I got my pills. I got to have my Cassie back.

Josie: Good morning ... do you mind if I call you back? Thank you. What pills?

Stella: My head isn't right.

Josie: You are taking prescribed medication? You've seen a doctor recently?

Stella: I don't remember. Maryport. No, Carlisle.

Josie: How long ago was this? What's the medication?

Stella: Stuff. I dunno.

Josie: You've been drinking.

Stella: You try sleeping on the beach without something to help, something to help you sleep, so I have a drink. Nobody can't smell it. They told me, get one of those hand-rubs with all the alcohol in and you wipe it around your mouth.

Josie: Someone told you hand-rubs would conceal the smell on your breath? You can't drink if I get you a room in a hostel. You do understand that?

Oh dear. I've a box of tissues somewhere.

There's a shower in the hostel. You obviously need some sleep. How are you for cash?

Stella: What about my baby?

Josie: Like I said, I'll need to do some ringing round, get hold of your records.

Stella: I got no money left.

Josie: Go back to Reception and wait. I'll ask for a cup of coffee for you, some biscuits. I'm sure we've plenty.

I'll organise an emergency pay-out and see you

	when I've dealt with my appointments. Please don't make a fuss in Reception. Other people are as upset as you are. Be more considerate.
Stella:	You never had people look down on you all the time. People treat me like muck.
Josie:	Well, let's see if we can help to change that. I'll see you in an hour or so.
Stella:	You're getting rid of me.
Josie:	I'm sorry, I don't mean to end this interview so soon, but you came in here shouting and you've been telling me I'm out to get you. I want to help. There's so many people to see today. Sorry, you'll have to go but I will catch up with you as soon as I can. Take a handful of tissues. Oh, good gracious. Sit down. I'll meet my next client in another room.

Four: Wednesday 23:19

> **We're waiting for your call.**
> Whatever you're going through, a Samaritan will face it with you.
> We're here 24 hours a day, 365 days a year. Call 116 123

F123: *Samaritans, how can I help you?*
Caller: You lot got a script or something telling you what to say?
F123: *You've rung Samaritans before?*
Caller: I bet you all sit in in your office having a laugh. I hate this hostel. Silly bitch next door crying all the time.
F123: *Everything you say is confidential –.*
Caller: My heart is breaking. It's real, having heartbreak. A woman in the hostel said. It's not right, people breaking my heart. Cassie's mine. I'm not making it up. They say I'm making it up and they're wrong. They took all the others but they said I could keep her and then they took her and it breaks my heart.
F123: *The others?*
Caller: I told you, they took them. You're not listening.
F123: *You're telling me several very distressing things.*
Who are the others?
Caller: They say I tell lies and I don't, my dad wouldn't let me tell lies, he had his ways –.
F123: *Is there something you want to say about your dad?*
Caller: You got a dirty mind, you just do this for the

filth, I know your type.
Gone all silent on me now, have you?

F123: *You began to say something about your father –.*

Caller: I got nothing to say about that pervert.

F123: *Let's focus on what's important. You say your baby has been taken away.*

Caller: There was a notice in the office, it said, Call free day or night.

F123: *What you say about your missing baby sounds urgent. Have you reported this to the police?*

Caller: They won't believe me.

F123:: *I'd like to establish what's happened, how you feel about it, whether there's any way in which I can help.*

Caller: You could make them give her back.

F123:: *I'm afraid that's not in our power as Samaritans, but we can signpost you to another agency for help.*

Caller: Get fobbed off again? I'm gonna into that stupid office and kill that woman thinks she knows better than me.

F123: *Is there nobody in the office you can talk to about your baby?*

Caller: I want something done, I've got a knife. I never let anyone find it.

F123: *You have a knife?*

Caller: Said so, didn't I? What's the big deal? Lots of people carry a tool.

F123: *Do you believe carrying a knife will help you to get your child home?*

Caller: You're having a laugh. All I got is this room, and it's tiny and the window rattles and you can hear the bitches either side farting. I lost everything.

F123: *What you describe sounds difficult. How does carrying the knife make you feel?*
Caller: I'm fucking furious.
F123: *Do you feel furious all the time?*
Caller: They don't know anything about me. They got lists of things they got to do, they just go through their lists, they call us clients, I'm not a client.
F123:: *The office you talk about, is that the one with a notice about Samaritans?*
Caller: They think shiny desks and glass doors make them look important. They make us wait outside. The chairs wobble and there's this plastic box of kiddy toys. They're all broken and we sit there in a row till it's our number. I hate them. It's all fake.
F123: *Maybe you hate the situation you're in?*
Caller: They make me into nobody. I'm Stella Fenton. I'm a proper person. I'm not a number on somebody's fucking list. I'm not somebody's caseload.

Caller rings off.

Cassie
Five: Thursday: 17:56

It was teatime, with scones, and last year's home-made strawberry jam. Cassie had never eaten home-made jam. The glass jar was sticky with twins' fingerprints and the yellowy scone crumbled when she spread it with butter. Nobody grumbled about mess on the floor.

Paul said he would grab the fine weather to carry on building the twins' climbing frame. 'The forecast's for rain tomorrow. It's the mountains that bring the rain. We live in one of the wettest places. Oh well. I wouldn't live anywhere else.'

Lucy told Freddy to get a dustpan and brush for the crumbs.

Cassie went upstairs to the room they said was hers and stood near the window. She still felt like someone who'd woken up from a dream and found herself in the wrong house – except her small blue wheelie suitcase stood in the corner by the chest of drawers, and the books Lucy lent her were arranged along the top. She ran her fingers across the spines. *To Kill a Mockingbird*, *The Catcher in the Rye*, *The Great Gatsby*, *Red Dust Road*, *Clay*. Lucy said she might like these novels but Cassie was nervous of opening them in case she got dirty fingermarks on the pages. Her own red book was under the bed. She hadn't decided whether to put it with the new ones. It might look stupid, fairy tales next to proper stories.

Paul wanted to store the suitcase in the loft but Cassie wasn't sure.

She moved to the window and opened it. Down below, on the lawn, Paul stood with his hands on his hips, prodding a complicated-looking mound of metal bars and netting with his toe. The sweet smell of lavender drifted up.

Funny, how the smell of lavender made a kind of link between Dr Hume's room at school and this cottage. She took another deep breath, letting the scent fill her nostrils. Maybe Lucy would let her have a pot of lavender. There was space on top of the drawers. It was a nice chest, painted white. The drawers didn't stick. The walls were white, too. Lucy said white paint brought light into the cottage. Cassie never had her own suitcase before. Samuel brought it when he collected her from the emergency carers. He said Eskdale was a wonderful valley, he wished he could live with the smell of the mountains. It made him feel alive. It was a peculiar thing to say. Did he mean being a social worker made him feel dead? Cassie was never going into social work.

'Hang on, Luce – ouch – damn and blast it, nipped my finger.

Okay, that's done it.'

'I can't hold this netting up much longer. Don't be a baby.'

Cassie found herself smiling, and she leaned out, to see them better. It was such a relief, not having to stay with perfect grown-ups. Did everyone swear if they nipped a finger? *Don't be a baby.* She couldn't work out how old most grown-ups were. Paul's face had a kind of lived-in look. Samuel's skin was smooth.

Samuel was new at social work and Cassie felt very old at it, but he'd been right about Paul and Lucy. Being taken to another placement usually made her feel sick. There had been so many. This time, something about how new he was had made her almost hold her breath. On the drive into

Eskdale, he had to pull over, drag a map out of the glove compartment to check the map. His sat-nav had sent them in the wrong direction. He said, not looking at Cassie, making it casual, 'I think Mr and Mrs Robinson might be just right for you. They haven't fostered before but – see how you get on with them. I like them a lot.'

Cassie didn't answer. She wondered why they'd given her a social worker who didn't understand Cassie's placements always fell apart – yet she wanted this to work for his sake. He'd told her the carers had children of their own, but nothing had prepared her for the twins. They were now screaming so loudly the whole village would hear them. Lucy had managed to fix the netting to the rail and she picked up Freddy, swinging her round and round while Tommy headbutted Paul. Cassie heard him say, 'Gently, sweetheart. I'll fix the swing tomorrow.'

Samuel said Lucy and Paul would be 'just right' for Cassie but she thought it couldn't last. The twins filled the house, overflowed into the garden. Why did Paul and Lucy ask for a foster-girl when they had the twins?

'Freddy's got to leave my teddy
alone.' 'I'm not touching your teddy.'
'You kicked him.'
They were arguing that first time Cassie met them.

'Freddy, say hello to Cassie. And this is Tommy. Don't squabble, girls, please. I told you, Cassie's coming to live with us. Cassie's part of our family now.'

They had been dressed almost identically, in blue denim shorts and tee-shirts, though one had a rainbow on her tee-shirt and the other's had a balloon, all sequins. The little girl had stroked them up and down, making the colours change.

At least the twins weren't identical. The twin called Freddy had thick, red hair tied back in a ponytail, and the other had straight brown hair, bunches sticking out above her ears. Their dad stood in a corner of the kitchen. He didn't say much, that first afternoon. The girls had bony shoulders, like his. He wore jeans and a tee-shirt with some kind of logo. It made him look – what was it? Samuel had leaned against the wall, next to him, in a jacket and tie, sort of uniform for him. Some of the social workers came in tee-shirts or long skirts, whatever, but it wasn't the clothes that made the difference.

Cassie had said, 'Freddy a boy's name.'

Lucy had tugged her nose. Maybe she thought it would fall off. 'Why must names be male or female?'

Cassie had stared at the twins. They stared back. Their pale skin was so fine her finger had twitched. She could stroke their cheeks, check how soft their skin was. Her own hair was mouse-brown, dragged back in a ponytail. She'd been desperate to wash it before meeting them but there wasn't enough shampoo. She knew she looked like a ragbag.

Lucy said, 'Freddy was baptised Frederica. My grandfather was Wilfred. He died last year.' Lucy patted the top of Freddy's head, smiling at Cassie. 'He absolutely adored them. And Tommy was baptised Tamsin. Paul's middle name is Thomas. My mother won't call them anything but Frederica and Tamsin.'

'Nana has to call me Freddy.' Freddy had twirled around on one foot, almost colliding with Cassie.

'I don't think you'll be able to persuade her, sweetheart.'

'If she won't, I'll say Grandma Grandma Grandma,' this said to stamping.

Lucy had raised her eyebrows. They were brown even though her hair was red. 'She won't like that.'

'I like Freddy.'

Lucy said, 'I know you do and so do we, but Nana doesn't. We just must accept it.'

The little girl stuck out her chin and opened her eyes extra wide. She meant to get her own way about choosing her name. Names were important. She was so young. She wasn't afraid of anything.

'You're a big girl.' Freddy had run at Cassie and stood so close the top of her head met Cassie's chin, smelling of grass and sunshine. 'I'm six. How old are you?'

'Fourteen,' said Cassie, stepping back. Had the child expected a hug? Cassie had stuffed her hands into her pockets in case she got it wrong.

'Let Cassie get used to us, poppet. I expect she'll have lots of grown-up ideas and it's going to be great having her around.' Cassie's shoulders tensed as Lucy reached towards her, but Freddy grabbed her mother's arm, hung off it, swinging. 'Cassie will be fifteen soon and we can have a party for her, like we do for you. Freddy, you'll topple me over.'

Cassie had bitten her tongue. Lucy was being kind but *party?* By the time July came, and her birthday, she'd be with another family. Why had Lucy said she would have lots of grown-up ideas? Until recently, everyone said Cassie looked about twelve. They had treated her like a kid, even though her body was different every time she looked in the mirror, growing taller, rounder, breasts pushing out so that her bras frayed.

'Let go of me, Freddy, please, I'm not a swing. Where's Tommy?' Cassie had glanced at Tommy, hiding behind the kitchen table, thin brown arms tight around a small teddy bear with a red and white hat sewn to the top of its head. The bear's striped trousers swung from Tommy's little finger. Tommy's lips had been pursed. *She's deciding about me. Shit.* Cassie had felt her nostrils tightening.

'Tommy, bring your ted to say hello to Cassie.'

Tommy had not said hello but when they went for a walk down to the river, before tea, she had grabbed Cassie's hand.

Without warning, Freddy burst into the room. 'I got her first.' A small, gritty hand snatched at Cassie's arm, tugging her away from the window. Cassie hadn't noticed them running out of the garden. Paul was still screwing bits of the climbing frame together.

'That's not fair, you cheated, that's not fair.' Tommy shoved Freddy aside, grabbed Cassie's other arm. 'I want Cassie more than you.'

Lucy said, 'Sorry, couldn't stop them.' She leaned in the doorway, her red hair falling over her face and her blouse untucked from her jeans.

Cassie shook off the children's clutching fingers. 'Stop it. I'm not listening till you calm down.' The girls had got into the habit of shouting for her to play with them as soon as she came in from school. 'I've got homework.' From the corner of her eye, she saw Lucy tuck her hair behind her ears and nod. Her breathing eased when she realised Lucy wouldn't criticise. There'd been too many times in other foster-homes when the carers' own children complained about Cassie. She'd become used to making her face go blank.

'You always say that.' Freddy stuck out her lower lip. 'No, I don't.'

'Is homework nice?' Freddy took hold of Cassie's hand and pretended to trace a pattern in the palm.

Lucy coughed.

'It's okay.' Cassie glanced at the little wooden table

near the window where her school bag lay. She couldn't quite get used to having such a smart backpack. It was navy-blue, with tough white stitching, a compartment for a laptop and plenty of room for books. The straps were padded. 'Actually, I'm supposed to do some reading. Only I've already read the book. I could –.' She caught Lucy's eye.

'It's almost their bath time,' said Lucy. 'Their fingernails are filthy.' She walked into the room and straightened the mirror. 'No more than half an hour?' Sunlight poured through the window to light up her hair. She tipped her head on one side. 'Half-term, would you like a haircut? I don't know what you prefer.'

Cassie went hot and cold. Lucy would get fed up with her soon. She'd say or do something stupid. 'Okay, twins, I'll play one game. What games have you got?'

'I didn't mean – Cassie, you don't have to, we'll get you a nice haircut anyway.'

'They've got great toys.' They really did.

The choices were, laying out the racing-car circuit, dressing-up in the new ambulance kits, starting on the rebuild of the wooden castle, or playing the game of finding Postman Pat's hat and Jess, his black cat.

Cassie chose racing-cars. In all the houses she'd stayed in, only boys had racing-cars. The track was made up of curved pieces which snaked around the twins' bedroom, under stools and even around the legs of the beds, as long as the green and white bedspreads were folded up out of the way.

When Lucy arrived to say she had run the bath, Freddy kicked at the track, breaking it up. 'I want Cassie. You got to come.'

While it was explained to Freddy that kicking her toys was bad, and Freddy had burst into tears, Cassie scrambled around the floor, picking up the pieces. Tommy enjoyed being the good twin and putting them back into the box. Cassie couldn't put off any longer going into the bathroom, knowing a naked body would be in the bath.

She wound up the speckled frog and the deep-sea diver, worked out how to get the two red power-boats zipping along, blew bubbles, drew extra water into the sink for rinsing shampoo out of soapy hair, anything to distract herself from remembering that other pale body in a bath.

When Lucy said, 'The water's getting cold. Time to get out,' Cassie was taken by surprise. How long had she been hanging over the edge of the bath, swishing and blowing bubbles? 'Sorry, Cassie, forgot Freddy's towel, it's on the rack behind you, the green one.'

Tommy stood up so fast she sent a surge of bathwater on to the tiles. 'Me first.' Her eyes fixed on Cassie, she lost her balance and slithered sideways. Cassie grabbed her elbow, steadied her as she straddled the edge of the bath and hopped on to the big yellow towel Lucy had thrown down. She fell against Cassie, wet arms brushing across Cassie's shoulders.

Lucy reached out, wrapped her in a tight yellow bundle. 'Your turn, Freddy.'

Cassie leaned back for the green towel and stared at the reddish-gold strands of Freddy's hair, floating on the surface of the bathwater. She recalled a drawing she had seen in a poetry book. A girl drifted on a river, wearing a floaty dress, her face almost under water and her long hair spread out on the surface. It looked pretty but it was all wrong. Somebody trying to drown herself could not look pretty. Cassie knew. She had seen a nearly-dead body in a bath.

Then Freddy stretched her arms above her head, twisted, grabbed the edge of the bath. 'I'm the queen of the castle!' As she pushed herself upright, she splashed water into Cassie's face and on to the tiles. Cassie lunged at the squirming, slippery body, heaved Freddy out of the bath and wrapped the green towel around her. Freddy rubbed her fists into her eyes and sang. Tommy joined in.

'I'm the king of the castle, You're a dirty rascal.'

'Don't see what that's got to do with having a bath.' Cassie scrubbed at herself and Freddy. 'I'm soaked.' Her wet blouse stuck to her skin. Freddy's hair smelt of vanilla shampoo.

'Tell us a story from your red book.'

Lucy raised her eyebrows. 'The red book?'

Freddy shouted, 'I want the giant goes stamp-stamp-stamp and he bashes the little boys' heads till their brains come out all over the place.'

'A homely tale of cruelty to children, Cassie?'

'It's just an old book I have. It's fairy stories, sort of.' Cassie pushed Freddy away. 'The story's called *Nix-Nought-Nothing*. They like the actions.'

'Of course they do. Where did you get your red book?'

'It was a present,' said Cassie, grabbing the edge of the towel. 'Look, you've soaked me, Freddy. I might as well have got in the bath with you.' She wiped the splashes from her cheek. She was not going to remember Rod's smile when he gave her the book. She was not going to remember Sarah crying and crying and crying after Rod died. She was not going to think about Sarah saying she couldn't cope any more with being a foster-carer.

Stella

> **We're waiting for your call.**
> Whatever you're going through, a Samaritan will face it with you.
> We're here 24 hours a day, 365 days a year. Call 116 123

Six: Saturday 09:57

L202:   *Samaritans, how can I help you?*
Caller: Why won't you ring the police for me?
L202:   *I'm afraid we don't do that. What's troubling you?*
Caller: I want them to get my baby back.
L202:   *Something has happened to your baby?*
Caller: I thought you Samaritans did good turns.
L202:   *Have you rung the police?*
Caller: I'm fed up people telling me what to do like I'm stupid, poking their noses in, telling me I've done it all wrong. I'm sick of it. I got my rights.
L202:   *It sounds as if you've had a lot to deal with –.*
Caller: You got no idea. Nobody helped me when I went to work in the bar and I had to sleep on the beach and I went into that office and I told them he said if I wanted to keep the room I had to do him favours.
L202:   *Who was this?*
Caller: Bar owner, pervert. Men only think about their dicks.
L202:   *You reported this, is that what you mean?*
Caller: Grit gets in everywhere. The sea stinks and your hair's all sticky.

L202: *You mean, sleeping on a beach? It must be very uncomfortable. You say you went into an office?*

Caller: I wanted to get the police on him only I knew they'd take his side. He'd say I was making it up or I was coming on to him. That's what they all say. He thinks, he gives me a room and I'll be his tart.

L202: *Can I go back to what led you to call us? You are worried about your baby?*

Caller: Nobody pays me any attention unless I'm pregnant. I got fussed over every time I was pregnant, and then they take my babies and nobody cares. It's a crime, tell you what, if a social worker turned up and took your babies you'd get the police on them but you won't ring the police for me.

L202: *We can't approach the police on your behalf, but we can advise you who to ask.*

Caller: I'm not ringing any police, they're out to get me.

L202: *You've had contact with the police before?*

Caller rings off.

Cassie

Seven: Saturday

Cassie flattened herself against the wall of the kitchen. She had heard the shouting upstairs, one twin screaming at another, but louder still was a hard, furious voice, a voice she scarcely recognised. Somebody stamped down the stairs and Lucy banged into the room, slamming the door so hard that the china mugs on the stand clinked.

'I swear I'm fucking going to kill them.' Cassie tried to be invisible.

Paul looked around from the stove, where he was making some sort of meaty sauce to go with spaghetti. 'Steady on.'

Lucy dragged a chair away from the table, sat down with a thump, and laid her head on the table mat, scattering the knives and forks and spoons that Cassie had been about to set out. Her fists drummed on the wood.

This scene played out in other houses where Cassie had stayed, but usually she was the one who started the argument. That's what they said, anyway. The script wrote itself across her mind. Her lips felt numb. She didn't want to hear the words, not here, not this time. She didn't want to say, *"I don't fucking care anyway, I hate it here, I hate you, go on then, ring up, get them to take me away."*

'Don't look so worried, Cassie,' said Paul. She hadn't noticed him stepping from the oven to lean over Lucy. He was massaging her shoulders.

'Oh God.' Lucy's words were muffled. 'I am such a cow. It's okay, Paul, I'm okay now.' He stood back and Lucy stretched out her arms as if she wanted to touch the ceiling. Then she drew a deep breath. For a moment, Cassie thought

Lucy was going to cry and her throat felt tight. Lucy was not allowed to cry. She couldn't work out what she wanted to happen except for everything to be right between Lucy and Paul.

Paul glanced across at Cassie. 'Happens to both of us, sometimes.' He wasn't pretending to smile. 'I could kill them. I have to get out into the garden and chop wood.'

Lucy twisted round in the chair. There were tears on her face. 'I was hoping to God this wouldn't happen so soon after you got here, Cassie. I mean, me having a meltdown.'

Paul said, 'I'll just rescue my sauce before it burns a hole in the pan.'

'You can be a self-righteous prick sometimes, Paul Robinson.' Cassie's mouth fell open. Did Lucy really call Paul a prick?

'Are they actually drowning or what?' Paul threw the spoon on to the worktop.

The kitchen door opened, very slowly. Freddy, draped in a green towel, came in sideways, angling her head. A red scratch-mark ran down her left cheek. 'Tommy started it.' Her voice was high. She was ready for another fight.

Lucy began to stand but Cassie jumped in front of her. 'Freddy, go upstairs, put on your pyjamas, and tell Tommy to do the same. I'm going to read you a story about a fight.' She felt super-electric. Paul and Lucy swore and fought and made up. She wanted to throw her arms around them.

Cassie raced to slide out the red book from its hiding place under her bed. By the time she reached their room the little girls were in their beds, still rather wet. She sat on the end of Tommy's bed and slapped her hands over her ears when the bickering started again. 'Lalalalalala not listening not listening.'

As soon as they finished wriggling, she began the story of

Mr and Mrs Vinegar, who lived in a bottle. Mrs Vinegar swept so hard that she broke the bottle house. This turned into jumping off beds and trying out the action.

Lucy came in. She had been watching from the doorway and Cassie had not seen her. 'Time you calmed down, my pigeons.'

'Not a pigeon, read it again, read it again!' Freddy bounced, hair flapping.

'Just the end, Cassie.'

Cassie had never read bed-time stories to anyone before staying with the Robinsons. It was so important she could burst. She turned to the last paragraph.

> As he drew near to the wood where he had left his wife, he heard a parrot on a tree calling out his name: "Mr. Vinegar, you foolish man, you blockhead, you simpleton; you went to the fair, and laid out all your money in buying a cow. Not content with that, you changed it for bagpipes, on which you could not play, and which were not worth one-tenth of the money. You fool, you – you had no sooner got the bagpipes than you changed them for the gloves, which were not worth one-quarter of the money; and when you had got the gloves, you changed them for a poor miserable stick; and now for your forty guineas, cow, bagpipes, and gloves, you have nothing to show but that poor miserable stick, which you might have cut in any hedge."

'What's a blockhead, Cassie? What's bagpipes?'

'Tommy, I told you last time about bagpipes.' Cassie shook a finger at Tommy, same as she'd seen Mr Hetherington do. The action made her wrist flop. 'It's practically the end so no more interrupting.'

Tommy leaned over, pressed her forehead into the duvet and pretended to sob. Cassie knew about fake crying. She carried on.

> The bird laughed and laughed, and Mr. Vinegar, falling into a violent rage, threw the stick at its head. The stick lodged in the tree, and he returned to his wife without money, cow, bagpipes, gloves, or stick, and she instantly gave him such a sound cudgelling that she almost broke every bone in his skin.

'Whack whack whack.' The girls banged their fists into their duvets, sending out tiny white feathers which floated in mid-air before drifting down to the floor. Cassie flicked a glance at Lucy in case she didn't approve of whacking duvets. She might think Cassie was a bad influence reading them a story with whacking in it. 'Don't get any ideas, you two.' Lucy stood up to close the spotty dog curtains, straightened duvets. 'I don't want any playing at Mr and Mrs Vinegar.'

'But Mum, he was a big silly, Mr Vinegar.'

'Yes, he was.' Tommy reached for Lucy, wound her arms around Lucy's neck, whispered into her ear.

Freddy sat up straight and said to Cassie, 'Mrs Vinegar, she broke their house, I think she did so she's a big silly too.'

Lucy kissed her on the forehead. 'Good night and God bless, darling.'

Cassie's throat tightened. It was Tommy's turn next for *Good night and God bless darling*. Had Sarah kissed her on the forehead? For years she was sure of it, could picture Sarah leaning forward to tickle her earlobes. Cassie put a finger to her right ear, touching the small lobe. Somebody once nibbled her right earlobe. Was that Sarah? Memory was so unreal, all tangled up with dreams and pictures in books. Fake memories. Was that what authors did when they wrote novels, make fake memories?

'Come on, dreamer,' said Lucy, taking her elbow and leading her out to the landing. 'The way they attack each other sometimes, it drives me scatty because I don't seem able to stop them and then I get mad at myself and then – well, you saw. I wish you hadn't but maybe it's just as well because I'm not going to be able to guarantee good behaviour forever. My good behaviour, I mean.'

Cassie did not know what to say. Lucy's blue eyes seemed deeper set in her face than ever and there were lines on her face Cassie had not seen before, under her eyes and beside her mouth. She wanted to touch them.

Lucy stroked the red cover of the book under Cassie's arm. 'Great story. What a collection. Who's is it?'' She tilted the book to read the title. '*Joseph Jacobs English Fairy Tales.* Wish I'd had them told to me when I was a kid. There's nothing sentimental about stories like that, is there? Is the cover okay? Looks as if it's coming off.'

'There was this foster-family I lived with.' Cassie stared at the book. Lucy must not see her expression. 'Rod read to me every night. I learned to read with Rod. I hated reading at school.'

'How old were you?' They were back in Cassie's room and Lucy was adjusting the gathers in the curtains.

'Not sure. Six or seven? At school they said I was special needs because I couldn't read, but the stuff they gave us was boring. I read so fast with Rod. He gave me this book.'

Lucy opened the bedroom window and a small breeze lifted the curtains. They were patterned with birds. 'How long did you stay with Rod?'

'Rod and Sarah. Till I was eight.'

Lucy didn't ask any more and Cassie wouldn't have told her anyway. It was like a dream, a time she would never describe in case words twisted the memory into a different shape and made it something that it wasn't. Even thinking about the nearly-two years with Rod and Sarah made her feel so sick and angry she wanted to break windows – like Mrs Vinegar, smashing the walls of her bottle house.

Maybe it would be better for everyone not to live with their true parents but with other people who wouldn't think, *"She's my child, she's mine,"* like a handbag or a car, and then get upset if they fought, like Freddy and Tommy. Maybe everybody having foster-carers instead of parents would make people happier.

Cassie was beginning to appreciate being with sisters who bit one another, scratched, and kicked. If Freddy wasn't in the room, Tommy went to find her. If Tommy got a cut, Freddy tried scratching her arm or knee so she had a cut in the same place.

Could foster-sisters get as close as real sisters?

Dr Hume's idea about writing about all her different foster-placements was interesting. Dr Hume said it might help Cassie to see her life in perspective.

She reached out for the bookshelf to touch wood and crossed her fingers as well. There was something about the way the twins treated her, as if she were special, not Special Needs. Their lives would be totally different from hers. They'd been baptised, christened, whatever it was. God-stuff. Paul explained but Cassie couldn't get her head round it. At night, Lucy knelt between their beds and they said a prayer together, and when Cassie went into this room they said was hers, definitely hers, for as long as she wanted, Lucy called out, 'Good night. God bless.'

Paul and Lucy both said, 'Good night and God bless, Cassie.' She understood the words but she had no sense of what they meant. If it was like touching wood and crossing fingers, she'd have called it fairy-tale superstition, except Paul and Lucy weren't stupid. They were more like Rod and Sarah than any other foster-carers – well, until Rod died, and Sarah wouldn't stop crying.

How was it different, being a parent, not a carer? Maybe some parents weren't carers and some carers weren't parents. Cassie banged the edge of her hand against the bookshelf. She had a totally clear memory of a parent who wasn't a carer. Her hand hurt.

The atmosphere of supper with Lucy and Paul, later that evening – spaghetti and meat sauce – was so calm that Cassie began to wonder if the shouting had actually happened, until Paul said, 'I'm sorry about earlier, Cassie. It isn't just our kids. We have our moments.'

'Don't get confessional,' said Lucy, stacking the dishwasher. 'He's getting bloody holy, starting this course.' She looked back at Cassie. 'You know Paul's training to be a vicar.'

'You said you wouldn't mind,' said Paul, standing up, folding the napkins. Cassie followed the movements of his wide, strong hands. He was tall and thin and broad-shouldered and his eyes were tired. 'What do you think, Cassie?'

Cassie stared at the dresser, covered in boxes labelled *Freddy* and *Tommy*, their crayons, pencils, erasers, toy scissors, doodle-books, all tidied away. She remembered Paul swinging a twin in the air without dropping her, catching Tommy before she screamed.

'I don't know about vicars.'

Paul tossed the napkins into a drawer. 'Go on, tell me the truth. I bet you know more than you're saying.'

'Leave the girl alone,' said Lucy, but she glanced across at Cassie, half-smiling.

Cassie took a deep breath. She would try not to gabble. 'Well, I don't really get what accountants do. You look like someone who likes being out of door for a run or something, not stuck indoors with books. But being a vicar, is that all being inside too?' Her cheeks were hot. Was this a test?

'Don't bully her, Paul. Cassie's right, anyway, you do love being outdoors.'

'Accountancy's more interesting than people think.' Paul ruffled his hair, and half-grinned. He had even, white teeth. 'But I'm ready for something new. I've been thinking about getting ordained for years.'

'It would have been nice to know that, years ago. Don't expect the rest of us to get holy alongside you.' Lucy wound her arms around him and pinched his nose. 'And no coming back from those courses thinking we're going to do all the chores because you'll have assignments to write.'

Cassie expected to feel left out. They were so tight, so wound around one another, their heads so close – yet Paul winked at her over Lucy's head. Did all vicars wink? She had never met a vicar but she had a picture in her mind of men with white collars and black clothes though Paul had already told her there were women vicars. Cassie wondered if they would wear white collars and black clothes too. She'd have hated only wearing black.

After supper, she sat with her elbows on the small table in her bedroom, flipping back through the pages of *Jane Eyre* to the part they were meant to have reached for homework. She had already finished it. She loved how Jane escaped from the horrible school, but she was not at all sure about Mr Rochester. He was playing games with Jane. He wasn't honest. It was a sort of bullying. Cassie sniffed out bullies even when they looked like heroes.

What would Rod and Sarah have done if they'd suspected she was bullied at school? Even when she was seven there were kids who pretended she had a bad smell. If she had carried on living with Rod and Sarah, would the bullying have stopped? She was so young ... but there were girls who ... was she the sort of girl who always would get bullied? Was there something about her so different that kids would always know, like she had the plague?

Cassie had read in one story about how plague houses were marked on the outside and nobody went into them to help the sick people. There was this saying, "avoiding people like the plague". Plague victims were left till they died and their bodies were dropped into big pits and covered with soil.

Maybe Lucy was worried Paul would smell different once he was a vicar.

Cassie stroked a page, half-seeing the black print on white paper.

If she believed the god-stuff he and Lucy believed in, she'd say to their god, make it different this time. Make it different.

Stella

> **We're waiting for your call.**
> Whatever you're going through, a Samaritan will face it with you.
> We're here 24 hours a day, 365 days a year. Call 116 123

Eight: Sunday 00:14

D204: *Hello, Samaritans, how can I help you?*
Caller: These pills are doing my head in.
D204: *That sounds rather worrying. Are you all right?*
Caller: I feel all strange.
D204: *Your doctor gave you these pills?*
Caller: You saying I got them on the street?
D204: *You sound very anxious. Do you have any support, anything to help you?*
Caller: She's going to make me go to a doctor. What's a doctor going to do?
D204: *Do you mean someone is trying to help you?*
Caller: Fucking social worker, poking her nose in. They're going to find out about the vodka and my little girl.
D204: *You have a little girl?*
Caller: Nobody's interested in me.
D204: *What makes you feel that nobody is interested in you?*
Caller: Those times they took my babies and never came back to see how I was. It was fine when I was expecting, oh, let me take you to the doctor, oh, I'll sort out that gas bill, oh dear, how are your ankles today? Going on and on and then nothing.

D204:	*When you say "nothing", what is it you feel?*
Caller:	I'm on my own. I'm on my own.
D204:	*You sound very distressed. Can you tell me a little more about your babies?*

Caller rings off.

Nine: Monday 10:30

Josie: Can I come in, Stella?
Stella: Can't stop you.
Josie: I'm sorry the room is so small. It was the best I could find right now.
Stella: What are you doing here?
Josie: Stella, you came into the office and said you wanted to get back on track so you could find your baby. You said you'd been sleeping on the beach.
Stella: Yeah, well. Don't sigh at me like I'm a bad kid.
Josie: I'll try if you try. Do you mind if I sit down? No, it's okay, you keep the chair, I'll just perch here. Gosh, this mattress knows how to bounce.
Stella: You saying I get punters in?
Josie: Don't be so touchy. I know you're aware it's a condition of staying here, no drugs, no alcohol, no adults unless the warden approves.
Stella: Might as well be in prison.
Josie: I hope not. I've been doing some research and I've been able to talk to one of the social workers who tried to help you before. I didn't realise you were born here in Whitehaven. And Cassie was born here too but you left when she was still a baby.
Stella: How much you got in those records? Does it say how often I fart or fuck?
Josie: I can see the situation is complicated. Your daughter is nearly fifteen. She's within her rights if she refuses to see you. You don't go to the planning meetings?

Stella: Why do I care about plans for her? What about me?

Josie: Well, we can make a plan to help you get back on track.

Stella: What does that mean?

Josie: You should register with a local GP practice, see a doctor and sort out that medication. Are you still taking a benzodiazepine? You really shouldn't be drinking. I can't see the doctor with you. They will ask how much you drink.

Stella: None of their business.

Josie: There are programmes to help people stop drinking.

Stella: Do-gooders, they make me sick.

Josie: They won't think badly of you.

Stella: They can just fuck off if they do.

Josie: All sorts of people drink too heavily, and can't stop without help and support.

Stella: What the fuck do you know about me? Now what are you sighing about?

Josie: I wish you would try not to swear so much.

Stella: You think you're better than me.

Josie: I don't, Stella, really I don't. I can see from the records you've moved all over the county. I know records don't tell the whole story. They don't show how you feel, Stella. I'm sure lots has happened to you that you don't tell anybody.

Stella: Oh, you're that kind of know-everything expert. Not just a fucking wanker. You're sighing again. You don't like being a wanker. Now what? You going now? Pushing off when you don't like what I say?

Josie: Stella. If you want to reconnect with your daughter you are going to have to make some tough choices about your own behaviour.

Stella: I'm here, aren't I?

Josie: Well, your body's here but everything about you says

	you don't want to be. Don't interrupt. You're angry and fed up and hostile. I suspect you've been feeling like it so long it's turned into a habit. It's not a habit that helps you and it certainly won't help with your daughter, not now she's nearly fifteen. She's not a child.
Stella:	I don't have to put up with this. You think you're so much better than me, you – everyone hears everything in here. These walls are like paper.
Josie:	Please don't kick the wall. Sit down. Stella, sit down. Right. Have you a tissue? I don't mean to make you cry. We've only known each other a few days. You want to see your daughter, but you're not prepared for it.
Stella:	You wouldn't put up with it in here. They're always screaming. I'm gonna go screaming mad in here. It's like going deaf and blind.
Josie:	I'm trying to get more help for you. I've put in for some funding – my budget doesn't have much left, and I'm sure as sure there's nothing in the local mental health budget, but we've access to a good local charity for counselling and therapy. They might agree to provide some funds. You need help. A good therapist might make all the difference.
Stella:	Someone else to interfere and tell me where I'm all wrong?
Josie:	Someone with deep experience of understanding emotional upheaval. Good heavens, that face you pulled, makes you look about twelve. Will you register with a doctor tomorrow?
Stella:	Might do.
Josie:	You could try drafting a letter to your daughter – Cassie, is it? Or writing down how you feel. If we can

	get you in to see a therapist they'll give you strategies. You could record on your phone? You do have a mobile?
Stella:	Got no money on it. Course I got a mobile. You think I can't write, I can tell by the look in your eye, you think I'm stupid. What do you mean, strategies?
Josie:	I don't think at all that you are stupid or that you can't write. I do know that sometimes, people who've lived through difficult times, they choose all sorts of different ways of expressing themselves. Like, I once had a client who drew all the time. Whatever suits you, Stella. I don't know enough about your talents.
Stella:	You're sighing again.
Josie:	Good heavens, is that the time? I've another client to see.
Stella:	Same old same old. Can you get me some decent soap? Stuff in here is crap.
Josie:	Goodbye, Stella. Talk to the warden, see what she can find for you. I'm sure she'll want to help. You can use the computer in the common room if you want to, she tells me. Do you know how to use one?
Stella:	I did a course once. Why do I want a computer?
Josie:	Might help in finding you a job that pays. I'll be in touch. Stop snivelling. You don't mean it. It won't help you.

Ten: Monday 11:42

Phone recording

I'm fed up ringing those Samaritans. All they say is they want to listen and they never do anything and that social worker keeps telling me I got to sort myself out. They got no idea. She says write down how I feel or draw or shit like that. It makes my hand ache writing. It don't sound like me on this recording.

If I had a better phone I could get more apps and sound better. My voice sounds all funny. How I feel. Fucking dumb ideas she has. Maybe if I pretend I'm talking to Cassie it will sound better.

One two three Cassie. Are you listening?

I got to tell you about Luke.

Makes my skin crawl remembering.

I hope he burns in hell.

He was my dad's brother.

He had a great fat belly hanging out and a tiny dick.

I don't know how he found it to piss. He must've grobbled around to find it and point it. Actually he kept pissing on our bathroom floor. I think once he pissed in the bath. How do I know it was tiny? He poked it in my mouth.

Cassie, whatever you do, don't let men make you do blowjobs, it's vile. You feel sick with this slimy stuff in your mouth and you can't swallow it only you have to and then you want to throw up.

Recording clicks off.

Cassie

Eleven: Tuesday afternoon

School was getting worse. Taylor Lawson said she knew about Kyle. Cassie didn't believe her but she couldn't risk it. She gave away her packed lunch. She wasn't hungry, anyway.

When Paul picked her up from the bus, she pretended to read a textbook, and then, telling Lucy she had lots of homework, she bolted upstairs to the small room under the eaves and opened the window. The cool afternoon scent of lavender floated in on a soft wind. Taylor's comment about Kyle made her feel queasy. She could not bear the smell of food.

How did Kyle's stepmother get to be a foster-carer? She wasn't just a useless carer, she took all the care in the world not to notice what Kyle was doing to Cassie. Maybe they were so desperate for foster-carers they'd take anybody who rang up and offered. *They.* Somebody high up in the social services offices?

Samuel wasn't like *them*.

What if her mother suddenly turned up? It wasn't possible.

She paced around the room. Was now the time to start on the storybook Dr Hume had suggested? Among the other books on the shelves Cassie had found a notebook with blank pages and a gold and red cover. Paul said, when she asked, that it was a spare, and nice notebooks were always handy. Cassie was welcome to have it.

The paper was so smooth that at first Cassie simply turned the pages, stroking them. 'Can I write in it?'

'You can draw in it if you want.'

'I'm no good at art.'

'Just don't let the twins get hold of it. They'll only scribble.'

She rooted in her backpack for her bag of pens, sat down, opened the red and gold notebook, and wrote her name on the first page.

Cassie Clearwater.

It was such a great name for a writer.

Somebody scratched on the door and Paul's head appeared. 'Are you free, Cassie?'

Her stomach knotted. She did not want to answer any questions. 'Cassie?'

She got up, went to the door and opened it.

Paul's hair hung in damp strands across his forehead and his cheeks were pink. 'I can't get any sense out of them. Something about Mr and Mrs Vinegar?'

'I told them the story the other night.' Cassie's fingers twitched at the thought of the red and gold notebook. Its blank pages called to her.

Paul pushed hair out of his eyes and smoothed out his frown with long, thin fingers. 'I know you've got a lot of homework – Lucy's fallen asleep – head down on the kitchen table. Something at work and now the girls are fighting, but a story from you? Do you have time for this? Feel free to say no. It's my problem.'

She took a deep breath. The twins wanted her again. Her heart beat a bit too fast. It was dangerous to want them so much. 'I'll come.'

The twins were sitting up on their beds, poking out their tongues at one another.

Paul followed Cassie into the room and sat down on the floor with his back to a bookcase. 'It's nearly eight o'clock. I'm fed up with the pair of you. You have promised faithfully not to get out of bed or do anything horrible to one another's toys if Cassie tells you a story.' He looked up, and Cassie noticed the smudges of grey shadow under his eyes. 'It doesn't have to be a long story. They should have been ready for sleep at seven o'clock.'

The little room had a sloping roof and a view of the garden through its small windows. The sweet smell of roses was strong, and another scent that made her think of honey. The fragrance of the air drew her to the window. On this side of the cottage was a view of the green and purple hills they called fells, outlined against a deepening blue sky. It was more beautiful than she had a right to expect. She didn't deserve to live here.

Inwardly shaking herself, she leaned against the window ledge, folded her arms, and began. 'This is my very favourite story. It's about a girl called Catskin.'
'Nobody's called that.'

'I don't want a story about cats.' Tommy stuck her forefingers in her ears, but she was watching Cassie.

'Well, Catskin wasn't her real name,' said Cassie, settling down with a wriggle to find a comfortable position on the deep sill. 'I don't know what her real name was. You can decide after, if you can think of one. Don't mither, Freddy, you haven't heard anything yet.'

Freddy stuffed a thumb in her mouth and grinned around it.

'She's dribbling,' said Tommy, but Cassie ignored her.

'Well, this girl's father was a rich man and he really wanted a son. When his wife had a daughter he didn't want to see the baby. He didn't pay any attention to her, not ever, till she was fifteen, that's the same as me, well I'll be fifteen soon, and he thought he could get her out of the way if he could find a husband for her. People sometimes got married when they were fifteen, lots of years ago.'

'Why aren't you reading the story? Read it, read it.'

Tommy jumped up and down her bed, and Freddy joined in. 'Read it, read it.'

Cassie folded her arms and did her best scowl. 'I don't have to read it. I know this story off by heart.'

'Really and truly?'

'Really and truly. Will you both shut the f – shut up and let me get on with it.'

She dared not glance at Paul. 'A nasty old man came and said he'd marry the girl. She completely didn't want to marry him but she didn't know how to get out of it so she went to see the lady who looked after their hens, and asked her what to do.

'What was her name?'

'I don't know. The story doesn't say.'

'She got to have a name,' said Freddy, removing her thumb.

'Well, what?'

'She's called Dorabelle,' said Tommy.

Freddy opened her mouth to object but Cassie said, 'You can make up the next name.'

Tommy picked up her Peter Rabbit toy, tucked it under her chin and poked out her tongue at Freddy.

'That's not nice, Tommy,' said Paul.

Cassie wished he would not interrupt. 'Dorabelle said the girl should go to her daddy and say she would not marry the old man unless he gave her a dress made all of silver. Well, she got the silver dress and it was very beautiful, but she still didn't want to marry the old man so she went back to Dorabelle. Dorabelle said, "You've got to say you won't marry him unless you get a dress made all of gold." So the girl went to her daddy and asked for a dress made of gold, and he gave her one, and she still didn't want to marry the old man. Dorabelle said she had to ask for a dress made from feathers from all the birds.'

'Yucky-yuck,' said Freddy. 'Feathers stick in. I got feathers in my pillow from Nana and she said they're duck feathers and that's horrible.'

Paul said, 'We changed the pillow, Freddy, so don't interrupt.'

'It was a bit tricky getting the feathers.' Cassie caught Paul's eye. She really could do without his interruptions. 'The rich man – you know, he was the girl's father – well, he had to get a man to throw a huge pile of peas on the ground, and the man shouted at the birds that each one could take a pea in exchange for a feather.'

'I don't like peas,' said Freddy.

Tommy sat forward, clutching her Peter Rabbit toy. 'The feathers might get blood.'

There was noise from Paul, who was wiping his eyes. His face was red with the laugh he was trying to swallow.

If he didn't like the way she told stories he could fuck off.

He waved his hands and blew his nose like a watery trumpet. 'You are a fantastic story-teller,' he said, blowing again. 'It's the literalness of my daughters that gets me.'

'Oh. Okay. Birds like peas, well they like peas in the story, okay, Freddy? So she got this very pretty dress made of feathers. No, there wasn't any blood and the ends of the feathers were really soft and not prickly at all and he still didn't want to marry the old man. Dorabelle told her to ask for a coat made of catskin.'

'That's horrible, that's cruel, I don't want to hear this story any more.' Tommy turned over, covered her head with the pillow and made sobbing noises.

Paul said, 'Oh, Tommy.'

Cassie spoke over him. She knew fake when she saw it. 'The cats were dead before their skins were taken off. Anyway, that's the story.' She had almost said that Tommy's favourite red shoes were made from dead cow-skin but stopped herself in time. 'Sit up, Tommy, the good part comes next.'

There were two or three more loud sniffs. Tommy wriggled on to her side and pulled a veil of filmy brown hair over her eyes. She looked like a cat hiding under a bush.

'Okay, so as soon as the girl gets the coat of catskin she puts it on, ties her other dresses into a bundle and runs away into the woods.'

'What did she tie them with?'
'Well, Freddy, what would you use to tie up your dresses?'
'Were the woods like our woods?'

Cassie realised that if she answered all the questions she would never get to the end of the story. 'She keeps on walking through the woods till she gets to a wonderful castle and there isn't a doorbell or a knocker so she shouts through the gates, and a man comes. He's sweeping up dead leaves.' Cassie straightened up, coughed, and spoke in a deep, pretend-man voice. "What do you want? No beggars here." She asks for a job and the lady in the castle comes out and says, "You can work in the kitchen if you like." So the girl goes to work in the kitchen, and it was huge. All the pots and pans hung down from the ceiling. There was a fat woman who did all the cooking and she didn't want the girl coming into her kitchen. She called her Catskin –. '

'Is your name Catskin?'

'No,' said Cassie, with a start. She stared at Tommy's wide-open brown eyes.

'Well, I'm called Tommy but really I got this stupid name Tamsin, and you're called Cassie and it's a bit like –.'

'No, my name isn't Catskin.'

'Is your proper name Cassie?'

'Freddy, can I go on with the story?' 'What's her proper name?'

'What do you mean?'

'Before she got called Catskin, what was she called?'

Cassie stared at Freddy's pale face. A smear of white from toothpaste lay in the crease beneath her mouth. 'I never thought about it.' She recalled that it was Freddy's turn to invent a name. 'What name do you think?'

Freddy waved her hands. 'I know, I know, she's called Kayla.'

'I don't like Kayla.' Tommy's fake frown was as obvious as her fake tears.

'A girl in their class is called Kayla,' said Paul, raising his arm like a school kid.

Cassie ignored him. 'Let me think a minute.' The picture on the wall above Freddy's bed was of a large black cat with deep green eyes. She'd noticed before that it came from an art gallery. When she lived with Rod and Sarah, Sarah had showed her how to mix paints. Something prickled at the back of her nose. 'Her name is Emerald.'

'Your voice has gone funny,' said Freddy, pointing at Cassie. 'It's my turn to choose. Emerald's a silly name.'

Paul tugged Freddy's ankle. 'It's the name of a precious stone. Don't argue. Go on, Cassie. I don't know this story and I want to know how it turns out.'

Cassie didn't believe him. She wondered if Lucy would've called him a holy prick if she'd been there. 'Well, the horrible cook gave Emerald all the dirty jobs but she didn't care. At least she didn't have to marry a horrible old man. One day everybody in the kitchen started saying the Lord of the castle's son was coming home and there was going to be a ball. Emerald said she would love to go. The cook threw a bowl of dirty water over her.'

'Why? That's disgusting,' said Freddy. She had stopped sucking her thumb and was chewing a strand of curly hair.

Cassie felt a frown coming and rubbed her forehead.

Catskin had turned into Emerald, and somehow giving her a name meant she was changing from the Catskin in the story that she loved. 'I think she wanted Emerald to believe she was dirty and disgusting like throwaway water but Emerald had a plan. She'd already found somewhere to hide her dresses so she sneaks off into the woods, gets into a tarn and has a proper wash.'

'We go in the river and it's cold,' said Tommy, pretending to shiver.

'Is it?'

'We'll take you soon,' said Paul. 'It's beautiful. Well, we think so.'

'Thanks,' said Cassie, thinking that nothing would get her into a freezing cold river. 'Anyway, she puts on her silver dress and goes to the ball and the young Lord sees her and he has to dance with her and he falls completely in love with her.'

'Where did she hide her dresses?' Tommy folded her arms and tipped back her head.

She looked so like Paul that Cassie wondered if she was imitating him, or if Paul had tipped back his head in the same way when he was six. She bit her lip, trying to remember pictures in her old book. 'She found a hollow tree in the forest and hung them up inside. No, she didn't have hangers, it's a story, okay?'

'Well, that man who dances with her, what's he called?'

'He's called – he's called Trevor,' said Freddy, kicking her feet.

'Trevor?' Cassie's picture of a Trevor wasn't a handsome young Lord.

'Our friend's dog is called Trevor.'

'What sort of dog?' Cassie was suspicious.

'He's all black and shiny and he loves getting in the river.'

59

'Labrador,' said Paul, his voice shaking again.

Cassie scowled at him and carried on. 'At the end of the dance she runs off so she can change into her old clothes and get back into the kitchen.'

'I wouldn't have put my dirty old clothes on,' said Freddy.

'She doesn't want to be found out. Well, the young Lord, yes, that's Trevor, told his mother that he would die if he couldn't marry the beautiful girl in the silver dress, so they arranged an other ball. They thought she would turn up again. In the kitchen everybody was talking about it and Catskin – Emerald – said she wanted to go but the cook screamed at her and told her she was a slut. I think that's a very rude word to call someone. Anyway, Emerald sneaked out of the castle and ran back into the wood –.'

'And she got in the tarn and got washed all over,' said Tommy, who had taken off Peter Rabbit's blue coat, to scrub his back with it.

'And she put on the gold dress and went to the ball. And this time, at the end of the dances, she ran off again.'

'So next time she put on the feather dress?' Freddy tilted her chin. 'I know this story.'

'I'm telling it,' said Cassie, putting on a cross voice.

Freddy giggled.

Cassie sighed. They knew so many tricks, these little girls. 'Yes, but it's different, because Trevor follows her from the ball and watches her change out of her feather dress into her catskin dress, and then he knows who she is. And he is so excited because he's found her. He goes back to the castle and tells his mum that he wants to marry the kitchen maid. Well, his mum gets cross and says, "No way" and she loses her temper.'

Tommy said, 'Our mummy loses her temper and then she has a cry and Daddy gives her a cuddle.'

Paul stared at the ceiling.

The image that flashed through Cassie's head almost broke the thread of the story. She hurried on. 'Well, Trevor gets so poorly after that, he goes to bed and he won't eat or drink anything and he gets paler and paler and paler. His mum gives in.'

'Our mummy gets cross when we don't drink our milk,' said Tommy. She had managed to force Peter Rabbit's legs into the arms of his blue coat.

Cassie was distracted by another flash, this time of memory. Had her mother once given her a mug of milk with a chocolate straw? She ran her fingers through her hair, and wished it were as thick and curly as Lucy's, as Freddy's would be.

'Emerald went out into the woods and put on her dress of gold before she went to see Trevor's mum, and Trevor's mum thought she was so beautiful it would be fine for Trevor and Emerald to get married.'

She fell silent.

Paul stood up, rubbing his calves and wincing. 'Cramp, Great story, Cassie. Bed for you, Freddy.'

'Oh, that's not the end, there's a bit more.'

Freddy yawned as Paul pulled the duvet under her chin. 'I want the end.' She chewed her thumb.

'It won't take long,' said Cassie, stretching. 'Trevor and Emerald are very happy and they have a little boy, and after a few years, Emerald starts wondering about her daddy, and if he's okay.'

'He didn't want to see her,' said Tommy, smoothing out her pillow. She yawned too.

'Trevor got his big coach and horses and they all got into it, and their little boy – no, I don't know what his name was. Stop interrupting. They drove through the woods to the house where Emerald used to live.' Tommy opened her mouth and Cassie held up both hands. 'What did I say? Do you want to know the end?' Tommy pursed her lips. 'Trevor went to the big house to meet Emerald's daddy. Well, it was very, very sad.'

'I don't like sad stories,' said Freddy, sticking her thumb back into her mouth.

'It's not sad at the very end so wait till I finish.'

Paul took the teddy bear away from Tommy and laid it at the end of her bed. 'Hush up, the pair of you.'

'Well, it's a bit sad because Emerald's mummy had died, and her dad was all on his own. Trevor asked him if he used to have a daughter, and he said, "I did a really bad thing. I let my daughter run away and I didn't look for her and now I really, really want to see her again." So Trevor took him to the coach, and Emerald's daddy cried and said he was truly, truly sorry, and he went to live with Trevor and Emerald and he was so, so glad –.' Cassie had to stop. Her eyes were prickling.

Paul gave each girl a kiss on the forehead.

'Cassie, you got –.' Freddy's words were muffled by the pillow. Cassie frowned at Paul.

'I think she means, will you give her a kiss.'

'Oh.' Cassie shrugged. She leaned down, found a small, warm ear, and pressed her lips to it. This was far, far too dangerous.

'And me,' came the voice from the other bed.

Tommy's hair smelt of the open air from their games in the garden. When Cassie bent over, she turned on her back, lifted her arms and grabbed Cassie around the neck.

'Nighty-night,' said Cassie, using the Lucy formula as she was pulled closer and closer.

'Sleep tight.'

'I will if you will.'

'All right.' A body-shaking yawn followed. When the arms dropped, Cassie was surprised by how cold she felt. The twins could get fiery hot.

As she followed Paul to the door, Tommy said thickly, 'Little boy's name?'

'Wilfred?'

'That's not nice name. He's called – he's called Thomas.' Freddy's voice was sleepy.

'No, he isn't,' said Cassie. 'He's called Trevor Junior.' She followed Paul to the upstairs landing.

He left the door ajar and shook his head. 'You're a natural born storyteller, Cassie Fenton.'

'It's not my story,' said Cassie, flushing.

'You made it yours. I disturbed you. Go back to your homework and I'll bring you something to drink. Not a cup of milk.'

'I like ordinary tea,' said Cassie, feeling bold. Her throat was dry.

'Tomorrow they'll want you to tell them all about Trevor Junior.'

Cassie went into her room, sat down at the small table, and drew the new notebook towards her. Her hands shook. Paul was wrong – the girls made up details for the story, so now it was their story as well as hers. She did not know how to feel about that.

Maybe she could write a story about what happened afterwards, like, did little Trevor want to see his new grandpa or did he start whingeing? Small kids were always whingeing. They had qualifications in whingeing, though the twins were not too bad, really. What if Catskin's dad got jealous about her nice kind husband? Emerald's dad. How odd the story felt with the names in it – Dorabelle and Trevor and Emerald. At least they hadn't asked for the name of Catskin's father.

Cassie would never have forgiven the parents, who let their daughter go away. That mother couldn't have loved her. Whatever the horrible father thought, if the mother had loved Catskin, she'd have looked for her, found her. She would definitely have searched for Emerald.

Squashing a pang, she wandered to the window and leaned out, inhaling the smell of lavender. It was like medicine for the pain in her chest. Why didn't Catskin's mother try to find her? Cassie hung over the sill and imagined letting go, floating out across the garden. Some bird or other was kicking up a fuss. It was very loud, very annoyed. Was it annoyed? Was it happy? She didn't understand bird language. Maybe there was a book about it.

Someone knocked at the door. Paul said, 'So sorry. I got side-tracked. Your tea. You haven't eaten any supper. I've put cheese and biscuits on the tray, and a packet of crisps and an apple. Luce says you have to eat the apple. It's getting late. Don't stay up too late.'

Cassie realised that she was hungry, after all. 'Thank you. Oh – chocolate.'

'We thought, well, you could do with a treat.'

She ate everything but the bar of chocolate before turning back to the desk and fingering the notebook again. The pages were beautifully smooth. It must have been quite expensive. The lines were very faint but she was glad of them. Her handwriting tended to straggle. They hardly ever wrote by hand at school. Time to get on with it. She opened the bar of chocolate.

Twelve: Tuesday evening

> MY FOSTER-PLACEMENT STORYBOOK
>
> My mother fell down in our flat, and I cried so much the woman in the flat across the landing came. I was too little to open the door. She said she was ringing 999. I don't know how the door was opened.
>
> FOSTER-PLACEMENT NUMBER ONE
> A lady took me away to stay with a family and I tried not to cry in case they rang 999 and I was taken away again. I know now that wouldn't happen.

Cassie read over what she had written and felt a twinge of panic at the idea of Freddy and Tommy being taken away because Lucy was too drunk to get up from the floor. She rubbed her eyes. What made her own mother drunk? The neighbour must have been awfully worried, listening to a little girl crying, not being able to get into the flat. She could remember the letter-box flapping, and blue eyes staring at her, as if it happened yesterday. She was sure that's what happened. She thought she could remember it. Perhaps it was a fake memory, like fake news. When had she discovered her mother had been drunk?

> I did not remember much except being cuddled by another lady. I was sent back to my mother after a few days, and could not forget how horrible she smelt when she was lying on the floor and being sick. I was still very young. I had just started going to school.

It was very odd to recall it all so strongly. Here she was in a really nice room, in Paul and Lucy's house, and her mind was full of another world, like in a dream. Was she a different girl in that world, in that flat? She stood up, took a couple of steps, sat down again.

> One day I could not wake up my mother. I knew it was time to go to school, so I got myself dressed in the scratchy pinafore and white blouse. The cuffs were a bit dirty and the blouse was all creased. This time I knew how to open the front door. I stood on the landing and stared at the opposite door. It was painted blue. I stood on tiptoe and rang the bell. The woman came out in a hurry and got upset, but I did not cry. She called the ambulance and a social worker arrived even before the ambulance. She was a different social worker from the last one. The neighbour said my mother had done

> it before but she already knew, the lady who came. She had what I thought was a sort of cardboard book and kept turning the pages. There must have been stuff about my mother from before. People had notes about me and my mother in a file.

When did she find out about social workers? They kept records but they never told her what was in their file. No wonder she got so angry sometimes. And when did she find out that her mother had drunk a bottle of vodka and taken a lot of her pills all at once?

Cassie hated being sick. Vomit tasted horrible and her throat hurt afterwards. It was too hard at the moment to think about her life as if she were an author telling the story of Cassie Fenton. She'd never be Cassie Clearwater if she didn't find a way of escaping from Cassie Fenton.

FOSTER-PLACEMENT NUMBER TWO

> I was placed with different foster-carers this time. The social worker taking me said they would look after me till my mother was well again. I stayed with them much longer. Their cat had kittens, little black and white ones. I loved cuddling them. They said I was good with small animals.

She chewed the end of her pen. Didn't some animals play tricks when they were scared, trying to protect their babies? It was not like lying, not exactly, but didn't some birds fly up high and make a lot of noise so people wouldn't find their nests or tread on their eggs? The people with the cats said the cat kept picking up the kittens in her mouth and trying to hide them. It was like a game, working out where she'd put them.

Either her mother was an evil cow or she was mad or deranged because if animals looked after their children then humans would. Humans were animals. Kyle. She chewed her lower lip.

> I wanted to go to the school I started at but the school couldn't take me. I wasn't in their area. The carers lived a long way from where I used to live, and their children were older than me. They went to secondary school. I had to go to school near where they lived. I remember the front door of the new school and we weren't supposed to go in without a receptionist letting us in. I couldn't manage the lessons. Nobody wanted to be my friend. Sometimes the social worker took me back to the old flat to see my mother. She drove me herself. It was a long journey, I was travel sick and once I threw up in her car. I think I wasn't truly travel-sick but frightened my mother might be ill again, or that the social worker

would decide I ought to live with her again.

Cassie put down the pen and shook her hand. It felt tight. She was supposed to be getting used to writing down answers, ready for exams, but this was different. She was writing about herself, and social workers, and the woman who was supposed to be her mother.

My mother cried very noisily, her nose was red and she shouted at the social worker. It didn't feel like I was going home. I didn't want her to cuddle me. I remember her nose was soggy. The social worker told me my mother was getting treatment. I think I stayed about two school terms with that family. I wonder now if my mother was given anti-depressants.

Cassie frowned. How had she known the people with the kittens lived in Barrow and her mother lived in Whitehaven? She picked up the pen again, hesitated. Why couldn't she think "we lived in Whitehaven"?

She thought about it again. There wasn't "we" or "us". It was me and her.

I always have to write 'my mother', I can't say 'my mum' or 'Mum' because that makes her sound as if she's important. Writing 'my mother' makes her sound as if she was almost

> separate from me. In the old days rich kids were looked after by a nanny. They were taken to see their mothers when they were clean and tidy.
>
> We talked about this in a history lesson. Some teachers in this school are quite good. A boy asked about kids who go to child-minders, who don't see their mothers much. He asked if child-minders are like nannies. Taylor got into a fight with him in the school yard after. Her mum is a child-minder.

Cassie stared at what she had written. How did she know what grown-ups were thinking when she had been a little girl? Her eyelids felt heavy, but she wanted to write at least one more entry before she went to bed. The black ink winked at her from the cream page. It was a beautiful book. The words seemed important because she was writing them out with a proper rollerball pen, even if her writing wasn't very neat. It was different on a computer.

> Anyway, I did go back to live with her again. On my 6th birthday she took me to a café for a treat. We had fish and chips. I didn't much like the taste of the fish. A man in the café came and stood at the table. He leaned over and touched my mother on her boob when he thought I wasn't

> Looking. He followed us home and she said I had to play on my own. I had a teddy, I think, but not much else but I knew I had to stay in the kitchen. I heard my mother shouting and the front door slamming. She made me stay in the kitchen. After a while I wanted to tell her I was bored but she wasn't in the sitting room or her bedroom. I found her in the bathroom. She was lying in the bath with her eyes closed, the water running and turning pink. Blood was running out of cuts on her wrists. I saw a big, empty bottle on the floor by the bath and I picked it up. it didn't have much smell. This time I knew how to use the phone. We learned at school.

Outside in the garden the birds were still calling, but more calmly now, properly singing to one another.

Did she really have to write down what came next?

Dr Hume said, "Sometimes, finding the words to say what we remember helps us to discover what we think."

> I rang 999. The operator asked my name and said I was a good girl. She asked if I was on my own in the flat. I said only my mother was there. The operator told me to wait till the

> ambulance came. I went back in the bathroom and turned off the taps. I pulled out the plug so all the water ran out. The plug was under my mother's feet so it was easy to get it. Then I opened the door for the ambulance people. I had tried to wrap towels around my mother's wrists. I remembered a foster-carer putting a bandage on my arm when I fell over so I had an idea about stopping blood.

She leaned her head on her hands, listening to the birds, letting the pictures from the past drift back as if they belonged to someone else, someone in a story.

> Blood smells so strong. I knew because of falling over. Also I had cut myself on the lid of a baked bean tin, and once I tried cutting bread. The neighbour came in when she heard the sirens. The neighbour tried to tie a knot in the towels but it didn't work because the towels were soggy.

Cassie's head drooped. She was back in the bathroom with the neighbour standing in the bathroom doorway, wiping her hands on her scarf and telling the ambulance ladies that Cassie's mother had done it all before, and it was disgusting when she had her little girl still living with her, and she shouldn't be allowed to have children. Her scarf was red, red as blood.

The pen rolled out of Cassie's hand towards the edge of

the table and she started, grabbed it. The picture in her head was as clear as if it she had seen the red scarf yesterday.

> One of the paramedics said I should go into the sitting room. The neighbour took me, made me sit down. Then she went back to the bathroom.
>
> There were two women on the ambulance. They told me they were first aiders, and said I was very brave and clever. But I felt cold. I didn't know why my mother had cut herself. Nobody asked me about the knife she must have used and I hadn't seen it. I suppose she dropped it over the side of the bath or something like that.

Cassie stood up, knocking back the chair as yet another memory clawed its way out. She had been afraid her mother would turn the knife on Cassie. The very thought was a monster in the back of her mind. She almost lost her balance as she dropped back on to the chair.

> I don't know why the neighbour left me on my own and went back into the bathroom. Maybe she wanted to see everything, maybe she was bit scared. She didn't have any children herself. Maybe she was afraid to stay with a girl whose mother had cut her wrists

and made blood run into the water.

Some grown-ups were like that, frightened of children, not liking them. Cassie had stayed with foster-carers who didn't much like children. They were the ones who rang up the duty team. "You've got to take her away today. I can't cope with her running away nonsense any more." Cassie knew about the duty team, the social workers who took the calls and had to stay late, sorting out somewhere for her to stay over the weekend. Four times – she counted on her fingers, to be sure – four times the foster-carers had rung up and said they couldn't keep her any longer, and Cassie had ended up outside the council offices with her clothes in a black bin-liner or stuffed into old carrier bags. Just once she'd been given an old suitcase. She couldn't remember what had happened to it.

She couldn't write any more, not tonight. There was too much fuzz in her head. The monster was still there, hiding. Still, Lucy was nearby, and Paul. She sat on the bed, picked up the bar of chocolate and finished it. She would be able to sleep.

Stella

Thirteen: Wednesday 10:00

Dr Fleet: Good morning. Take a seat. I see you've just registered. What can I do for you?
Stella: Social worker said I'd got to come.
Dr Fleet: I see. It'll take a while for your records to come through. Tell me why you're here.
Stella: That social worker said I've got to come. She says it's my pills.
Dr Fleet: You've been prescribed medication? For what condition?
Stella: I got all screwed up and I couldn't sleep. I need something so I can sleep.
Dr Fleet: You want more sleeping pills? I can't just issue a repeat prescription, you know.
Stella: Benzo-something.
Dr Fleet: Benzodiazepine?
Stella: That's the one.
Dr Fleet: We usually only give a short course. How many were you prescribed?
Stella: I can't be doing with this, I'm going.
Dr Fleet: Wait a moment – come back and sit down. You look very tired.
Stella: What are you doing?

Dr Fleet: I'm going to take your pulse. No, don't talk. Relax your arm.

Okay.

A bit on the fast side. Why did your social worker suggest you should come to see me?

Stella: I told you, I can't sleep.

Dr Fleet: I can't just issue drugs without good reason, without knowing your history.

Stella: That's my business.

Dr Fleet: We aren't going to get far if you lose your temper. Which practice gave you the prescription? Do you recall the doctor?

Stella: Can't remember. Maryport. I had a cleaning job, caravan site.

Dr Fleet: Was that the first time you were prescribed Diazepam?

Stella: That's the name. I've had it before.

Dr Fleet: Before this recent episode? Where was that?

Stella: I don't remember.

Dr Fleet: You should have been regularly monitored. How often did you go back for a check-up?

Stella: I never.

Dr Fleet: Were you having panic attacks? That's one reason for the prescription.

Stella: Might have.

Dr Fleet: You're still very tense. Sit back a bit, relax. What makes you so on edge?

Stella: I don't have to tell you.

Dr Fleet: Why did a social worker suggest you should register as a patient here? It can't have been simply to give you access to drugs without monitoring.

Take your time.

Stella: You keep looking at your watch.

Dr Fleet: I'm sorry. The waiting room is full. We've a lot of patients today but I'm not sending you away without helping you.

Stella: They took my baby and I want to see her.

Dr Fleet: How old is the baby?

Stella: They took all my babies. It's not fair.

Dr Fleet: Oh dear. Look, I can give you something for the next few days to help you relax and sleep but you'll have to come back. How often have you been pregnant?

Stella: Lots. I dunno.

Dr Fleet: I'll wait for your records to arrive. There's a box of tissues by your elbow.

Stella: You men like it when us women cry. It makes you feel like you're in charge.

Dr Fleet: I think we need a blood test. Ask at Reception for an appointment with our specialist nurse, please. How long have you had a social worker?

Stella: Years and years, off and on. All different. Only just got this one.

Dr Fleet: You still haven't exactly made clear why she has referred you to me.

Stella: She said she couldn't force me. Said she wouldn't know what I said. She don't know much anyway. What do you want blood for?

Dr Fleet:: I'm writing a prescription for enough tablets to last three days. Make another appointment as soon as possible for the bloods. They'll know at Reception.

Stella: You're a bit young.

***Dr Fleet*:**: I am, of course, getting older by the second. Here you are. Good morning.

Fourteen: Wednesday 23:14

> **We're waiting for your call.**
> Whatever you're going through, a Samaritan will face it with you.
> We're here 24 hours a day, 365 days a year. Call 116 123

M65: *Hello, Samaritans.*
Caller: Are you writing stuff down about me? I bet you got this call switched on loud so everyone can have a big laugh.
M65: *Only you and I are on this call. Have you called Samaritans before?*
Caller: What's it to you?
M65: *You sound rather agitated.*
Caller: You all say the same things, you got a script. Somebody tells you what to say.
M65: *We listen to you. That's the most important thing.*
Caller: Yeah, that's what you all say, like there's a script. I bet there's only two or three of you and you change your voices and accents so you sound like you're different.
M65: *You rang tonight. Something is on your mind. What would you like to tell me?*
Caller: I wish I hadn't told about Shane. It brought it all back and I don't like it all back.
M65: *It brought back memories, is that what you mean?*
Caller: Why you asking about Shane? I said I didn't want to talk about him.
M65: *You've talked about Shane on another call?*

Caller: I can't stand the women in the hostel. They give me the creeps.

M65: You're in a hostel? Can you explain how you feel about that?

Caller: Told you didn't I? Told you I can't stand them.

M65: What does 'I can't stand them' mean to you?

Caller: They look at me funny. The woman in the next room, she took my nice shampoo and stuff. We haven't got locks on our doors, I told the woman in charge, the warden is it, I told her we ought to get padlocks.

M65: What did she say?

Caller: We got to trust one another. She's bollocking arsehole mad.

M65: You don't trust the others?

Caller: You never lived in a hostel, did you?

M65: Your experience is what matters to us.

Caller: Oh yeah? Well, I'm getting back at them. Did a bit of lifting today.

M65: Lifting? What do you mean?

Caller: Lifting, that's going in a shop and taking what you got to have. Not stealing, not thieving, not creeping into somebody's bedroom when she's got no lock for her door, when she's never going get hold of one – you tell me, is that the same as just lifting a couple items from a shop when they got masses and nobody's looking. If they looked, that'd be different.

M65: You took something from a shop. How do you feel about that?

Caller: They never pay attention in charity shops. And that jacket, it kind of sang to me when I went in the shop. It was so pretty. It said take me so I did. Label said £20.

M65: *Why do you think the jacket sang to you?*
Caller: I'm wearing it now. It's like patchwork only expensive. It got an expensive label in it. Some rich bitch bought it. I got it free. I'd love to swing it under Shane's nose.
M65: *Shane?*
Caller: I told the other one about Shane. I'm not doing it again. If you lot can't organise yourselves ...
M65: *You sound upset when you mention Shane.*
Caller: If that woman in the next room gives me funny looks again she's for it.
M65: *Funny looks?*
Caller: You must've had funny looks. Everyone gets funny looks.
You doing that silent thing?
M65: *What sort of look is it that you call a funny look?*
Caller: They look at me sideways, like I was dogshit on their shoes. They move off when I come in the kitchen to make my toast. I feel like punching them in the throat.
M65: *They make you feel unimportant?*
Caller: Yeah – I feel like, like I'm all squashed flat, like I'm pressed down on the pavement, like –
I don't want to talk about this any more.
M65: *Do you want to finish the call?*
Caller: Yes. No. Wait. No.
M65: *Do you have anyone to help you?*
Caller: She's fucking useless.
M65: *Have you shared with this person how you feel about being in a hostel?*
Caller: She said I'd got to stay there till she finds me another place to myself, if I get my baby back.

M65: *You have a baby?*
Caller rings off.

Fifteen: Thursday 02:33

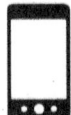

Phone recording

Cassie, remember this, it's dead important. Men are all wankers. They stick it in some bit of you can't fight back. My dad's brother, my uncle Luke, he was all over me, he said I was his special little girl, well, I bit his dick once only he clobbered me so hard I couldn't hear out of my left ear for weeks.

I just played this back and my voice changes when I talk about him. This woman sounds rough, like she drinks too much but I don't drink much.

Where are you? What are you doing? Why won't you talk to me? You're never ever to see your granddad nor his friends. Nor Luke. They're all in Whitehaven still. Don't come to Whitehaven. It was good sometimes when we all went on the beach. We went at night. My dad never knew. I felt safer on the beach. At school they told us to take care when we were out at night, us girls. I could have told them, what's the point? Home's the worst place. They lock the doors and they can do what they want.

I like Whitehaven really. I remember bad things, that's the trouble. You got to find ways of not remembering bad stuff. I can't get it out of my head. I have to say it over and over and over. It's not fair. Nobody should of taken you away. They should of left you with me. I was a brilliant mum.

Cassie

Sixteen: Thursday morning

Mr Hetherington handed out the books and when she got her copy Cassie almost shouted. It was *The Great Gatsby* and she had already started it. Lucy said it used to be one of her favourite books. The writer had a way of describing that Cassie wanted to try out for herself when she rewrote her story.

> The wind had blown off, leaving a loud, bright night, with wings beating in the trees and a persistent organ sound as if the full bellows of the earth blew the frogs full of life.

Cassie didn't know what bellows were and had to ask Paul. To her surprise, he poked about beside the grey stone fireplace in the sitting room and pulled out a gadget that puzzled her. It was made from two pieces of wood, shaped like the ace of spades in a set of cards, with leather sides and a nozzle at the end. 'Try it,' he said, swinging it between his fingers. Cassie discovered that if she flattened the wooden paddles together, air shot out through the nozzle with a farty, wheezy sound that made her snort. It was like the kind of fart that gets away from you.

Paul brushed his flyaway hair out of his eyes. 'We use it to get the fire going, sometimes, if we run out of breath.'

Cassie hadn't paid a lot of attention to the fireplace. She noticed now that someone, probably Paul, had added to the pile of logs on either side of the small black stove with windows in it. The bellows leaned against the stones, beside the fire-irons. She had to ask what they were when she first saw the little brush, shovel, and pair of tongs.

'Why are you interested in bellows?'

She had shown him the copy of *The Great Gatsby*.

* * *

Mr Hetherington was an old man with white hair thick as a brush and wide red cheeks. Taylor's best mate, Bagsy, was in a different English group but even all by herself Taylor could set the whole row of desks clattering. She had some kind of psychic power that helped her get other people to do what she wanted, like lifting their desks on their knees so that the metal legs banged against one another. Today she sat in the middle of the back row, sharing her desk with a boy whose face was so pale his spots were like red paint blotches. Most people sat two to a desk but nobody sat with Cassie. Taylor did not allow it.

Mr Hetherington said, 'Anyone seen the film of the book? There's an old version. As a matter of fact, I believe there are at least two but a new one came out not so long ago. It's a story that film directors keep coming back to. While we read it, I'd like you to imagine what scenes and characters you would pick out for a film version, supposing you were the director.'

Something small and hard smacked into the back of Cassie's head. She did not move, even when a second short, thick screw skidded off the edge of her desk and rolled across the floor tiles. Mr Hetherington sighed, put down his copy, and began to walk slowly forwards. Cassie stiffened and dug her fingernails into the palms of her hands. It was going to happen again. It so was not fair. He bent down – his knees creaked – scooped up the screws, and walked past Cassie without speaking, until he stopped in front of Taylor and the boy. After a moment Cassie turned around. Everyone else was staring. The boy, Jason, was in Taylor's gang because his dad had a garage with a lot of old cars on the forecourt. He knew how to drive already. His dad was teaching him to do brake spins. That's what everybody said.

'Thank you, Taylor. I'll take the bag to enlarge my collection of Taylor souvenirs. By the time you leave the school, I'll have enough memorabilia of you to set up my own auction house.'

Taylor's face cracked. 'Dunno – I don't know what you mean, sir.'

'Oh dear, really? This is so tiring. I hoped I was not going to have to Feng Shui my classroom for you every time you come into it, but I see that there is no alternative. Back here at the end of school today, Taylor. You can rearrange the desks. I'll give you the floor plan and of course I'll be watching to make sure you don't disturb the energy flow.'

'I got – I got an important thing after school, sir, you can't make me.'

'No, I do apologise, you are right. I'll ring your parents tonight to make sure they understand the situation and you can rearrange my room tomorrow after school. The rest of my students will cope, I'm sure, with an energy flow that harnesses your – um – your forcefulness.'

People laughed and Taylor glared at Cassie, narrowing her eyes. She shook her head in a barely noticeable way that made Cassie's stomach muscles tighten.

'And the bag, please?' Mr Hetherington held out his hand.

Squinting through thick black mascara, Taylor said, 'What?' Then she said, 'Sir?'

Jason's spots were bright red. Cassie guessed that the evidence had been shoved in his direction. She'd often had stuff dropped on her in the past. She knew how it felt to have something slimy and wet arrive in her lap or be shoved into the arch of her back, but it would be different for Jason. He was in it, whatever it was.

They got to the end of the lesson without anyone else kicking off. Mr Hetherington was popular. He coached football in the winter and athletics in the summer, and hardly anyone – apart from Taylor, who was sometimes too stupid to work it out – messed about in his classes. He didn't shout, wasn't sarcastic, much, knew everybody's names, knew their parents and their aunts and uncles and cousins. He had been teaching at the school forever.

As they filed out for the mid-morning break, he touched Cassie lightly on the shoulder, holding her back. 'You looked almost pleased when I gave out the books. I don't think I've seen you smile since you started here. What – five weeks, six weeks ago?'

Cassie shrugged.

'I see what's happening to you, Cassie. I don't have to wait for anyone else to tell me. I also see how you write. We've only had a couple of assignments so far, but you have an interesting turn of phrase that suggests to me you enjoy writing.'

She was afraid to answer.

'I do not allow intimidation in my classes.'

'No sir, I noticed.' The words were out before she could stop them, and to her relief, he threw back his head in a cough of laughter.

'There's more to you than meets the eye, I am quite sure. Have you met *The Great Gatsby* before?'

'We – I got a copy at, at –.' She could not say, at home. 'Where I'm staying.'

'Yes,' he said, scratching his head. 'Your Mrs Robinson is

the chief practice nurse at my doctor's. She can put the fear of God in me if she thinks she ought. My waistline.' He slapped his stomach. It wasn't bulging over the top of his waistband. 'Yes.' He eyed Cassie and smiled again. 'I hear their kids are rather a handful. Did Mrs Robinson give you the novel?'

'You know about the twins?'

'You realise everybody knows everybody else round here.'

'The twins ... I mean, they're not bad or anything.' She was surprised by the urge to defend them.

'I'm sure they are not. Any household handing out *The Great Gatsby* to you must have lots of character in it. I like pupils who ask a lot of questions, sensible questions, obviously. That's all I meant about them being a handful. It's okay, Cassie, my daughter teaches at the primary school they go to. You'd better get along or you'll miss break.'

Cassie didn't know what to say. He talked to her as if she was just another ordinary person, same as Lucy or Paul. He had a daughter.

'Off you go,' he said again, making pushing movements with both hands.

She went outside into the corridor and stood for a moment in front of the notices, wondering where Taylor would be for break. The bell would ring soon. It was safer here than with the others. Her gaze flickered over the notices about theatre trips and good films to watch on TV, and best-selling books. Mr Hetherington really believed some kids would read his notices. Well, she supposed she was paying attention now. She tried to imagine what it was like to be Mr Hetherington's daughter, talking to her dad about kids in her school. He talked to Cassie about the nurse at the doctor's. It was like gossip, only not. They said nice things about other people. What would he say if he knew Lucy said about the twins, "I could fucking well kill them"? She didn't mean it, though. Probably not.

Maybe it was useful, getting angry like that, like having a roaring beast inside you, no, a racehorse, and you let your racehorse out when you have to get somewhere really fast, but not in a supermarket.

Seventeen: Thursday lunchtime

Taylor and Bagsy were waiting in the girls' toilets after lunch. As soon as Cassie pushed through the swing door, the other girls squirmed away, apart from the two who grabbed her arms and hauled her inside.

Cassie did not struggle or speak. The sooner this was over, the better. She knew exactly how to keep her face straight and smooth, even when her heart was banging so hard she was afraid they could hear it.

Taylor said, 'This shithole, this load of crap had a go at our Kyle. She grabbed his dick, tried to get the pants off him.'

'Trying to give him a blowjob was she? Cocksucker. They're all cocksuckers, girls like her.' Bagsy was enjoying herself.

'She's been in hundreds of places, nobody wants her, nobody can't bear having her in the house, my aunt's cool, the kids love her, but she couldn't have this one in the place not with the others. They're all vul – vul'nable, they got to be looked after like specially, like my aunt does.'

A small plastic bag of screws thudded on to the tiles at Cassie's feet. 'Swallow them, right now, or we'll shove them down for you.'

She only had to swallow one. A passing teacher heard the cheering and banged into the cloakroom.

Cassie's throat was sore but she had managed to bite Bagsy's fingers.

Obviously, nobody was going to tell the teacher what was going on. She sent them off for afternoon classes, after the usual lecture about poor punctuality leading to poor results and how if there was one more episode like this they would be in supervised isolation, on individual learning plans, with every lesson reported to parents. Did they understand?

Cassie hung back from the others when they scuttled along the corridor. She was panicking about the small brass screw sitting in her stomach. Then she remembered one of the houses where the mum thought her little boy had swallowed a pin and made him eat bread and butter. He was okay afterwards. Cassie crept into the empty dining room where dinner ladies were still cleaning up. A bowl of biscuits had not yet been cleared away, so she grabbed an individually wrapped pack of four digestives, guiltily dropped a fifty pence coin beside the bowl, and slid back into the corridor. She would be late for the next lesson, but frantically swallowed four biscuits as fast as she could.

She wished she could tell someone. Dr Hume said she should.

They were not going to beat her this time. If she told, they'd come after her again. It never worked, telling the adults.

Her throat was sore. It wasn't as bad as anything Kyle did, though.

When Paul picked her up from the bus she felt too sick to talk. A biscuity mess lay heavily in her stomach, the back of her throat was sore and her wrists hurt. Lucy spotted the red marks as soon as she got in from the surgery. Cassie didn't tell about the screws, but she said a bit about the gang of girls in the toilets. Paul had to stop Lucy from ringing up and leaving messages on the school's answerphone. He said there had already been a phone call from school but he wasn't going to talk about it now.

That night, after the twins had gone to bed and Lucy and Paul were out in the garden doing something to the climbing frame, Cassie pulled out the red and gold notebook. It was time to write about Rod and Sarah.

FOSTER-PLACEMENT NUMBER THREE

It was only one night but I suppose I have to count it as a placement, the night after my mother cut her wrists. The social worker drove me to the new place. It was good at first because I knew them, I had stayed with them before but they didn't want me to stay for more than a night because they had another foster-girl and they didn't have room for me. Her name was Rosie but she was horrible. She pinched me. The kittens had all grown up and gone away and the cat was old and didn't want to be picked up.

FOSTER-PLACMENT NUMBER FOUR

I don't know why people think if you have a pretty name like Rosie you must be nice. But it was lucky they didn't want me because the social worker took me to stay with Rod and Sarah. Everything changed with them. They rescued me. That's how I remember it, even though I had to go away from them when Rod died. After that everything was bad.

Nobody was as kind and good as Rod and Sarah.

The other foster-carers were nice in their way but Sarah and Rod made me feel important. My mother, I couldn't unremember her lying on the floor, or in the bed or the bath, and though she did take me to school, mostly, and make sure I cleaned my teeth, she was so miserable it was like I wasn't there, she didn't see me. It wasn't as if her eyes didn't work. I was invisible.

Why is 'unremember' a better word than 'forget'? When you forget, it's like you don't choose, whatever it is you forget disappears, but when you don't want to remember something you have to undo your brain.

Anyway, I got angry with her. Why did she have a baby if she didn't want to be a proper mother? I wanted to kick her but I didn't. I told her I hated her and I was never going to see her again. The social worker said I shouldn't say things like that to my real mother. I wanted to say she was not my real mother, Sarah was like my real mother, except she didn't want me after Rod died. It was like something dried up inside me, like a —

What had she felt when Sarah said she couldn't be Cassie's foster-carer any more? She leaned her forehead on her hands. Why was she remembering Stella Fenton when she'd started writing about Rod and Sarah? She put the cap on the pen, gripped the edge of the table and tried counting backwards from thirty. Who was it who'd told her about counting back to get in charge of herself? Cassie had seen so many people she forgot what their titles were, especially after a social worker said there was too much turnover in the staff.

Cassie had a label. She was a young person, and there were old people and mental health people and homeless people and disabled and children and too much turnover.

Writing by hand in this beautiful notebook about horrible things was very strange. She half-wished she could use a computer instead.

Eighteen: Friday evening

Lucy poured tea into a fat white mug and gestured to Cassie, who was in charge of the plate of thick yellow cheese. The plate had a picture of Muncaster Castle painted in the middle. She followed Lucy into the sitting room where Paul sat at a small table pushed against the window. It was his work desk.

Lucy patted the top of his head, where the hair was thinnest. 'Cassie and I had omelettes. I'll make one for you when you're ready, if you fancy it.'

'That's nice.'

'The twins had chimpanzees to tea.'

'That's nice. What?' Paul's elbow jerked and papers floated off his desk.

'You've had a long day, Paul. You ought to eat something.' Paul picked up the tea, gulped, gulped again. 'This will be fine. I grabbed a sandwich at five when I knew I was going to be late.'

'It's going to be okay, is it, combining work and all these assignments you've got to write?'

'I had to finish those accounts. They brought the deadline forward. I've got to take this assignment with me.'

Paul was going away at the weekend for his training course. Cassie had never seen an adult doing homework before. He kept scratching his head and sighing.

'Paul, is it going to be as hard going as this for the next three years?'

'What do you mean?'

'You keep sighing, my love.' Lucy fingered the little gold cross sitting in the hollow of her neck.

'Oh well, us accountants don't go in for writing essays.'

'What's this one about?'

'Tell the story of my journey towards ordination.'

'What does that mean? You can't get ordained till you've finished the qualification.'

'I've got a framework for writing it, they gave us one, some suggestions anyway. It'll be okay, but I wanted to get some ideas down now, before I forget them.'

'How much longer, do you think?'

'Give me five minutes, then I'm done. Cassie, you look as if you're bursting to ask something.'

Cassie stared at the framed photos of the nearby fells. Lucy said she took the photos years ago, when she and Paul camped in the valley and climbed the mountains. Her favourite was Great Gable but Scafell Pike was a good one, too, all craggy on top. It was one of the highest mountains. Cassie couldn't tell from the photos whether one mountain was higher than another. They all looked similar to her.

She asked the question. 'Can we go up a mountain at half-term?'

'It would be fun,' said Lucy. 'We ought to get the twins up somewhere not too challenging.'

From the corner of her eye, Cassie watched Lucy tighten the soft green silk scarf around her curls, pulling them into a bunch at the nape of her neck. 'I don't think we're on Cassie's wavelength this evening. You should have seen us in the shop this afternoon when I took the plastic off the shopping. I really embarrassed her. I swear you thought the shopkeeper was getting ready to shout at me, didn't you? He's an eco-freak too, honest.'

Cassie's fists tightened. They'd stop thinking they knew all about her if she chucked the cheese over the floor or puked up a screw. Well, the screw was in the bottom of the toilet bowl now.

'Sorry.' Lucy tried to straighten her face. 'Let's go back in the kitchen till Paul's finished. We're distracting him.'

She led the way out of the sitting room but stopped by the open door. 'You weren't to know he's on the village eco-shopping team. Mike, I mean, in the shop. He's got those big tanks in now, Paul, so we can take empty plastic bottles, like washing-up liquid, and washing liquid for clothes and just fill up. It's good, isn't it? I thought we'd take a bottle for shampoo next time. What d'you think, Cassie?'

Cassie glared at the doorknob. They always did this, they kept on asking what she thought. Is it better keeping this old fridge or getting a more energy-efficient one? Cassie, one of the doctors at our practice is getting rid of his daughter's bike, it's too small, would you ride one if I brought it home?

It was like they saw gates to open where she saw great big stone walls. 'Suppose.' The kitchen table was still covered in shopping. Lucy used rough brown bags – she said they were made of jute – and recycled practically everything into bins in the shed. The twins had jobs to do, like carrying newspaper and empty cardboard boxes and tins and bottles, out to the shed, but after watching Freddy drop a pile of shredded paper, which blew everywhere in the garden, Cassie found herself jumping up to open doors, or collect whatever fell out of their arms.

At least Lucy didn't tell Paul that she, Cassie, had hidden behind the shelves while Lucy was stripping off all the plastic wrapping and dropping it into the waste bin. If the shopkeeper had lost his temper and shouted at Lucy, Cassie might have had to step out and give him a slap. Already, after only six weeks with them, Cassie wanted people to like Lucy.

It was not a feeling she was used to.

'Cassie, did you have a chance to check out the shampoo? Would we like it?'

Paul wandered into the kitchen, flapping sheets of printed paper. 'Done. I'm done. I can't write another word. If my supervisor doesn't like my life-story ....'

His life-story must be so different from hers. She bet he wouldn't be remembering a black plastic bin liner dropped on the pavement outside the council offices, a cardboard box dumped on a desk, breaking along one side so that a pair of her knickers fell out on the floor. Once she'd taken the whole lot out into the corridor and pissed on it. She'd been twelve. There'd been a row. Paul said his story was supposed to be about his journey to ordination, so did he only write down parts, not everything? She wished she could write her imagined story instead, only she hadn't got another notebook.

'Cassie, you look as if you're about to ask another question. Oops.' Paul caught a couple of oranges as they rolled towards the edge of the table and carefully put them in the fruit bowl.

'I wasn't.'

'Go on,' said Lucy, shifting the fruit bowl to the dresser. 'You do look as if you're brooding on something.'

Cassie took a deep breath. 'Could I borrow a laptop for a bit?' Paul and Lucy exchanged glances. Paul said, 'That's a perfectly sensible request. We did wonder, didn't we, love? You can borrow mine.'

'What — you mean, right now?'

'Don't sound so incredulous,' said Lucy. 'I've a few jobs for the holy man to get on with.'

'Like what? No, save it, let me set up for Cassie. I can give you a separate log-in. I expect most of the kids at school have their own laptops or tablets.'

He was right. There was plenty of boasting at school

about flatscreen tvs in bedrooms, playstations, gaming consoles – even the kids with hardly any money in their pockets had top-end haircuts, and smartphones. Cassie would rather have the money. One day she might have to run away for good and she'd need money, not stuff. Stuff was what other people decided she should have.

'I'll set you up with a username.' Paul grabbed an apple, took a deep, splashy bite, and went back to his laptop.

'Go,' said Lucy, giving her a gentle push. 'He means it.'

Cassie followed him back to the sitting room. Looking over his arm, Cassie saw that the username he typed into the box was Catskin. 'Oh. Thanks.'

'Set your own password. Don't make it easy for us to guess. I've already set the internet protocols so you shouldn't get into trouble.'

Cassie made up a password, settled herself in the chair made warm by Paul. He adjusted its height before going back into the kitchen. She was alone with the blank screen. At school, the blank screen often made her feel panicky but this evening she was excited.

The program was the same as on the school network. She opened a new document, selected her favourite Comic Sans and began to type.

> Once upon a time there was a small girl whose parents began to quarrel. She could not cry where they might see her. She could not cry if they could hear her. And then they were angry with her, just because she knew they were quarrelling.
>
> 'Leave this house and wait in the garden,'

said the father in his deep, hard voice. So the little girl ran out. She was afraid, because it was the middle of the night, and the wind was angry and the rain made her nightdress very wet. She stood under a tree, touching its bark with her fingers, while her feet grew colder and colder and the dark grew blacker and blacker, like black paint dripping on black cloth.

Suddenly a little bird flew down from the tree and landed on her shoulder. It twittered softly into her ear, dug its tiny claws into the soft place on her neck, and flapped its wings. When the feathers brushed her cheek she heard it speak in a squeaky sort of sound.

'You do not belong here. They are not your true parents. You must go seeking through the wide world to find your real mother and father. They are crying because they have lost you.'

The girl curled her toes into the moss under the tree and wished she had remembered to put on her shoes. 'How will I know them?'

The bird's words sounded a bit like a song. 'When the time comes, I will fly to your feet and tell you.'

'But where must I go and how will I travel? The wind is so cold and the night is so dark. When do I start?'

The bird flew down from her shoulder to

perch on the back of her hand, and the stars and moon came out. They turned the garden silver.

'The next breath you take, the next beat of your heart.'

Cassie pushed back the chair, frowned, saw her reflection on the screen and scowled at it. She wanted the bird to give a rhyme to the girl, a rhyme the girl could remember and use every time she faced a challenge and had to move on to the next place. But what words rhymed with 'heart'?

She tried words out under her breath.

'Start, part, depart, upstart, dart, cart, fart –. '

'How are you doing?'

Paul had wandered into the room.

Cassie hit esc, her heart thundering.

'Don't do that – did you save? Did I set up the autosave? Move over, Cassie.'

'It doesn't matter.' She bit her tongue so hard that her eyes watered.

'You've been at least half an hour concentrating on whatever you're doing. I came in twenty minutes ago for my book and you didn't flicker.'

She got up, blinking. As he sat in the chair, lowering it to suit his long legs, Cassie stared at him. He seemed normal enough, an ordinary dad, always brushing his fine brown hair away from his eyes. Why didn't Lucy didn't nag him to get a shorter cut? Maybe it was because his forehead was so high and bony and he wanted to hide it. He had a long, straight nose and a short upper lip that he was chewing at the moment, looking for Cassie's document. His ears were like Tommy's, flat against his head.

Would Tommy grow up with wide bony shoulders, like his? Tommy's shoulders were wider than Freddy's already. Would that make her more like a boy than a girl? Cassie hadn't ever given much thought to twins, though kittens in the same litter could have completely different markings — but only because the female would have mated with different toms. She shifted weight from foot to foot, uncomfortable about where her thoughts were taking her. Fathers had to trust the mothers to tell the truth about their babies, unless they went for DNA tests ...

She must have made a sound for Paul swung round. 'It's okay, don't worry, I found it. I'm saving it to a USB pen drive, so you won't lose it again.'

'Thanks. Thanks. It's a story I'm writing.' Her face screwed into a scowl. It was stupid, giving away stuff like that. The heat rose to her cheeks.

'Of course, you're a great reader. Are you going to be another F Scott Fitzgerald?' Cassie stiffened. Was he poking fun? Again, her face must have given her away, for Paul stood up quickly and set the chair back at the right height. 'I'd better get on, all those jobs Lucy has. Need to get stuff together for my course.'

'You keep saying.'

'I must be repeating myself. You'll have heard Lucy complaining.'

Cassie felt mildly apologetic. 'I don't get that god-stuff.'

Paul said, 'It doesn't matter.'

'Your god's a man.'

Paul scratched his head, sighing. 'That's one of the myths I have to dispel.'

'I thought it says he and him and father in all the stories.' Cassie sat down, glaring at the screen. The icon for the USB winked at her.

'Not all of them,' said Paul. She heard him move

towards the door. 'Myths are pictures of the truth. Aren't stories like that, too? You don't take them literally but they speak to your experience.'

Cassie could not think of what to say. The tone of his comment surprised her. He was looking at her. 'I didn't realise you wrote your own stuff as well as telling stories to the twins. Maybe you'll let us read your stories one day.'

'It's not like your story.'

'I sincerely hope not. Mine's for me and my supervisor. But proper stories change lives.'

Cassie wanted to say that nobody else's story ever changed her life, except the story of Catskin, obviously. 'What you're writing for your supervisor, is it about being an accountant?'

'Well, a little, of course. I'm still doing some work for the firm.' He leaned in the doorway, arms folded. She saw new lines on his face. 'I've to go into the Whitehaven office but I'll probably have to keep on at our branches in Carlisle and Penrith too. I'm keeping my options open. I might want to carry on working as an accountant when I'm ordained. You're frowning. I mean, I don't know yet whether I want to be attached to a church, have us all live in a house next to a church, or carry on like now, still living here, but taking church services and helping out.'

'You might all leave here?' Cassie did not mean her voice to crack.

Paul cocked his head. 'In three years, when I finish, you'll be nearly eighteen.'

A cold shiver ran down Cassie's back. When she was eighteen, she'd be on her own for ever. That was what she'd been told. Actually, once she was sixteen they might move her into a flat and leave her. She had been telling herself for years that she couldn't wait to be on her own. That would mean living alone next year – in a year's time. She shivered.

'You'll be able to decide exactly what you want to do, Cassie.' Choice? After all these years of being told? 'Lucy and I hope you choose to stay with us as long as you want. Imagine, after three years living with Freddy and Tommy, they'd hate it if you went away.'

She glanced at his bony face, the blue eyes watching her.

'Cassie? You okay?'

She shrugged, struggling with the new sensation of a carer wanting her to like him.

Stella

> **We're waiting for your call.**
> Whatever you're going through, a Samaritan will face it with you.
> We're here 24 hours a day, 365 days a year. Call 116 123

Nineteen: Saturday 08:22

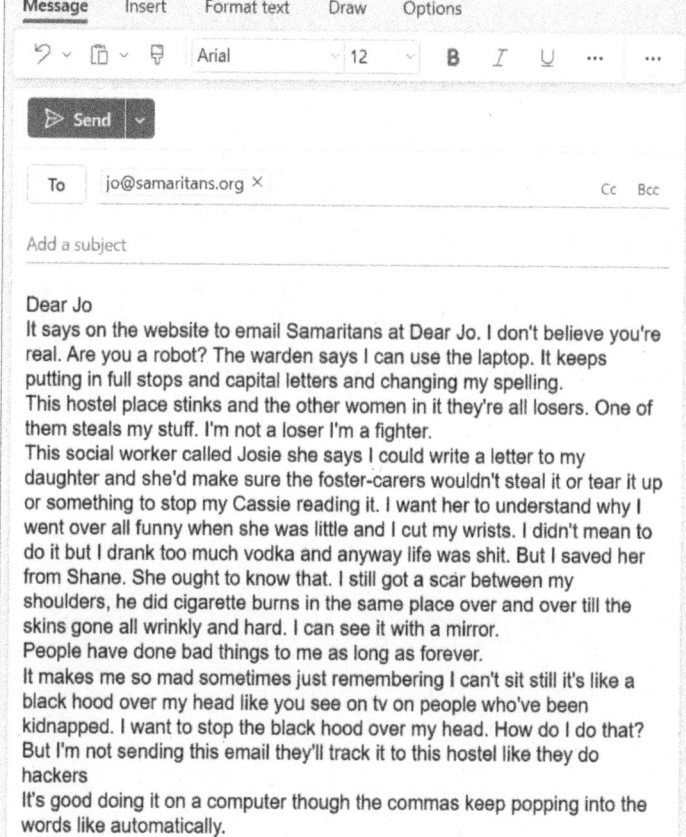

To: jo@samaritans.org

Dear Jo

It says on the website to email Samaritans at Dear Jo. I don't believe you're real. Are you a robot? The warden says I can use the laptop. It keeps putting in full stops and capital letters and changing my spelling.
This hostel place stinks and the other women in it they're all losers. One of them steals my stuff. I'm not a loser I'm a fighter.
This social worker called Josie she says I could write a letter to my daughter and she'd make sure the foster-carers wouldn't steal it or tear it up or something to stop my Cassie reading it. I want her to understand why I went over all funny when she was little and I cut my wrists. I didn't mean to do it but I drank too much vodka and anyway life was shit. But I saved her from Shane. She ought to know that. I still got a scar between my shoulders, he did cigarette burns in the same place over and over till the skins gone all wrinkly and hard. I can see it with a mirror.
People have done bad things to me as long as forever.
It makes me so mad sometimes just remembering I can't sit still it's like a black hood over my head like you see on tv on people who've been kidnapped. I want to stop the black hood over my head. How do I do that?
But I'm not sending this email they'll track it to this hostel like they do hackers
It's good doing it on a computer though the commas keep popping into the words like automatically.

Twenty: Saturday 08:49

Dear Cassie
I want you to come and live with me like we did when you were little and it was ok. We had a nice little flat didn't we, and I can get one again if you live with me. I am starting on a clinic so I wont take the pills any more

I don't see men a lot now though a womans got her natural urges but I cant have any more babies something went wrong after they took you I got another fellow but the baby didnt come out properly and they had to take it all away. I mean I havent got the bits any more they botched it up. They treat you like muck

Shes not going to let me write that so I cant give her this letter but it makes me feel good writing it down, the world is full of fuckers and the sooner you know it the better for you girl. Anyway my handwriting is terrible

Twenty-one: Sunday 02:46

> **We're waiting for your call.**
> Whatever you're going through, a Samaritan will face it with you.
> We're here 24 hours a day, 365 days a year. Call 116 123

P162: *Hello, Samaritans.*
Caller: I want to talk to a woman.
P162: *How can I help you?*
Caller: I talked to a woman last time. I'm not talking to a man.
P162: *If you prefer you can ring back.*
Caller: Feel like stopping it all, just getting a knife and stopping it. I won't, though, not giving the fuckers the satisfaction.
P162: *Getting a knife? Can you tell me what makes you feel so unhappy?*
Caller: They think I'll give in, sit in some bloody therapy group. I'm not doing that.
P162: *Who are they, the people who think you'll give in?*
Caller: Bloody social workers, therapists, waste of time.
P162: *What would you like to happen?*
Caller: I want my baby back. I can be a good mum, I had a nice little flat. We were okay after Shane went.
P162: *You said, 'we were okay after Shane went.' Do you mean, you and your baby?*
Caller: Course I did, why don't you listen better? Shane went off and it was all better. He was the devil. He dressed nicely but he was bad.

	Nobody believed me when I told them, not till he broke my arm again.
P162:	*How do you feel about not being believed?*
Caller:	I didn't expect anything else. Aren't you gonna ask me about it? You don't believe me about Shane, I can tell.
P162:	*What would you like to tell me about Shane?*
Caller:	He liked it when he hurt me. He fucked me nicely and then he hurt me when I wasn't expecting it. Aren't you going to ask me questions now?
P162:	*I wondered if you had more to say.*
Caller:	He was a good-looking bugger. He had a lovely smooth bum. Stripped off – used to walk about the place all nude, like. Hips, like, he could get into my jeans. I was a 10. Course, the legs were too short for him, too tight. That was kind of sexy though. Thighs – yeah. And his gear all outlined. And six-pack, oh yeah. He used to do 60 press-ups, 60 sit-ups first thing every day. I hadn't to get in the way, I hadn't to breathe in the same room even. White teeth. He had them whitened. He used to bite me. I still got marks. You wouldn't see them. On my belly. Not my boobs, like, he knew I might go to get my boobs scanned.
P162:	*You mean a mammogram?*
Caller:	That's the one. After Cassie was born I wanted to do everything right, like, blood tests, everything.
P162:	*Cassie?*
Caller:	My baby. You wouldn't call her a baby.
P162:	*I wouldn't?*

Caller: She's nearly fifteen. They haven't let me see her since she was eight.

P162: You said she was taken away when she was a baby?

Caller: I was on the drink, I was so unhappy. They should have let me die, busy-body interfering neighbour turned up, got in the flat, I had the pills.

P162: You still feel they should have let you die?

Caller: They got a psych doctor on it, and there were all the forms, and meetings and hospital, I got locked into a hospital. And social bloody people, kept changing.

P162: Do you mean that every time there was a different social worker?

Caller: They look down their noses at me, honest to God they do, all of them and they dress like old tat some of them. But I stopped Shane from belting her when she cried, I did, I got in the way. Got a scar on my neck.

P162: Shane is her father?

Caller: I told you about Shane, you stupid? He said he didn't believe me but he did really. She looked just like him for a bit till she went off her feed and got skinny.

P162: That must have been very worrying for you.

Caller: He wouldn't believe she was his. Well, he knew about the others. Nobody sticks with just the one, do they? I know she's his, she got his big brown eyes, like so dark they're practically black and she got a dimple in her left cheek like him and – well anyway I wanted him to stay, the fucker. He brought in a big mirror, put it by the bed so he could look at us. He said he'd put one on the ceiling but he never got round to it. Why are you asking all these questions? You've no right asking about fucking sex, are you dirty-minded or what?

Caller rings off.

Twenty-two: Tuesday 14:30

Teresa: Come in, do sit down. I think I've some notes from your social worker.
Stella: All lies anyway.
Teresa: Let's talk about it.
Stella: Social workers are fucking useless.
Teresa: I'm sorry you feel like that. Would you like a cup of tea?
Stella: Don't mind.
Teresa: I've just made a pot. I'll let it brew for a bit. You like milk and no sugar?
Stella: Notes say that, do they?
Teresa: The chair by the window, that's very comfortable. There are some things I must establish with you. The first is that everything you say to me is confidential, unless there's something you want me to discuss with someone else.
Stella: Who you going to talk to about me?
Teresa: Well, for instance, you might want me to organise something for you, something only a social worker or doctor can sort out. I will do nothing without your agreement. Do you want to be here in this session, Miss Fenton? Or would you prefer me to call you Stella?
Stella: Call me what you like. What's the difference?

Teresa: It's a big difference. If we agree to work together, you choose whether I call you Stella or Miss Fenton. My name is Teresa Stainton and if you prefer it, you call me Dr Stainton.

Stella: Work together? Eh?

Teresa: When we talk, we think about the meaning of what's said. Sometimes it can get emotional. People rarely come for therapy without bringing a big bag of emotion with them. Does that make sense?

A shrug doesn't tell me.

Stella: All right.

Teresa: So, am I Teresa and are you Stella?

Stella: Like we're friends? We're not. I suppose you can call me Stella.

Teresa: You agree to come here for an hour, each time? I can make notes or I can switch on this recorder so we both remember what we say. Whatever you decide, you can have a copy of the notes or the recording.

Stella: Sounds creepy.

Teresa: I can see it makes you uneasy but it's my job to make sure I do the very best for you. People tend to remember how they feel rather than what's said. Memories come with feelings. People remember the feelings more than the details of what happened. Memory can very creative.

Stella: Don't know what you're talking about.

Teresa: If you aren't ready, we can stop. You don't have to be here, or you can come another time. Josie has agreed for six sessions to begin with and this

	is the first.
Stella:	All right, okay, I agree to everything.
Teresa:	You can always ask me again, later, if you're not clear.
Stella:	Nobody never asked me things like this in all my life.
Teresa:	For the time we have, you are the most important person. That surprises you? If you're ready? I'll switch on the recorder. Can we talk about why you say social workers are fucking useless?
Stella:	You think I look a mess. Yeah, you do. I got bags under my eyes and I got lines on my forehead, I know how I look. I need a haircut but I got no money for it. Go on, how do I look?

    Told you, I look crap.

Teresa:	No, no you don't. You look as if you haven't slept much recently, Stella.
Stella:	I got crap skin. I should've give up smoking years ago.

    Calms my nerves.

Teresa:	I often walk around the Marina – I love the smell of the sea, even on a rough day. I find that very calming.
Stella:	Okay if you got warm clothes on.
Teresa:	It's warm outside today.
Stella:	Are we talking about the weather now?
Teresa:	Tell me why you dislike social workers.
Stella:	I never said that. I said they eff off soon as it gets hard.
Teresa:	Are you ready for tea? Are you happy with this mug with the sheep on it? I love these mugs. If it's

	too strong, there's hot water still in the kettle. I'll pour. Milk in that little jug and there's biscuits, chocolate or orange. Oh dear.
Stella:	Bollocks.
Teresa:	I'll fetch a cloth. It doesn't matter. Did it go on your jeans? I don't want you scalded before we start.
Stella:	It went on the floor.
Teresa:	I think that's everything mopped up. Let's start again. You've had several social workers?
Stella:	Why you asking? You got notes.
Teresa:	I'd prefer to establish what you think.
Stella:	These orange biscuits are quite nice.
Teresa:	My daughter makes them. She's a great cook for a twelve-year-old. I think it would help if you told me exactly what you want to say in the words you normally use.
Stella:	You got a nice room here, nice flowers. Nice sofa. You got no mirrors though.
Teresa:	Stella, you make me feel as if you are pushing against a door that keeps trying to open when you want it closed.
Stella:	Why don't you talk straight? You're bad as social workers, all talk. Least those effing Samaritans listen. That's all they do, they go and on about listening and asking how I feel and if I knew I wouldn't be ringing up would I.
Teresa:	Please sit down, Stella. You ring Samaritans, you agree to see me. There's something important you want to say.
Stella:	Am I interested. Do I care.

Teresa: What is it that you don't want to say?
Stella: Samaritans don't pretend – least, I can't see them and they can't see me so they don't – I'm in a muddle now. You got me muddled. You're not supposed to get me muddled, you got to sort me out.
Teresa: I gather your social worker found you somewhere to live?
Stella: You changing the subject?. You got it in your notes. You're trying to catch me out.
Teresa: You really are shoving hard against that door. It's a very heavy door. Is it a door in or a door out?
Stella: She won't see me.
Teresa: Who is she?
Stella: I'm her mother, it's my right.
Teresa: My mistake. You are trying to break in, not keep the door closed.
Stella: You making fun of me?
Teresa: What do you think the rights of a mother are?
Stella: I got rights. Why won't she see me? She's mine.
Teresa: You speak of her as a possession.
Stella: Fuck off. She was in my body like all the others. I had her inside me.
Teresa: Like all the others?
Stella: You being nosy again.
Teresa: I haven't met your girl. I haven't seen you together and even if I did, I still would not know the answer to your question, why won't she see you. You have the answer.
Stella: What, like in my head?

Teresa: Where do you think it is?

Stella: You're the shrink, you tell me.

Teresa: I'm not a psychiatrist, Stella. I'm trying to help you understand your own feelings.

Stella: I know how I feel, I don't need anyone to help, I feel so fucking angry I could kill. How do I know it's true she won't see me? They tell me, they say she won't see me but till I watch her say it to my face I'm not believing anything they say.

Teresa: You don't trust what other people tell you?

Stella: Too fucking right I don't. I got no reason to trust them.

Teresa: It feels to me as if you are carrying a heavy weight on your shoulders, like a rucksack full of stones.

Stella: You and your "it feels to me" — you make me laugh.

Teresa: It must have been very hard work to reach my door when you're carrying such a load.

Stella: Huh.

Teresa: You agreed to come, Stella.

Stella: I got no choice.

Teresa: Well, your social worker made this appointment but she isn't standing outside, checking. She didn't put you in handcuffs to get you here. You made the decision.

Stella: They treat me like a circus animal, and I got a turn to do, like, stand up on a box and twirl round in circles.

Teresa: Do you feel like a circus animal?

Stella: Fucking stupid question.

Teresa: My mistake. These days, circuses tend not to

	include performing animals, but people. Really skilled acrobats, trapeze artists, high-wire performers, clowns – oh, perhaps sometimes they have performing dogs and their trainer. The trainer loves the dogs, I think. The acrobats are amazing, very gifted.
Stella:	Nah.
Teresa:	If you were a circus performer, what act would you be good at?
Stella:	Now what you talking about?
Teresa:	You said that you feel you are expected to stand up on a box and do a turn.
Stella:	I never said that.
Teresa:	Hang on – I'm going to get out my toys. Sorry to rattle about but I have a special box for these. Here we are. Here's my model donkey, my Luke Skywalker, Yoda, here's my favourite Siamese cat. And the medieval Queen. Not sure how this gun got into the collection. Butterfly, tractor – well, which one speaks to you?
Stella:	They're kids' toys.
Teresa:	They can be helpful to adults too. Do you want to dip in?
	Like a lucky dip?
Stella:	You got a clown in the box? Don't want a clown. I had a model farm for Cassie. She liked the horses. This a wolf? And little wolf cubs? They're quite nice. And a red dragon. Is this a unicorn? Tiger. That model tiger got huge shoulders.
Teresa:	You've picked up the dinosaur. Is that

	tyrannosaurus rex?
	So it is.
Stella:	They died. They all died, didn't they?
Teresa:	They were superb creatures in their day. Such tiny forelegs, such huge jaws.
Stella:	Sometimes I feel like I'm scrabbling and scrabbling and I can't reach. Can't get through.
Teresa:	When you come back, we might explore that sense you have of not getting through.
Stella:	Is that it? Have you done with me?
Teresa:	My next appointment is in fifteen minutes. I need to prepare. We'll meet soon. Sorry, you can't take the T-rex away.

Cassie

Twenty-three: Friday morning

'Mr Collins is an expert in digital photo-manipulation. He'll encourage those of you who haven't had a lot of practice.' The teacher smiled so widely that Cassie glimpsed a glittery gold filling in a molar. She wondered how the teacher could afford it. 'Mr Collins used to be a student here. We are very proud of his success. He'll be especially helpful to you.'

'Thanks,' said Mr Collins. He didn't look comfortable being Mr Collins. The men teachers in this school all wore ties and proper shirt collars, and jackets and trousers. Usually, the shirts were plain and the trousers were grey. Probably there was a notice in the staff room that told them exactly where to buy their stuff. The Collins expert chose to walk into the computer room in bright pink tight trousers – were they jeans, even? – and a purple tee-shirt with a pink and white logo.

> If you like nerds, raise your hand.
> If you don't, raise your standards.

He'd been at the school and they were proud of him?

'I'll come around individually to see how you're doing, but in essence, this is it. Use the webcam to take a portrait of yourself, passport-style.'

Cassie stopped listening. She didn't have a passport, had only ever seen the photos outside the photo-booths in supermarkets and they made everybody look like a criminal. Digital manipulation? WTF? He was going to show them how to make fake pictures, not real ones so the crapheads in the room could fake it without actually having to smile?

Real pictures were painted with oils and water colours and acrylics.

The memory made Cassie wince. She shouldn't have written their names last night in the red book. Even though Rod was dead, he was alive in her mind. He had to be alive in Sarah's mind too. Rod taught her to read and Sarah helped her to choose library books, when she wasn't busy, but mostly Sarah was a painter, a proper painter with a studio in the attic, where the light streamed in through a special window they'd installed. Sarah let Cassie clean the oil paints off her brushes once she'd shown her how to do it, and how to mix colours.

Cassie loved the smell of Sarah's paints. She was hopeless at drawing, couldn't be bothered to practise though Sarah used to say women always learned to paint – they were the well-off women who didn't have to scrub floors or wait at table or work in the fields. It was Sarah who found the story of Catskin in the book of fairy stories, who said that Catskin was clever. Catskin made her own future instead of letting her father force her into something she would have hated.

Cassie had to stop thinking about them or she would snivel.

'Cassie, please stop daydreaming. You've been given the task.'

The teacher's hiss into her ear made her jump.

'Take the photo of yourself with the webcam, find the photo of somebody else you admire – were you even listening? You don't know how lucky you are to have Mr Collins here to help. He's got his own company now.'

'Sorry,' said Cassie. It was the only way to make the woman take her gold tooth somewhere else. Nearby, a boy said, loudly enough for Cassie to hear, but not the teacher,

'Give him a blow job. He's dying for one.'

She gritted her teeth. The boy had no idea what he was describing. He thought he did. It was nothing to what Cassie had been made to do in a place she swore she was never going to write about.

The task was to upload a self-portrait, and redesign it, using the software tools in the school network, like in English they were supposed to write a report as if they worked for a newspaper, so the self-portrait would be like somebody else – like, a TV reporter, or a solicitor, or whatever ....

On one side of Cassie the girl had found her favourite vlogger and was faking herself into a fashion celeb. On the other side, the lad was busily uploading photos of a footballer. He kept up a running commentary under his breath. They forgot to pretend that Cassie smelt so disgusting they'd have to walk on the other side of a corridor, or press themselves against a window, poking fingers down throats.

Cassie pulled a face at the screen, took a shot, slid the image into the top right corner and thought about the stupid task. Then she fumbled in her pocket for the USB pen drive Paul had given her and slid it into the port. As long as she didn't try to upload anything into the network, she ought to be okay working on her story.

> Once upon a time there was a little girl whose parents fell into a quarrel. 'Leave this house and wait in the garden,' said the father in his deep, hard voice.

Cassie looked at what she had written before.

So, the little girl ran out.

The little girl shouldn't run off till she had a plan. Catskin asked the woman who looked after the hens. Cassie decided that a bird would turn up and ask about the little girl's plan.

Suddenly a little bird flew down from the tree and landed on her shoulder. It twittered softly into her ear, dug its tiny claws into the soft place on her neck, and flapped its wings. When the feathers brushed her cheek she heard it speak in a squeaky sort of sound.

'You do not belong here. They are not your true parents. You must go seeking through the wide world to find your real mother and father. They are crying because they have lost you.'

The girl curled her toes into the moss under the tree and wished she had remembered to put on her shoes. 'How will I know them?'

Cassie stared at the screen. This girl was sounding like a wimp. She deleted, 'How will I know them?' and wrote instead, 'That's stupid,' said the little girl. 'They were supposed to be looking after me. If they're gonna cry, fuck them. Anyway, I'm not wandering all over to find them either. If I'm so important, they can start looking for me.'

'This isn't a session for word-processing.' Mr Collins leaned past Cassie and gestured at the screen. 'Where's the image? Is that it? Are you trying to make the image from words?' He was wearing a very powerful after-shave. Cassie hit ESC.

It might have been okay if he hadn't seen the USB pen drive, yanked it out and started waving it in mid-air. 'You could have infected the whole network.' Cassie grabbed at it, missed, but connected with his chin. He dropped the pen drive and she snatched it.

After that, the sky fell in. As she shot up from the stool, sending it rolling across the floor with a clatter, she remembered telling the story of Henny-Penny to the twins. They loved the nastiness and invented extra twists of torture. Henny-Penny ran around telling everyone that the sky was falling, and then Foxy-Woxy made his move. He'd been biting off heads and now he was coming for Henny-Penny's. Cassie ran out of the classroom, skittered along the corridor, almost losing her footing, feeling a bit like a headless Henny-Penny. The teacher caught her when she fell down the stairs, and marched her off to the headteacher's office, her long, red-varnished fingernails digging into the flesh of Cassie's arm.

She could overhear the headteacher talking to Dr Hume about the trolling. She appeared more interested in trolling than Cassie slapping a grown-up, even if she hadn't meant to.

The door from the outer office to the head's study had been left half-open. 'Can't we do something about it? Poor kid. She's only been here a few weeks. What's she done to attract so much vitriol?'

'Word travels,' Dr Hume said. 'She's been all over the county. That's in the social worker's report. But she did slap Adam Collins.'

'Do we need to know more about it? What does Adam say?'

'Not a lot. The class erupted. I'm afraid they thoroughly enjoyed it.'

'Taylor Lawson's in that class, isn't she? Can you ring Cassie's social worker? His name's in her record, is it? Or is it a woman? Maybe you should ring the foster-carers first.'

Dr Hume made a sound – a sigh, an exclamation? Cassie wasn't sure. She was holding her breath. 'It worries me to bring social services into this so quickly. I read her file, and the foster-mum's been in to see me. Nice woman, level-headed. She's a practice nurse and you can always rely on them not to over-react.'

'I don't want us to over-react either. Kids can be vile.'

'Well, yeah,' said Dr Hume. 'Diane says they've got some evil game they've been running for days to make Cassie lose her temper. Taylor Lawson is up to something. I wonder if Cassie even knew she hit Adam Collins, if she was just on edge.'

It always gave Cassie a shock to hear a teacher's name. It made teachers sound like ordinary human beings. Diane must be the name of the teacher with the gold filling.

'You'd think after all these years I'd be used to casual cruelties in a classroom, wouldn't you? I really wanted to knock it on the head.' 'You've set the tone very clearly,' said Dr Hume. 'The staff are behind you but – well, truly, it takes time. We've a whole community of families to convince that we mean it, and a few others so used to ignoring us they assume we'll give up.'

The headteacher said, 'What I can't stand is parents who say their children are a fucking nuisance. It makes me feel almost violent. How can they describe their own children like that?'

The secretary, busy with her files, looked up for a moment, shrugged, and opened another drawer. She didn't pull a face at the swear word. She didn't glance at

Cassie, even though she'd seen Cassie being settled on a chair. Whatever was in the filing cabinet was more interesting.

Cassie slid out into the corridor, heading for the door that led to the playing field. She would avoid using the front entrance to get out of the school. There was a webcam.

As she sprinted across the field, she clenched her fists and shook her head, as if shaking would empty out all the misery and frustration. She ought to have known by now that just being in the school, just breathing the air, was enough to set them off, kids from those families that made even the headteacher swear. Cassie was like a disease.

All along the west coast there was this network with relatives in it, like a secret that only they knew. This school was near Egremont, but one girl in her class had relatives in Workington, another in Barrow, and if Cassie asked, she was sure they knew someone in Carlisle or Ulverston or Kendal or Sedbergh or anywhere else where she'd been dumped with foster-carers who weren't really interested, and the social workers were too busy, or over-worked, or hassled.

It should have been different in this school. She ought to have smelt right, being born in Whitehaven. Kids from Whitehaven came to the school. They got the bus to Whitehaven. There weren't any buses back to Boot but she would just have to work out how to get there from Gosport. The bus stopped at Gosport.

What if Paul got cross? She knew he could get cross. Lucy said she would fucking kill the twins, only she didn't mean it. Did the headteacher think the parents who said their kids were a fucking nuisance really meant it?

Her stomach lurched, and she glanced over her shoulder

at the playing field behind her. Nobody was chasing after her. The air was full of a clean, frothy smell from freshly mown grass. Green strands stuck to her legs and trainers. Men were still marking the field with white lines for a running track, for Sports Day. They were too busy to have noticed her sneaking across.

Walking more slowly now, she reached the narrow slit in the stone wall – it was meant to stop pupils rushing out fast, a sort of traffic control – and slid sideways through it to the pavement. The bus-stop wasn't far. She chewed the inner side of her left cheek, where an ulcer had opened.

What would Lucy say about her running off?

Twenty-four: Friday afternoon

Lucy met her at Gosport. Cassie had finally rung up, said she had run out of school in the middle of the day, that she needed money for the bus fare. She felt bad about reaching Paul's voicemail and even worse when Lucy picked up the call. She said she was finishing a home visit and it wouldn't be a problem.

In the car, on the way back to the village, Lucy said, 'Dr Hume called me.'

Cassie jumped and would not meet Lucy's quick glance. Lucy reached out and patted her knee. 'She says you're still getting bullied. She thinks you overreacted to something in class. That former pupil they're so proud of – he hadn't been briefed about you.'

Cassie wriggled under the seatbelt. 'I don't want people being briefed. I want to be like everyone else.'

Lucy swore quietly under her breath as two bikers overtook them, making her swerve towards the ditch. 'They'll be somebody's death one of these days. They think the speed limit isn't the same on a motor bike.' Cassie saw her knuckles tighten on the steering wheel. She hoped she would be able to manage if ever she got a driving lesson. Lucy said, 'I don't think you really want to be the same as everyone else. Nobody does, not in their hearts. You want equal treatment and that's different. I'm learning that, we're learning it, Paul and me, we're finding out the hard way with the twins.'

'I don't know what you mean.' Cassie was half-relieved, half-troubled. Was Lucy building up to having a go about her running out of school?

'You see how they are. They don't look alike, and even if they did it would be the same. They compete with one another all the time, they gang up against us, they have their own secret codes, and they're different. Everybody's unique. The knack is finding a way of making them feel they're getting equal treatment even when Tommy needs a good telling off about something because that's probably what she's been angling for, and Freddy wants to be taken into another room and talked to quietly. Equal doesn't mean the same. Do you understand now?'

Cassie shook her head. 'It sounds so complicated.'

'Bringing up children is extremely complicated,' said Lucy. 'That's why I go into a corner sometimes and scream. Well, you heard. They make me incandescent. I'd really like to spank them, but when I feel like it, that's when not to do it.'

'Spanking isn't meant to happen at all, is it?' Cassie tried to sound unconcerned. She had gathered bruises in her time.

'The problem is when children lose their tempers and play up, it's hard not to behave like a kid yourself and have a tantrum of your own. Sod it.' She braked hard as a sheep trotted out of the hedge into the middle of the road. 'I wish they wouldn't do that. We'll have to get it back into a field. Come on.'

Paul was at home, making something with spaghetti for the twins' tea. 'Samuel rang.' He rolled his eyes at Lucy, blinked at Cassie and nodded towards the kitchen table. 'Make a cup of tea for us all, can you? So, what did Dr Hume have to say?'

'She'd like us all to go in after half-term, maybe with Samuel, not sure. She wants to change Cassie's groups, put her in with different people, maybe think again about her subjects. How would you feel about that, Cassie?'

Cassie carefully spooned tea into the ladybird pot. 'Didn't know I had any choices. They just put me in groups, like in my last school.' Tea leaves spilled on to the table, gently floating into a grainy dark brown heap. 'Isn't she going to exclude me?'

'No,' said Lucy, calmly scooping the tea on to the flat blade of a knife, tipping it back into the pot. 'There's someone in school she wants you to talk to.'

'What, the counsellor?' Cassie could not keep the disbelief from her tone.

'Do you know the counsellor?'

'They say he's useless.'

'Who says so?' Paul wiped a tear from his eye. The act of chopping onions had turned his nose pink.

'I'd like to enjoy half-term,' said Lucy, lifting her red hair from her face and swirling it into a tight bun before giving up, letting it collapse on to her shoulders. 'No more worrying about what we can't change. It's done. Cassie swiped an adult in school, it was an accident, I think, but it's an issue for the school. It'll become an issue for us if Cassie swipes one of the girls which you aren't going to do, are you?'

'I'd die,' said Cassie, feeling the heat rush into her face.

'Come here,' said Lucy, sweeping her into a hug.

Twenty-five: Saturday morning

Cassie yelped when the twins landed on the end of her bed.

'You're sitting on my feet.'

'We like sitting on feet,' said Freddy but Cassie was already kicking.

'You're hurting me – get off – what the f – what are you wearing?' Freddy's bikini was very frilly around the straps and legs, and the flowers in the design were red and yellow on a blue background. Tommy's was checked, green and white, without frills.

The straps of her top slid down her arms so that Cassie saw her flat chest with its small pink nipples.

Tommy sniffed, tossed her head and tugged the straps over her shoulders. 'You can't look at my boobies.'

'You haven't got any boobs,' said Cassie. She knew she must not laugh. 'You won't get boobs for years yet.'

'Our mummy says it doesn't matter. We went in the river in our knickers before.' Freddy cupped a hand over her mouth as they both fell sideways into one another, giggling.

'We got swimmers for our feet,' said Freddy. 'Swimmers?'

'I can show you.' Freddy jumped off the bed and ran out of the room.

'You got to swim with us,' said Tommy, patting the back of Cassie's hand with soft fingers. Lucy did that sometimes.

Cassie's eyes prickled.

'Cassie, you got to swim with us.' Tommy prodded her arm. 'Ow.' She rubbed her arm and made a monkey face. 'You hurt me.'

'Did not.'

Freddy bounded back into the room, swinging a bright red flip-flop from each forefinger. 'We got these but

Mummy says we got to have proper swimmer shoes our feet have grown my feet are bigger than Tommy's. Mummy, Tommy's hurting Cassie.'

'I'm fine, shut up, Freddy. You don't mean swimming in the river?' The shouts brought Lucy into the room. 'Go away, girls, go downstairs. Daddy's getting breakfast ready and a picnic so go and say what you want in your rolls.'

'I don't want roll, I want sandwiches.'

'I don't like rolls. I don't want cheese.'

'Go away now before I get cross.' Lucy turned back to Cassie. 'I caught some of that. They love paddling in the river. It's cold but you get used to it.'

'Why do they wear flipflops in the water?' Cassie wriggled her toes into the white cotton of the duvet cover and wished everyone would go away. She wanted to go back to sleep or lie in bed with *The Great Gatsby*. She could even fancy *We're Going on a Bear Hunt* – anything to drift into another world, fall down a rabbit-hole, get sucked into a wormhole.

'Rock and boulders, lots of grit. Haven't you ever paddled in a river? Paul or I will have to go in with them, just in case.'

'You won't wear a bikini, will you?'

Lucy rolled her eyes. 'I've got a perfectly good pair of shorts and yes, I use swimmers. The proper name is deck shoes, I suppose, though these days so many people go abroad for holidays there's lots of different shoes to wear in the water. Now then, Cassie, I've been thinking about you.'

'I don't want to go in any river.'

'The twins are not going to let you off. You do understand that?' It was a bit like having Mr Hetherington in the bedroom, being very calm and positive and any minute now Lucy would Feng Shui the room.

Cassie looked it up last night. To Feng Shui a room meant organising objects like chairs and tables and other furniture so they made the room feel in harmony with nature. 'Feng' meant wind and 'shui' meant water. Very suitable for the Lake District, Cassie thought, since it was always wet and the wind never stopped blowing. Strangely, though, the room she was given was almost right. Lying in bed, she could see the door but it wasn't right in front of the bed and the table she used for a desk was diagonally opposite. It was calming.

It had to be calming. She knew that Lucy and Paul were waiting for the moment to tell her that Samuel was on his way to collect her because she couldn't be trusted. It wasn't only bunking off school.

Did they really understand about hitting the visitor?

'Cassie? You're not with me. Are you thinking about getting into a cold river?'

She shook her head. 'What then?'

'What happened at school.' The words spoke themselves before she could stop them.

Lucy had pulled out another drawer in the chest beside the little oak wardrobe. 'Okay. I was thinking you haven't got any shorts but those blue jeans you've been wearing are too short in the leg anyway, so why don't I hack them off, say, just above your knee? They'd do for a bit. That old tee-shirt you wore in bed last week, if I cut off the bottom you could get that bare midriff look. You'd look great.'

And that was that.

Maybe Lucy was keeping everything going till Monday morning and the twins were safe in school and she would get rid of Cassie when they weren't around to scream and kick. She could picture their faces, screwed up and red, with identical expressions even though they weren't identical.

***

They walked to the river. They had to go along the road first, which was a bit of a nightmare because the twins wanted to hold Cassie's hands and that spread them too far out for cars to pass. Paul said they had to practise walking in single file on the right-hand side of the road so all the drivers coming towards them could see their faces and pull out around them.

Paul always gave explanations, like a teacher. Maybe he would suit his new job, telling other people what to think. Was that fair? Mr Hetherington and Dr Hume didn't tell her what to think. They just asked questions she couldn't answer – not the sort of questions to do with getting things right or wrong, but big questions. She supposed they were about right and wrong too but not facts, or what she could remember.

As the tramped along the road, Lucy in front and Paul at the back, Paul started singing a nursery rhyme. Cassie discovered that if she marched in time to "The Grand Old Duke of York" she was almost in step with Lucy and the twins, and they sang at the tops of their voices so a gang of cyclists coming towards them stopped, wedged their bikes between their legs, clapped, and joined in with the song till the family and Cassie had passed them.

Lucy turned around, danced backwards. 'Sometimes I feel like I'm being videoed when Paul makes us all walk along in single file –.'

The twins began twirling and had to be stopped. Their bikinis were hidden by shorts and tee-shirts, but Cassie's bare midriff was slightly chilled in the breeze that riffled over her flesh. She could not imagine deliberately wading into a cold river, even though it would soon be the end of May. They would not get her into that water, whatever they thought.

Eventually Paul jogged past, turning right along a narrow road leading to the river. The road lifted left over a humpbacked bridge and straight ahead there was a track or footpath. On the far side of the bridge, the signpost pointed towards a farm and holiday places. The whole area was shaded by trees, but sunlight filtered down through the branches on to the surface of a clear, twinkling little river. Paul did not cross the bridge, but pushed through a gate, leading along the footpath until they reached the place where people often went for picnics.

'This is our paddling place,' Lucy said, swinging her bag.

The girls raced after Paul. Cassie meant to follow, but the hump-backed bridge was appealing. She wandered to the top of the curve, propped her elbows on the parapet, and gazed down at the water. How fresh it smelt, and grassy. If smell had a colour this would be somewhere between green and clear, though the colour wheel put blue and yellow on either side of green. Sarah had taught her that, six years ago, nearly seven. What was Sarah doing now?

She could not bear the idea that Sarah was fostering another girl and pressed against the parapet. The gritty stone scraped her bare midriff.

The river was not at all what she had expected. It was shallow, gurgling like little rivers did in books. The girl in her story deserved to find a river like this one. Maybe she could wash in it, after something nasty happened to her – like when Catskin got splattered in potato peelings when the Cook threw dirty water over her.

'You like it?' Lucy leaned beside her, stretching out her bare forearms. She had rubbed sunscreen over every inch of exposed skin before they left the house, telling Cassie that she hoped to beat the freckles, but Cassie noticed that her arms were even more freckled than her face. 'What do you think, Cassie?'

'It's quite nice,' said Cassie, taking a deep breath. Her heart always beat faster when she thought about her story. The smell of clean green water filled her lungs.

Lucy nudged her with an elbow. 'I thought you'd like it. We love it. This is Doctor Bridge. Don't ask me why, why it's called Doctor. Probably it meant something completely different in the old days, when it was built. They made bridges strong enough to carry a horse and cart, with this hump in the middle. Do you know about keystones?'

Cassie frowned. 'Is that the one in the middle? One of – I once had a game.' Sarah and Rod had given her the bricks. She had been able to build a bridge from curvy and straight wooden blocks and it would stay up – she didn't even have to glue it. To Cassie it was like magic. Sarah had showed her how the brick in the middle of the arch was the most important one, the key that locked the rest in place.

'Cassie? Are you all right?' 'Yeah.'

'You looked like – there's an expression about a ghost walking over your grave. You were remembering something bad, I think.'

Cassie said, 'It was something good only, only it turned into something bad.'

'I'm sorry. I shouldn't have asked.'

For a long moment Cassie stood still, listening to the burble of water and a bird with a red chest, not a robin, singing from a branch. She could see its open beak. 'What's that bird?'

'Bullfinch?'

'I don't mind you asking.'

Lucy rubbed Cassie's shoulder. 'Paul and I, we decided

to get married one day when we were standing here. It's always been one of our happy places.'

Cassie shifted, stood on tiptoes so that she could peer into the water. The stone of the parapet was warm, old stone, an old bridge. It made her feel solid. 'You've been coming a long time.'

Lucy said, 'We've been coming for years. When we were younger we used to camp, on that campsite by the railway station, you know, Dalegarth. We decided, soon as we could, we'd get a house or a cottage here. We knew it would be hard. We were lucky our cottage came on the market. It was practically a ruin. We had to do lots of work on it.'

'What, like, you and Paul did alterations?'

'Well, we had to find people who know what they're doing. It's not like building a house today. Even the mortar is different. I learned to make bookshelves. I put up the shelves in the room where you're sleeping and Paul did the tiles in the shower. They're a bit wonky.'

'Yes,' said Cassie. 'You noticed?'

'Yes I did only I thought it was the walls being all funny, I mean none of the walls – they aren't straight.'

'We like it.'

'It's nice.'

'You like it too?'

'It's a long way from – like, there's not many shops.'

'We wanted what it's close to, like mountains and the river. Do you mean that Boot isn't close to a big city? We didn't want to be near a town or a city. Whitehaven and Workington are big enough for me. I grew up in London. I am never going back. Paul's more local, he's from Kendal but it takes ages to drive there. The mountains are in the way. I love that the mountains are in the way.'

Cassie had practical thoughts. 'Freddy and Tommy, you

have to drive them to school. There's hardly any buses to get here. You have to take me to the school bus.'

'Do you mind?'

'Suppose not.' Lucy still hadn't said anything about Cassie running away and having to fetch her, even though it must have been a nuisance.

Lucy tugged at a strand of red hair and curled it around her finger. 'This isn't as remote as you think. People look out for each other, look after each other, like a safety net.'

'Like it's safe here, you mean?'

'Well. Not exactly. There was a dreadful incident here, few years ago, the summer we camped.'

'What happened?'

Lucy's eyelids drooped. 'I shouldn't have said. It's never happened before, won't happen again.'

If Lucy wasn't going to explain, she might answer Cassie's real burning question. 'Why did you decide to be a foster-carer? You've got the twins.'

'Let's go and find the others. Don't pull faces, Cassie, I promise to tell you.'

'I am not pulling faces,' said Cassie, following Lucy off the bridge and turning into the riverside path.

'You are pulling them in your head. I can see inside your head, Cassie Fenton.'

Twenty-six: Saturday midday

Cassie discovered there was no choice about paddling. Everybody paddled, even Paul. Lucy had brought a pair of old canvas shoes she'd meant to send to a charity shop, for Cassie to wear. They were disgusting, but the pain of stepping into the river, straight on to a sharp, flinty little rock, made Cassie change her mind. She staggered back to the bank and lugged the canvas shoes over her wet feet.

Sunlight flickered off the surface of the water, and little fish slid under stones. The twins tried to build the walls for a castle and gave Cassie the job of moving stones that were too heavy for them. Then Freddy fell over, cut her knee, bled, screamed, splashed back into the water when Lucy said she ought to change into dry clothes, after which it was Tommy's turn to bleed when she scraped skin off her elbow. They threw water at one another, briefly threw stones till Paul waded in with threats.

Cassie sat down beside Lucy on an old brown and white checked rug, waterproof side underneath. Rolls, and chocolate fudge cake carried in a bag that stopped the chocolate from melting, made her feel sleepy and full. 'My bum's sore. These stones dig in.'

'You get used to it, Cassie.'

'Why did you let me come when you've got Tommy and Freddy?'

'Ouch. Is now the best time to talk about this? Wouldn't you rather just enjoy the day?'

'I bunked off and you haven't said anything.'

'I wouldn't describe what you did as bunking off.'

'I hit that man.'

'Did you mean to hit him?'

Cassie picked at blades of grass in the bank behind her.

'Course not.'

'It was an accident, then.'

'You wouldn't have thought so the way everybody carried on.'

'Is now a good time to talk about it?'

'No.'

'Well, probably now isn't the right time to talk about fostering, either.'

'I'm going for a walk.'

'Don't be cross, Cassie. Don't spoil the day.'

Cassie stood up, dithering and Lucy reached for her hand. 'Promise I'll tell you when I'm not trying to concentrate on watching the twins. They're liable to do themselves damage when they're as excited as this.'

'Okay.' Cassie ought to be relieved they weren't talking about absconding from yet another school ... and Samuel wasn't about to turn up, ready to collect her ... and Dr Hume and the headteacher wanted to talk to her after the half-term holiday.

Tommy's voice was penetrating. 'Cassie, where are you? You got to come and play with me. Freddy's being mean.'

'Scoot,' said Lucy, gesturing. 'Along the path by the river's perfectly safe. I'll come and find you when they've stopped biting chunks out of one another.'

Cassie scurried along the path until she judged she was out of sight. If the children accused her of bunking off, she would not be able to hear them. Quite soon she reached a bench, and stopped, surprised by the metal plaque attached to the back of the seat. Instead of, "**IN MEMORY OF MAUD JENKINS, WHO LOVED**

WATCHING THE DUCKS", or something similar, she found herself reading a poem. It seemed complete.

Do not stand at my grave and weep
I am not there. I do not sleep.
I am a thousand winds that blow.
I am the diamond glints on snow.
I am the sunlight on ripened grain.
I am the gentle autumn rain.
When you awaken in the morning's hush
I am the swift uplifting rush
Of quiet birds in circled flight.
I am the soft stars that shine at night.
Do not stand at my grave and cry;
I am not there. I did not die.

Lucy came up behind her. 'You found it.'

Cassie was too engrossed to be startled. 'Who wrote it?' 'Nobody's sure. Somebody did a bit of research and said it was an American woman. She'd heard a story about another woman who couldn't stand by her mother's grave.'

'I love it.' 'Why's that?'

'I wish I knew really who wrote it.'

'Hmm. In my profession we're cautious about what we read online because there's so much false information around. Does it matter who wrote it?'

'It might.'

Lucy said, 'I do wonder how long the inscription has been here, or how often people stop to read it. It might make you think twice if you had bad thoughts.'

'I'm seeing inside your head now, Lucy Robinson. You're thinking about the dreadful incident, aren't you?'

Lucy slipped her arm through Cassie's. Her skin was warm and smooth. 'Let's go and find the others. Paul is shouting and he sounds awfully cross.'

'I can hear him too.' Cassie took a last look at the plaque on the bench. 'I'm going to learn this poem by heart.'

'That's a lovely idea. Have you copied it?'

'Not yet.' Cassie wriggled and fished out her small mobile.

'A photo's a good idea. We can print it out for you later if that's easier.'

'It's okay,' said Cassie, turning back to the path. She did not want Lucy to see her face crumple because Lucy was so kind, and she could not afford to want so badly to stay with them. Whatever Lucy said, the school might still decide to suspend her, and Samuel would say she had lost control and would have to go into another residential home.

After tea Cassie borrowed the laptop and searched for the dreadful incident. She inserted "*disasters Boot Cumbria" and a large number of weblinks quickly filled the screen. The most informative, to begin with, was in Wikipedia. A taxi driver called Derrick Bird went on a shooting spree in 2010.

'How's the research going, Cassie?'

Cassie looked up from the kitchen table, knowing her cheeks were red. 'I didn't look up the poem, actually.'

Paul stood in the doorway. 'You are being careful, Cassie?' The warning note was strong.

'I wanted to know about the dreadful incident,' said Cassie. Paul stared over her head, and she turned to see Lucy pulling a face.

'I haven't said much.'

'It says he was a taxi driver. You weren't in danger, were you?' 'Lucy, why on earth did you mention Bird?' Paul pulled out a chair and sat down. He had an empty glass in his hand. 'Thank goodness the kids are asleep. I don't want any nightmares.'

'It was the poem,' said Cassie, feeling uncomfortable. She did not want to be the cause of an argument between Paul and Lucy.

Paul scrubbed at his face. 'Poem? What poem? You're looking up Derrick Bird.'

Cassie said, before Lucy could speak, 'It's on the bench, I'm learning it off by heart, it's a really lovely poem, do not stand at my grave and weep, and Lucy just said she wondered how many people walking past it actually read it.'

'Thank you, sweetheart,' said Lucy, sitting beside her and lowering the laptop lid. 'But you're right, I did imply living in a beauty spot doesn't protect you from horrors. Well, words to that effect, I think.'

'It says he shot himself. I was thinking, how could you shoot yourself after reading this poem? It says he shot himself in Oak Howe Woods, above Doctor Bridge. Where we were, only on the other side of the river.' She waited.

'You're wondering if poetry can change someone's mood, I think.' Paul ran a finger around the rim of the glass, making it sing. 'Mr Hetherington says you have to change your own mind,' said Cassie.

'Does he now? Wise man.' Paul reached behind to open the fridge door.

'He's old.' She felt bad the minute she said it. He was old, yes, but he was wise, like Paul said.

'Do you want a beer, Lucy?'

Lucy said, 'I'm making a cup of tea. Tea, Cassie? I don't know how long the poem has been on the bench.'

Paul stared at the bottle of beer in his hand, peering through it at Cassie. His face was oddly distorted by the colour and curve, and for a moment he was a stranger.

Something in Cassie's face must have registered with him, for he put the bottle down. 'We ought to tell you what we know, now Lucy's mentioned it.'

Lucy sighed, switching on the kettle. 'Even if he'd read the poem. I don't think he'd have taken it in. He was very angry, he'd already killed so many people. It's a terrible story, Cassie. We remember because we were camping at Fisherground, that campsite, by the station. We drive past every day but maybe you don't notice the campsite.'

'I do notice.' Cassie didn't know why she had to insist. 'You often seem to be in another world.'

'What about the Bird man?'

'Well, he drove along the road from Eskdale Green and when he got here – near here – he stopped his taxi and shot people out of the taxi window. Just random shooting.' Lucy stretched, twisting her hair into a coil and letting it fall again.

'Why would he shoot, like, strangers?' Cassie could imagine wanting to shoot Taylor or Kyle, but not a total stranger.

'It was all much more complicated than that,' said Paul snapping off the top of his bottle. 'We didn't know most of it at the time, except the police were ringing people up and telling them to hide. They rang the station and the pubs.' He poured beer into the glass.

Lucy said, 'There was a helicopter buzzing around, and lots of police cars but by then he'd driven through the village, turned off to Doctor Bridge and crashed his car into the wall, you know, where we go. The wheel came off. Tourists were walking back. He got out of the taxi and he was holding a gun. That's what they said after it was all over. They asked if he wanted help and he said he didn't, but he didn't shoot them. He must have got past the murderous state. That's what we thought, talking it over afterwards.'

'It says here,' Cassie almost tapped the screen, 'it says he started out shooting his twin brother and then he killed other people he knew, in Whitehaven and other places, and then he killed just anyone.'

The freckles stood out on Lucy's face. 'I'll never forget that man on the campsite – you remember him, Paul? He said he was a journalist and he'd just got messages on his phone from other people about Bird heading into the valley. He tried to get families to shelter their children in the camp toilets but they said they didn't want to frighten their children. If they'd known about the school girl who just managed to get away – is there anything about that, Cassie? He shouted out, she saw the gun and ran off. We talked to another woman in Eskdale, years later. She said her little boy was sitting on their garden wall swinging his legs, and Bird drove past. He didn't shoot but he could have. Why are people so protective about not frightening children? The twins love your horrible fairy stories, Cassie, don't they? It's a good way to learn.'

Cassie said, 'If he was driving past the campsite, would they have been in danger?'

Paul leaned on his elbows, taking a long swallow from his bottle of beer. 'He would stop the taxi, open the window and call people over. They thought he was asking the way, and he shot them.'

Lucy flicked a glance at Cassie. 'He thought everyone was out to cheat him or do him out of his rights, that's what people said after. Cassie, if ever anyone was going to feel badly done by, it would be you.' Paul opened his mouth but she put out a hand to silence him. 'I don't know if he really was cheated, but you have been. Samuel told us about you, he had to do that so we'd understand if – well, we'd know it wasn't your fault. We knew you'd had all those foster-placements but we didn't really see how that might have affected you until you came to live with us. You haven't an ounce of self-pity, have you? I really admire that.'

Stella

Twenty-seven: Saturday 0:43

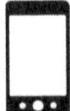

Phone recording

Cassie, I got to tell you about the knife. You think it's so easy cutting your wrists. You get in a bath of nice hot water, have a drink, have a lot of drink, really, it's not easy slicing yourself unless you're one of those kids cut themselves all the time. There's a woman in here says she always cut herself when she was a kid. It made her feel in control, she says.

You got to have a really sharp knife or a razor blade.

I'll teach you when you're living with me. It's a life skill. I listened to a lot of wank about life-skills but getting what you got to have without paying for it that's a skill. Rich people do it all the time so why shouldn't we? We got left out when the gifts were being handed out, we had to stand outside and pretend we didn't care.

First thing you got to understand is skin is dead easy to cut but what's underneath isn't. That's why so many kids cut themselves. I reckon they get scars and it makes them feel big but I got a tattoo on my left wrist to cover the scar and I wear one of those ethnic bracelets on my other wrist.

I nicked it from the Age UK shop. Old people don't want ethnic bracelets. I wish I had more tattoos. I'd like a big snake all round me, frighten off the wankers. I could make a design. In my head its head is between my shoulders at the back and it goes all round under my boobs and back again and finishes in the crease of my bum. I can see it in my mind. I'm going to get paper from that warden bitch's office and draw it before I forget.

Recording clicks off

Twenty-eight: Saturday, 0:59

Phone recording

Cassie, do you remember what hot blood smells like? It's sweet and sticks in your nose and it makes me think of copper bracelets. I got a copper bracelet. They never tell you when you read about it that it's so hard sawing across your wrist. There's stuff underneath, strong stuff, to make your fingers work. There's these dead easy veins under the skin but when you cut them not much blood comes out. It sort of oozes and turns the water pink.

I don't remember a lot because of the booze. I looked it up when they made me stay in the ward and they took you away. Nobody asked me why I did it. I wanted them to know you were the most important person in the world to me but they kept taking you off me.

Kids are fucking stupid when they cut themselves. They'll be put in hospital, locked up, they'll be told they're a danger to themselves so they got to be locked up, like they did with me that time. Don't you go cutting yourself, Cassie.

I thought if I nearly died, they'd let you stay.

They'd know you make life and death for me.

I can't write a letter to you.

She won't take it, that Josie.

I bet those foster-carers will take it off you if I post it.

I will find you.

Cassie, I promise I will find you.

Cassie

Twenty-nine: Saturday evening

Standing in the little bedroom later that evening, Cassie stroked the wonky bookshelves and tried to imagine Lucy with a saw, cutting up planks, drilling holes in the wall for the metal struts, hooking the metal brackets into them. Nurses would have to be very practical, though until she'd met Lucy she wouldn't have thought about it. Nurses were strong, too. They heaved people around in beds. Lucy had already mentioned turning people from one side to another, to avoid bedsores, or to change dressings. Yet Lucy said she admired Cassie who hadn't done anything yet except run away or hit a teacher.

Freddy and Tommy had been in the kitchen for the conversation about bedsores.

'How can a bed make you sore? My bed is all softy-soft.'

'Tommy, you never stop wriggling in bed.'

'I do too, how do you know what I do in my bed?'

'When older people have to lie in bed and they can't move because they're poorly, the blood can't circulate properly in the skin covering their bony bits. Yes, all right, Freddy, circulate is like going in circles. Your blood goes round and round inside your body.'

'Can you get bedsores, Mummy?' Tommy's fine brown hair fell into her yogurt as she leaned over the table to squeeze her mother's wrist. 'You got bony bits here.'

'No, poppet. And no, before you ask, Cassie won't either. She's much too healthy. Don't move, you've got strawberry yogurt in your hair and I don't want it spread about.'

* * *

Cassie looked at her reflection. What must it be like to shoot people in the face and watch all the bits of bone and flesh and blood spread everywhere? What was he thinking? He didn't want them to have faces any more? He wouldn't be able to remember people if he shot them in the face. And he killed his twin before anyone else, like, he was getting ready to kill himself.

There were lots of headlines from newspapers, saying how dreadful it was, how it was a one-off, that he was a truly evil man. Cassie lay down on the bed with her hands under her head. She had met some very nasty people. If they got hold of guns, would they shoot people, like in America? What did it mean to be evil?

She sat up and reached for the notebook and the story she was writing about her foster-placements. It was a kind of mirror, really, a picture of a girl called Cassie, and the last entry was about a little girl of eight. She had been putting off the worst bit.

She ought to write about Emerald, a girl who was nearly twelve, and what Kyle did to her.

FOSTER-PLACEMENT NUMBER NINE

Emerald was being moved again. She had been in an emergency placement after the nice people in Carlisle got flooded and she couldn't stay with them any more and she had been with them more than a year. They didn't have room for her in their flat, the one they were given till their house was mended. The emergency carers were quite nice and the social worker wanted her to keep going to the same school because she would be moving to secondary school next.

But Emerald said she wanted to go somewhere completely different where nobody would know about her. Everywhere she went — Carlisle, Barrow, Ulverston, Kendal, even Kirkby Lonsdale — people knew about her running away and being difficult and how foster-carers said she was too difficult. People passed on stories about her, their families knew.

The lady said what about Workington. It was still in the same county but she would go to a different school and it would be a fresh start.

FOSTER-PLACEMENT NUMBER TEN

Emerald went to foster-carers where they did it like a job. They had four kids from different primary schools and she was going to be the only one at secondary school. The woman was on her second husband and his son lived with them. He went to the same school as Emerald, the secondary school. He was a lot older.

The name sprang on to the page. It was like someone pinching your nose to make you open your mouth so you would have to swallow the medicine.

> The boy was called Kyle and he was sixteen and he thought he was hot. He wanted Emerald to suck his dick. She had a room to herself, it was a big house though the windows rattled and the carpet smelt disgusting. He came in the night when everything was quiet and got on the bed. He was tall and heavy and he did weights with his dad, and he lay on top of her and tried to stick his finger in her cunt.
>
> He said if she told he would say she started it, nobody wanted her, that's why she was being fostered. He knew she had been moved lots of times. He must have listened. Maybe they told him. He started coming every night. She got bruises on her mouth. One night he turned her over on to her stomach and tried sticking his dick in her bum but it was too tight. He still came all over her, sticky stuff running across her thighs. She got frightened about the sheet and tried to clean it off. The foster woman asked if Emerald's monthlies had started or

was she a bed-wetter, because if she was a bed-wetter nobody told her and Emerald would be going right back to the social. She didn't take bed-wetters.

Cassie had to put down the pen and walk to the open window. Outside, birds called, the pink and purple lavender was still in flower and trees were different shades of green. Somewhere a fox would be creeping up on its prey but that would be natural because foxes had to hunt to survive. Owls ate mice. Owls had huge, beautiful round eyes. She had never seen an owl in real life, only pictures. One day she would like to see an owl.

Her heart had settled into a steady thud. She went back to the little table, spread her fingers wide on the surface and braced herself.

Next time he forced her mouth open so wide it made her jaw ache and he stuck his dick in and she wanted to be sick. She would have bitten his dick if she could but he jammed his hand over her nose and she could not breathe. It was all salty the stuff from his dick. Semen. At least she would not get pregnant. She knew about getting pregnant. Everybody knew it happened when dicks got into cunts without protection, though Emerald was not quite sure about protection. There had been lessons at the last primary school but she missed some of them.

On the worst night he came in after he had been drinking beer with his dad. She was ready this time. She had two pairs of pants and her school shorts under her nightie and he tore them. It was only hearing somebody go past the room to the bathroom that stopped him. It was his dad. They could hear him throwing up, and shouting to know where Kyle was.

Next day, Emerald bunked off school and went back to the house when it was empty. She found the cooking oil in the kitchen cupboard, poured it over Kyle's sheet and pulled the duvet over it.

Then she packed a bag and took a bus to Kendal. She did not know what she was going to do. When she got off the bus, a policeman talked to her — she must have looked upset and a bit lost. He took her to social services in the town, and someone drove her back to the house in Workington. Her social worker came and then she was back in emergency foster-care (FOSTER-PLACEMENT NUMBER ELEVEN) because nobody would have her. She told the

> social worker about Kyle and she was kind but she said the foster-carers said Cassie was trouble.

Cassie put down the pen when the ink ran. Blobs of wet made the paper bubble. When did she start crying? Kyle treated her worse than a toy. He said she had been following him around the house grabbing his crotch, that she asked to suck his dick. His step-mum believed him. She didn't want trouble from foster-kids, just money.

Was Kyle wicked or evil?

Would Kyle turn into somebody like Bird, who shot people in the face? One thing was sure, his step-mum was Taylor's aunt. That's why Taylor thought she had such a hold over Cassie. She had no idea what Kyle was really like, because the foster-carers pretended not to know what he did to Cassie. Did that make them wicked or evil?

Thirty: Sunday morning

When Cassie woke up on Sunday morning, her eyelids were sticky. She groped for the drawer of the wooden bedside table, slid her fingers through the handle and jerked out the drawer. The notebook presented itself, red for danger. Breathing through her mouth, she yanked it out of the drawer and flipped it open. Her handwriting danced across the page. Quickly, she hoicked up the mattress and slid the notebook beneath. The mattress was heavier than she had expected.

She would tell Lucy not to worry about changing her bed. She would say that she wanted to help and changing her own bedding was simple. Lucy swore when she had to change duvet covers and kept experimenting with other people's suggestions for making it easier.

Lucy was clattering around in the twins' bedroom, her voice carrying. Cassie rolled over, falling out of the bed on to her knees. She hadn't woken up once in the night.

'Come on, Freddy, let go of the pillow. It's eight o'clock already.'

'No it isn't.' Tommy's voice carried with a clear note of victory.

'Mummy, our clock says eight-o-nine so you got it wrong.'

'Even more reason to get out of bed. Hurry up, into the bathroom, wash your faces and get dressed.'

Lucy lost the argument about the Snow-White dress and the pirate outfit. Cassie leaned by the window, listening to the chatter of birds outside. Lucy and Paul were taking the twins to church. Usually, Cassie went in the car with them but stayed outside, sitting in the churchyard, or waiting in the car. Last night, they said she could stay at home if she wanted to. 'We know you'll be sensible, Cassie, not go wandering off.' That was Paul. 'But soon you'll want to go out on your own. We'll show you the footpaths.'

A bird sang so loudly that Cassie opened the window wider and found the blackbird with a yellow-orange beak, perched on the end of a branch.

They had said "stay home".

She marched into the twins' room. 'I'm coming with you into the church today.'

'That's great,' said Lucy, pinching her nose. 'Are you sure?'

Freddy threw herself at Cassie's legs. 'You can come in our corner. We do crayons and sticking.'

'Sometimes,' said Lucy, pulling Freddy away. 'Depends which church we go to.'

Cassie was puzzled by the number of churches to which the Robinsons went. The nearest one she liked the best, so far, because they walked there, along the narrow road, and down a winding lane towards the sounds of the river. The church was hundreds and hundreds of years old. She didn't mind going inside to stare around, after the service had finished and people were standing around outside, chatting. She could wander down to the river and daydream. Nobody tried to talk to her.

Another church she quite liked was further away, and even older, Paul said. There was an old Viking cross in the churchyard and stone relics. Cassie wasn't interested in old stone carvings, and the stone cross was just a circle with a cross in the middle. She'd seen jewellery using the same design. The churchyard was peaceful and she could sit on the wall while she was waiting. They'd only been there once.

Today's church was much bigger and to reach it they had to drive for more than half an hour, following the bus-route. Cassie's school must be nearby. By the time they found a parking space, her thighs had glued themselves to the seat, a kind of terror.

'Are you coming?' Paul bent to peer through the window at Cassie.

'People from school – someone's sure to see me.'

Paul clicked open the door and held out his hand. 'It's not so bad where the kids go during the service. You'll be with Freddy and Tommy.'

He was right about the children's corner. She had to sit with Paul and Lucy for a bit, before the children were told to go to children's church, behind some pillars. The area was separated by bright red screens but that didn't stop a small child from poking his head around the edge of one and pulling faces at Freddy and Tommy. There were two corners, one for toddlers and screamers and one for older children, where the twins led Cassie.

It was not at all what Cassie expected. Green and blue plastic chairs were set out around tables on which were stacked boxes filled with strips of paper and safety scissors and felt-tipped pens. Printouts of men in long robes, Noah's Arks, flocks of sheep being chased by huge outlines that roughly suggested wolves — or maybe lions – Cassie never found out – lay ready for colouring-in. She was dragged by Tommy towards the nearest table and had to cram herself into a low chair. A boy squashed himself into an opposite chair, beside a little girl, and started to help her to organise her crayons.

He looked up at her and smiled. 'Hi. I'm Nick.' He had white teeth and a flop of black hair, falling thickly across his eyes.

Cassie's stomach lurched. She had recognised him at once. He was one of the prefects at school, a runner who won medals. Girls in her class talked about him, tried to get photos of him on their phones.

'You staying with the Robinsons? Don't do that, Millie, you'll tear the paper.'

'Sort of.'

'Like your outfit.'

For a wild moment she thought he was talking to her, but of course he was admiring Pirate Tommy, who had pulled the eyepatch over her nose.

Later, they all had to go into the main part of the church, to stand with the grown-ups while the vicar said whatever he was going to, and people sang hymns, and there was clapping and everybody sang "Happy birthday to you" to some old woman who was eighty and a little boy who was five in the last few days. Cassie had stopped listening. She was going to write a story, from the poem on the bench, about the grave and the person who wasn't there.

At the end, as they trooped out into the sunshine, the vicar said hello and goodbye to everyone. He knew their names, and when it got to her and she was trying to skip past, he said, 'Hello. You must be Cassie. Very nice to see you. Hope you'll come again.' He didn't try to shake her hand, didn't say anything over her head to Paul –

– well, he did. He said, 'How's it going? When do you start?'

'September? I'm looking forward to it.'

'I could do with the help.'

'I'll come and talk. I could do with some advice.'

The twins dragged on her hands, taking her away from Lucy and Paul and the chatty vicar, towards some kind of hall where they said there would be chocolate biscuits and orange juice.

In the car, on the way back, Cassie said, 'Why do you want to be a vicar, Paul?'

Lucy was driving. He turned to face her. 'It's a complicated story.'

'He never told me when we got married that he was thinking about it,' said Lucy.

'I didn't know I was – thinking about it, I mean. Freddy, stop trying to kick your sister, you're going to hurt Cassie.'

'It's boring,' said Freddy. 'Vicars are boring.'

'You were in the play area,' said Paul, reaching back with a long arm to tweak her nose, his eyebrows raised. He was smiling but Cassie wasn't convinced he was happy – something about an almost-wrinkle on his forehead.

'Yes but you never come and play. Vicars don't come and play.'

More wrinkles appeared. 'Not while the service is on, no. But I put up the climbing frame.'

'You don't come and play with us.'

'Enough,' said Lucy. Her hands tightened on the steering wheel. 'You're picking a fight when you don't need to, Freddy. You're choosing not to remember all the times when Daddy plays with you.'

Freddy was not giving up. She leaned against her safety belt and tugged at her rainbow-coloured socks, red curls falling into her mouth and muffling her words. 'He's got new books and he's not going to read to us any more.'

'When did I say that?' A sharp note came into Paul's voice.

Cassie pulled Freddy back, gripping her shoulders firmly. 'But my stories are much better than your daddy's.'

'Gee thanks, Cassie,' said Paul. She glanced at him. He shrugged. 'I'm not expecting you to stand in for me.'

Lucy said, 'Paul, you're going to be busy and it's fine. I'm ok with it.'

Cassie decided not to ask any more questions for a while, but she was curious, and in any case another idea for the story was running around in her imagination. Lucy had told her birds sometimes mobbed a bird they didn't want near them, like a whole lot of small birds ganging up on a hawk. She'd heard of birds mobbing a paint can on the ground because it looked strange, but the birds in the poem were quiet. *When you awaken in the morning's hush I am the swift uplifting rush of quiet birds in circled flight.* Had the person in the poem turned into a flock of birds? Was the poet telling the person by the grave that there wasn't a body in it?

She was sitting at the table in her room, after tea, trying to work out whether to write about the poor person standing next to the grave or the person who'd disappeared into the sky and turned into clouds and rain, when Paul rapped on the door jamb with his knuckles. 'Thought you could use this.' He held out a black rectangular case. 'I was going to wait till tomorrow but Lucy says I should give it to you now.'

'What is it? She need not have asked. Her stomach lurched. It was obvious a laptop case.

Paul cleared his throat. He was pretending not to notice her eyes had filled with tears. 'Got it refurbished from work. It's got an anti-virus package, the usual programs you're used to at school, I hope. You can use the internet here.'
She wanted to snatch the case, hug it to her chest.

'We thought – we know you won't misuse it. Write those stories, and I'll listen when you read them to the twins.'

'Thank you so much.'

Paul heaved the laptop on to the little table. 'It's a bit clunky.

Have you got a particular story to work on?'

Cassie felt a bit shy. 'I don't want to say – I mean, it's not worked out –.'

'You don't have to tell me. Is it for the twins? No, don't stress.' He hovered. 'I didn't want to give you the brush-off earlier about me being a vicar. I ought to say something because it will be a big change for us all. It's complicated because I've been years thinking it over and I can't say exactly what made me decide. Ask Lucy to give you her version. I've had to talk to different people, I've sat through interviews, asked myself lots of questions. There was a film made me think, once. Emotions.' Paul had stopped seeing her. 'It kind of grew inside me and I couldn't ignore it.'

Cassie had never thought of grown-ups trying to work things out when their lives changed – like the story in their heads getting a new plot twist. Mrs Vinegar was so mad at Mr Vinegar she hit him. The idea made her grin inwardly.

He looked at her directly. 'I did tell Samuel I was thinking about a change of direction and he seemed to think it would be fine.' Worry lines shot across his forehead. 'It's called having a vocation. Sometimes it just sneaks up on you. Lucy could tell you she never wanted to be anything but a nurse. You might have teachers at school saying the same.'

'Really?' At first she could not imagine it, but then she thought about Mr Hetherington and the time he spent putting notices on the boards that most people wouldn't read – or he wouldn't know if they'd been read but he put them up anyway. He did love the novels they were reading.

The idea made her feel hot and she sat down hard on her chair, running her fingers around the zip of the black laptop case. Her cheeks would be bright red.

'I'll leave you to play,' said Paul, closing the door. 'Hope you enjoy it.'

Stella

Social Services

Thirty-one: Monday 10:00

Josie: Good to see you, Stella. Thanks for dropping in. I thought this might be better than the hostel since you worry about being overheard.

Stella: I never said that.

Josie: Why don't we move to the chairs by the window. It's a lovely day. I wonder if we should find you some more summery clothes. We've got a stack of stuff.

Stella: I'm not wearing cast-offs, like I'm a refugee.

Josie: By all means complain to my boss. She'll explain how refugees deserve every respect and all the help we can get for them.

Stella: Coming here taking our jobs, our houses, taking all the money –

Josie: Stella, put a sock in it. I bet you've never said hello to a refugee. Let's get back to the reason you're here. You went to see Dr Stainton.

Stella: I swear it's like you put a tail on me.

Josie: She doesn't tell me anything you discuss. That's wholly confidential. But I have to know you've seen her. She sends in a bill.

Stella: She's diddling you out of your dosh. Bag of toys, like for kids. Not even decent toys either, all

	bashed in.
Josie:	She's a very experienced therapist, Stella. I'm sure she knows what she's doing.
Stella:	I'm not writing crappy notes just so you can read them.
Josie:	If you are recording or writing, that's for you. They aren't for me. I wouldn't dream of reading anything except, if you decide to write a letter to Cassie then I'll have to read it and so will her social worker.
Stella:	What I write to my daughter, it's private. I'm not in prison, like, you don't have to check all the time, it's not fair.
Josie:	Okay, so you haven't written to her yet. That's up to you, but my offer stands.
Stella:	What am I supposed to say to her? It sounds so pathetic, me saying you've got to come to the meetings, see what I look like now, so I can see you, see how you're looking now you're nearly fifteen.
Josie:	Is that what you want to tell her?
Stella:	I'm telling her she ought to see me, it's her duty and anyway I stopped her dad belting her when she was a baby. That ought to count for something.
Josie:	You think this would persuade her to come to a meeting?
Stella:	I can say what I want. That's the point, I can't write what I want because you're bloody going to stop me saying what I want. It's not right.
Josie:	Why don't you sit down so we can discuss this more easily? I'm getting a sore neck staring up at you.
Stella:	Get a taste of being looked down on. See how it feels.

Josie: Believe me, everybody working in an organisation has somebody looking down on them – well, over-seeing them. I must be accountable.

Stella: You got to fill in the forms like they tell you?

Josie: Well, yes, I do fill in forms properly because if I don't – look, that's not important. The main person I'm accountable to is you. It's my job to make sure things get better for you. Please sit down, Stella.

Stella: I sit down, you're gonna start on telling me stuff, I don't have to listen, I've had it with you do-gooders telling me stuff. What you mean, her social worker?

Josie: What? Oh, Cassie will have a social worker assigned to her.

Stella: She can fuck off and die.

Josie: We have a duty to protect Cassie. You're very angry, but it's not her fault.

Stella: You cunt, telling me how I feel – what the fuck do you know how I feel?

Josie: Pull yourself together, Stella. If all you can do is swear, you'll have to think again about seeing your daughter.

Stella: She goes to school. I bet she's heard everything. I'm not pretending to be someone else. I'm good enough to be her mother. I am.

Josie: Stella, I have other people to see today. I hoped that this morning we were going to make a plan for the next couple of months – improving your health, thinking about readiness for work –

Stella: Nobody's going to give me a job. They all look down on me, same as you.

Josie: Do you want to see Dr Stainton again? That's

what this interview is for. If you do, it goes into the plan. Was it worth it?
Stella: She's got nice biscuits.
Josie: So that's a yes?

Thirty-two: Monday 14:31

> **We're waiting for your call.**
> Whatever you're going through, a Samaritan will face it with you.
> We're here 24 hours a day, 365 days a year. Call 116 123

T112: *Hello, Samaritans. How can I help you?*
Caller: You ever talked to a counsel woman?
T112: *I think I need a little clarification. Do you mean your local council?*
Caller: People, they just sit there and look at you and you end up talking bollocks.
T112: *Do you mean it's sometimes hard to work out what someone else means?*
Caller: She's got these like toys and I'm supposed to pick one.
T112: *You don't know what to do in that situation?*
Caller: I said that didn't I? I talk bollocks. She makes me feel like scum.
T112: *Let's start again. Please, can you tell me why you've rung this afternoon? Something about your meeting with your counsellor?*
Caller: She talked a load of crap, wish I never went.
T112: *Why do you feel she talked a load of crap?*
Caller: She got me all het up, she says I'm like a dinosaur, who does she think she is?
T112: *Did you ask her what she meant by "like a dinosaur"?*
Caller: She went on about circuses too. She looks down

on me, I knew it the minute I saw her. Poncy mugs and fancy biscuits. Least I can't see the look on your face.

T112: *Let's concentrate on what is upsetting you.*

Caller: I can't say it.

L112: *Take your time. Really, take your time. I can hear the distress in your voice.*

This must be very tough for you. You're very brave to talk about something that hurts so much.

It doesn't matter if you cry.

Caller: I don't want to say.

T112: *If you're not ready, you can always ring another time.*

Caller: Yeah but you got a nice voice and it would be someone different and I'd have to start all over again and I couldn't, I really couldn't.

T112: *Well then. When you're ready, I'm here. I won't ring off.*

Caller: When I was little, my – we had this man over the road – over the road, he was my – he was my dad's friend, he was always round our house, well he pretended to be my dad's friend but really he was after ...

T112: *He was after?*

Caller: He was on at my mum, he fancied my mum and he got in our house so he could get at our mum.

T112: *You believe that your dad's friend, your neighbour, came to visit you because he was more interested in your mum than in being your dad's friend?*

Caller: He made my skin crawl. He was a monster.

T112: *Did you tell your parents you were worried by him?*

Caller: My dad would've thumped me
T112: *What about your Mum?*
Caller: You getting at my mum?
T112: *You said your skin crawled.*
Caller: It was worse. There was other stuff.
T112: *So you went to see the counsellor?*
Caller: She's like social workers, they don't fix anything.
T112: *You said you didn't talk at home about your feelings because your dad would have thumped you?*
Caller: I never said that. Did I say that?
T112: *I can hear the upset in your voice. Let's go back to what you thought might come from meeting a counsellor –*

Caller rings off.

Thirty-three: Monday 18:30

Josie: Can I come in, Stella? Gillian called me.
Stella: I hate it here.
Josie: I don't think we can do better for you, Stella.
Stella: They're lying scum in this place.
Josie: You got into a fight with the woman at the end of the corridor.
Stella: She pinched my stuff.
Josie: Yes, I heard that's what you said. What did she take?
Stella: Yeah, well. She stole my soap and stuff.
Josie: Your soap. Stella, isn't soap put into all the bathrooms for you to share?
Stella: My special soap.
Josie: What sort of soap was that?
Stella: It was like, it smelled of lemons and mint, that's what it said on the box.
Josie: I was under the impression you brought virtually nothing personal with you when you came into the office. You said you'd been sleeping on the beach.
Stella: You saying I tell lies?
Josie: Get a grip, Stella. You did present as someone who'd been sleeping rough for a few days. That's why I made such a fuss to get you into this hostel.
Stella: I slept on a park bench too.
Josie: Let's get back to the fight. What started it? She's got a black eye, Gillian tells me. Your cheek's red. She said it was hard work separating you both.
Stella: That Gillian bitch should keep her nose out. I had it all under control. I would have got my soap back and

	that stupid cunt in the end room should fuck off. She shouldn't be here anyway, she's got a flat to go to.
Josie:	And a man who broke her collar bone and her left wrist, as you well know. Stella, everyone here has had a hard time. If you've a few nice things of your own you want to keep private and safe, let Gillian store them for you – or let me get a padlock for the drawer in that little cupboard.
Stella:	You got no idea what they'll do in here. I ought to be in a little flat somewhere, why won't you get me a flat?
Josie:	At present, this is all that's available. Your soap sounds very nice. Did you – did she give it back to you?.
Stella:	You think I nicked it, you think someone like me never has nice stuff.
Josie:	I have to ask, Stella. Where did it come from? Was it a – a gift?
Stella:	You accusing me of lifting? I never, I got it for Christmas, I was saving it, it's special, everybody gets nice stuff for Christmas except me and I –.
Josie:	Okay, let's leave it. But if you want to me to send a letter to Cassie, or, well, I'd have to give it to her social worker, anyway, if you want a letter to reach her, you'd better sort yourself out. Don't pull faces, Stella.
Stella:	It's my right. She's my kid. Nobody else should have her.
Josie:	You're talking about her as if she's like that bar of soap. She's not a belonging.
Stella:	If you had kids you wouldn't say that.
Josie:	My life isn't important. I know you've registered with a GP and you've got another session coming up with Dr Stainton.

Stella: This is worse than being at school. You got a register? You giving me marks?

Josie: We want everything to work out for you. Stella, you've got soap but have you any shampoo? No, please, let me organise some for you. I know the hostel keeps a good store of shampoo and shower gel. You'd feel much better after a shower.

Stella: They take all the hot water. You're having a go at me again.

Josie: Really, I am not. Concentrate. When are you going back to your doctor?

Stella: Tomorrow. You come too, I'd go then, you come with me.

Josie: I wish I could but I've an enormous caseload – I mean, that's why I'm so late tonight. I've a day in the office to catch up on paperwork and the next day I'll be in court in Carlisle. Doesn't the practice say it offers a chaperone? Most do.

Stella: You're so overworked, it's a cushy number you're on, you can swan off, sit on the beach and nobody's gonna know, you're so important – it's not fair, if I had a little flat Cassie could come and live with me. I could get a proper job.

Josie: Keep your appointments with your GP and Dr Stainton. I'll see you soon.

Stella: What's a chaperone?

Josie: Ask the receptionist. Try to cooperate with Gillian. She worries about you. She's a decent warden. I must go. Try to work with Dr Stainton.

Thirty-four: Tuesday 10:00

Dr Fleet: Good morning, Miss Fenton. Please sit down. How are you doing?
Stella: Don't know.
Dr Fleet: Well, I have the results of the blood tests here. You'll be relieved to know your kidney function is acceptable. There's a marker on your liver. You must have been drinking very heavily for such a young woman. Give up now and you'll get your healthy liver back.
Stella: Don't care.
Dr Fleet: I suspect you do. You're depressed, and your history tells me you've been depressed on and off for years. It's not simply depression. You've had five pregnancies, your records tell me, and most of the babies were removed at birth. That's a lot to cope with.
Stella: Don't want to talk about it.
Dr Fleet: I don't suppose you do. I'm not a therapist. Depression's a physical reaction to something psychological. It isn't just a state of mind.
Stella: You think I can't do anything right. You're too young to understand. Now you're gonna sigh. People are always sighing at me.
Dr Fleet: You're anaemic. You're tired. You don't sleep well.
Stella: Say what you mean, why don't you.

Dr Fleet: I think you'd rather I did. This drinking. I don't want you to stop all at once, because that's going to leave side-effects. I'll slightly increase the prescription of benzodiazepine because that will help, but absolutely not if you drink at the same time. Can you halve your intake straight away? Will anyone help you?

Stella: I'm not doing that alcoholics anonymous stuff.

Dr Fleet: What's your incentive? What sent you here in the first place? Your social worker is helping you to do what?

Stella: My babies. They let me keep one but they took her off me when she was five.

Dr Fleet: You've a young daughter?

Stella: She's bloody fifteen practically and she won't see me. I haven't seen her for years and years but I want her back. She's mine. I got rights.

Dr Fleet: I see. What alcohol do you drink?

Stella: Vodka. Not so often. Cider, that's okay. Too sweet. Whatever. Cheap deals. Vodka's best.

Dr Fleet: Surely the expense affects what you can buy.

Stella: Sometimes I got to trade.

Dr Fleet: You're on the pill?

Stella: You're quick. No. They took all my bits out.

Dr Fleet: Let me have a look at the notes. Oh. Very unpleasant for you. But STDs?

Stella: I'm clean. I make them wear –

Dr Fleet: All the more reason to give up the drink so you don't find yourself trading, so to speak.

Stella: Am I gonna be okay?

Dr Fleet: If you make up your mind to follow advice.

Thirty-five: Tuesday 16:40

> **We're waiting for your call.**
> Whatever you're going through, a Samaritan will face it with you.
> We're here 24 hours a day, 365 days a year. Call 116 123

N135: *Hello, Samaritans.*
Caller: I don't want somebody being all charming, asking how I feel.
N135: *You've rung us before? Then you know I'm here to listen.*
Caller: I've said it in bits and pieces but I want to tell it properly, for myself, no interruptions. Okay? Okay? You still there?
N135: *Still here. No interruptions from me.*
Caller: It got worse when my mum moved out. My dad thought I could – I could be – I could do instead. I don't want to talk about it. Don't blame her getting out only she left me behind. His brother came round and the man over the road. I got pregnant. I don't know who it was. They took the baby away. He was so beautiful, so beautiful. My dad said I was always out with boys and he couldn't control me. I was sixteen so I left. Are you listening?
N135: *Yes, of course.*
Caller: You don't sound like you are.
N135: *Truly, I'm listening.*
Caller: All right then, I went to Carlisle. I had to nick his card. I got a job, sort of, stacking shelves.

Found a squat with a load of students. They were quite nice really, only the boys couldn't keep it in their jeans. They were nice to me. I fell pregnant again. The boys said it was nothing to do with them. I went on the streets for a bit till I got too fat and the social grabbed me. That baby was so pretty, big brown eyes. My baby. They stole her. If I could have kept her I'd have been okay. I'd have got a flat or a house or something but they said I wasn't fit. I got out of Carlisle anyway, students no fucking use, went to Barrow for a bit. There's a scene in Barrow, did you know? No, you won't, you lot are listening in from anywhere. Where are you? You in Scotland or something? London? Luton? Gravesend? I heard of Gravesend. Sounds like a place people go to get buried. I know you won't say. I got a job in a night club, got a room in a house, served at the bar. The bar manager, I thought his bum was neat. Thought if I had a boy baby he'd have a cute little bottom I could pat and — I did have a boy baby and they never let me see him. You lie there and some cunt in a mask and uniform tells you to pant or to stop pushing and keep panting and then all the pain goes and it slips out of you all wet and slithery and nobody lets you see and then you're empty. You're empty. You still there? You men get off easy.

N135: *I'm still here.*
Caller: The manager at the club turned nasty. I got cut up a bit. I kind of forget where I went next. I had to pimp, fell pregnant again. They wanted me to get jabs, like long-term contraception only I'm not having needles in me. It's my choice not

theirs. I got to be free to choose. Well, all right, I had my twins. There were six altogether if you count the monster. Six babies. I was back in Whitehaven. Did I say I was born there? Sounds all prissy neat and tidy, white. Should have been called Blackhaven all the coal mines. Then I met Shane. I told one of you lot about Shane. I'm not telling again. I fell pregnant and he said I was dead sexy, I turned him on, my big boobs, all that. My Cassie was born and I knew it was all okay and they let me keep her, because Shane lived with us. Then he said, there are cats, you stop them mewing by cutting their chords. He said he'd cut her chords, make her shut up. What do you think about that? You going to ask me how I feel about that? He went for her but I stopped him.

I did stop him. They said I was doing better with my Cassie and I could keep her. Then they took her away from me and my heart is breaking.

N135: *It sounds as if you were very courageous in protecting your child.*

Caller rings off.

Thirty-six: Wednesday 08:30

Teresa: Hello Stella, do come in. Josie asked if I could find you half an hour.

Stella: I don't know what the fuss is about.

Teresa: You had some sort of breakdown in the hostel? You threw your bedding out of the window and smashed a mirror in the bathroom.

Stella: You lot tell everything to one another but nobody listens to me.

Teresa: I'm listening.

Stella: You're being paid.

Teresa: That's true. It's a job I choose to do.

Stella: More than your daughter making biscuits.

Teresa: Of all the ways in the world in which I could earn enough for us to live on, this is the job I really want to do.

Stella: I'm supposed to be interested, am I?

Teresa: Hmm. I feel that door being slammed in my face again.

Stella: I'm not slamming. You got any biscuits left?

Teresa: You haven't had breakfast? In the tin on the table behind you.

Stella: They might as well have died. They're like all dead to me.

Teresa: I am so sorry I don't have long this morning.

	Josie seems rather anxious that you should get some additional support.
Stella:	I don't need crutches.
Teresa:	If I broke my leg I'd be glad of crutches.
Stella:	Are we talking about you now?
Teresa:	We've a cat at home. She's an active ginger, and she brought in a goldfinch with a broken wing. Our vet told us what to do to support the wing. Have you ever seen a goldfinch? I've the photo, on my phone. It's the most beautiful bird.
Stella:	I don't need to see your bloody photos.
Teresa:	The bird recovered. All that beauty is still alive in the world. We had to strap the wing to her body for a while, till the bones mended.
Stella:	Did you kill the cat?
Teresa:	I've put a bell on her collar.
Stella:	Why am I here?
Teresa:	You chose to come. It's early. Have you had breakfast?
Stella:	I'm getting out of that hostel soon as I can.
Teresa:	Coffee? I can manage a decent coffee.
Stella:	I suppose.
Teresa:	What's wrong with the hostel?
Stella:	Everyone wants to lock me up.
Teresa:	You can walk freely in and out of it, I think. You aren't locked in, are you?
Stella:	There's different sorts of free. Different locks.
Teresa:	That's a very interesting insight. What's the lock? What does it feel like?
Stella:	I saw a film with lasers and this woman, she knew where the lasers were and she kind of

	twisted and turned and never got hurt. Like a dancer.
Teresa:	Was this a heist film – someone trying to steal a precious object?
Stella:	You said that on purpose. She told you about shoplifting –.
Teresa:	Your social worker rang me at nine o'clock last night to ask if I could see you this morning, before my list. She told me you'd been in a fight at the hostel.
Stella:	You want a prize?
Teresa:	You want to see Cassie. She refuses to see you. I don't know her, don't know anything about her. About you, I only know what other people report and, most important, what I observe. I'm not sure that's knowledge. You still haven't explained your loss of control.
Stella:	It's like, in those films where somebody's captured and dragged off and they've got a hood over their head so they can't see. I can't see. I can't see. I can't see.
Teresa:	Stella. Hold it there. Breathe in – one, two, three, four, five. Hold it. Breathe out – really slow, really, really slowly – that's it. Drop your shoulders. And again. You've not been kidnapped. You want to see Cassie. You chose this. It's a good choice to look into your past and plan to meet your daughter. It's brave. Stella? There's water on that little side table. I'll put on the coffee machine. Okay? Take a break.

I'll ring and put off my next client for a few minutes.

* * *

Teresa: That's better. What do you want to tell me?

Stella: She's got to say she'll see me. If she won't, I've got to wait till she's eighteen. Then I can go and get her. I'm not waiting another three years. It's like a gripe in my gut all the time. The doctor told me it's the drugs but it's not. Gut-ache isn't the same — it's like somebody digging in with a knife, cutting out my insides.

Teresa: That's an image of violation. Rape.

Stella: I got raped when I was a kid.

Teresa: I haven't asked for access to your whole history, Stella. I don't want to hear you through the filter of so many other people's opinions. The key word I heard is 'digging.' When you spoke about your gut-ache, I felt, no, I saw a picture of someone with a spade, digging in a garden — digging a trench for planting a tree.

Stella: That's gross. Like a tree growing out of my guts? These foster-carers, who are they? Why do they want to get their hands on other people's children? They always put her against me.

I love my babies. I loved all my babies. Why did they take them away?

Teresa: The notion of your own fertility is very important to you.

Stella: You still got your daughter. She wasn't taken

	off you.
Teresa:	The box of models is by your chair, Stella.
Stella:	Kids' toys.
	Okay.
	That t-rex. Yeah. What's this? Is it a monkey? It's not a monkey.
Teresa:	I think that's an orang-utan, an endangered species, highly intelligent.
Stella:	It's got a baby on its neck. It's sort of cute. Ugly, isn't it? There's stitching or glue or something. I can't get the baby off.
Teresa:	I think the model is made with the baby attached. It isn't meant to be pulled off.
Stella:	If I was born an orang-utan nobody would have taken my babies away.
Teresa:	I'm not sure what your life expectancy would have been. The forests they live in are cut down. They raid local farms for fruit to eat and the farmers shoot them.
Stella:	I got nowhere to live.
	I like this black sheep. All the little black and white lambs. Once I heard lambs being taken away from the mums and they all cried and cried, you could hear it everywhere. Sheep want to be good mums and people take their babies away.
Teresa:	You found it very distressing.
Stella:	If you heard them all bleating, you'd cry too. You're doing that Samaritans thing, telling me back what I tell you. Fuck this.
Teresa:	You agreed to come this morning. You got up early, missed breakfast, got yourself showered

	and dressed – yes, I can smell the shampoo on your hair, it's very nice – and you got yourself here for half-past eight.
Stella:	What you trying to say?
Teresa:	You can and do make choices. You've observed Josie Graham and me. You've seen a doctor too, I think. I suspect you've made mental notes on us.
Stella:	Can I take a model with me this time?
Teresa:	I'm sorry..
Stella:	I like this fish. It's got a really long tail. It's got the whole sea to swim in. It's a lovely yellow. It, like, it fits in my hand. It looks like a little baby horse.
Teresa:	I think it's a seahorse.
Stella:	It's nice here. This room is nice.
Teresa:	Will you come back?
Stella:	Suppose. I might. What's special about seahorses?
Teresa:	I'll tell you next time. I'll find you a model you can keep.

Thirty-seven: Wednesday 11:23

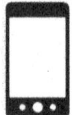

Phone recording

Why won't she let me have the fish? It's only tiny and the way the tail curves into my hand it's lovely. It made me think I could swim and swim and swim and the sea would be all salty and I could get clean again. I don't remember when I felt clean.

In the bath when I cut my wrists only the blood, there was so much and I didn't reckon on the water going pink. It was like in long trails and when I moved my arms ...

If I could go in a shop and buy a little fish ...It wouldn't be the same.

I want that fish. Other people must of got hold of it and stroked it.

I looked up seahorses and it's the males has the babies. If the dick jobs we have to live with had to have the babies they wouldn't ...

Makes me laugh, bloke with a tiny dick and a huge belly and it's not fat it's the baby inside.

Can't think of a single fella I know would take proper care of a baby. Their hands don't work right for looking after babies. Their hands are too big.

Dr Thomas might be nice with babies.

I really really didn't like it when the baby lambs cried and the sheep cried. It's not right taking babies away from their mums. Animals don't like it and they cry. Why have I got to get better from crying? It's natural getting angry

Recording clicks off

Thirty-eight: Wednesday 12:03

> **We're waiting for your call.**
> Whatever you're going through, a Samaritan will face it with you.
> We're here 24 hours a day, 365 days a year. Call 116 123

B94: *Hello, Samaritans.*
Caller: That counsellor woman says I'm free, I can choose anything. It's crap.
B94: *You don't feel free to choose anything?*
Caller: Didn't I just say it was crap?
B94: *What makes you feel that?*
Caller: Nobody let me choose. My dad wouldn't leave me alone and then he got his brother in and the perv over the street. I got all used up and I was just a kid and they were so big and heavy and they had huge dicks well not as big as they thought. I know that now. It's a fucking evil world. I think I should have killed them all, soon as they were born. They shouldn't have to live in it. If I get to find my girl, my Cassie, I might have to kill her so she don't go through what I've been through, everyone taking over, nobody listening, like using me like I'm a toy, bastard men I got a knife, I tried doing myself in, I'm useless. I got no willpower, it's not my fault they made me like it. Cassie, though, if they don't let me have her, nobody else is getting her. Nobody.

Caller rings off.

Cassie

Thirty-nine: Wednesday morning

Cassie tried hard not to grin but going through the village with a twin hanging off each hand, talking non-stop, made her heart beat faster. The sweet air, fresh from the mountains, blended with the soapy smell of small girls sent back to the bathroom after breakfast to wash their faces and clean their teeth properly. They were following Paul and Lucy towards a friend's garden, to water the vegetables while the friend was away. They'd been told they could pick beans and peas if they were ripe enough. Cassie had never seen fresh peas growing in a garden. Lucy said there was nothing as good as eating peas out of the pod.

Tommy was learning a poem by heart, called "My Shadow." It began,

I have a little shadow that goes in and out with me,
And what can be the use of him is more than I can see.
He is very, very like me from the heels up to the head;
And I see him jump before me, when I jump into my bed.

At every rhyme word Tommy gave a small skip, swinging the clown doll she took to bed each night. She'd given up her teddy. Someone at school had told her cuddling a teddy bear was baby stuff. Cassie noticed the teddy tucked under Tommy's duvet and guessed Lucy had sneaked it there.

'Tommy, shouldn't you be saying, "And what can be the use of her is more than I can see" – because it's your shadow and you're a girl?'

'That's not the words.' Tommy stopped skipping. 'You changed my story when I was telling it to you.'

What might have been a discussion between Cassie and Tommy turned into a fight when Freddy dragged at Cassie's other hand and began to sing at the top of her voice, all the while trying to hit Tommy with her lion.

'Row, row, row your boat gently down the stream,
If you meet a crocodile, everybody scream.'

Tommy swung in front of Cassie, ready to scratch. Cassie braced herself, tightening her grip on their hands and wrenching them apart.

Freddy broke off screaming to complain. 'You squeeze too hard.'

'You scream too much.'

Cassie shook them off, but Freddy seized her wrist. 'You got to tell us a story.'

'I got a better idea. You tell a story.'

'I can't tell stories.' Freddy produced a careful whinge. Tommy waved her clown in the air and skipped ahead. 'My Bendy can tell stories, he tells really good stories.'

'About his circus?' Cassie reached for her arm. They were approaching the road.

'He don't tell stories, Lion tells stories.' As Freddy tried to flourish her lion, it slipped out of her hand and rolled into the gutter. Both children dived after it and Paul's voice sounded from behind them, loud and cross.

'Get out of the road, twins, what have I told you.'

Cassie seized them, heaving them upright before snatching the toy from the gutter. As she dusted it against her jeans before handing it to Freddy, she wondered if she should stop thinking of Lion as "it." 'Is Lion a boy or a girl?'

Freddy frowned, tucking the toy under her chin. 'That's a silly question. Lion's not neither, Lion's a – a – Lion's just Lion.'

Cassie decided not to ask about lions and lionesses.

'Okay, tell me a story, Bendy first, then Lion.'

'That's not fair.'

'Freddy, B comes before L, is that right?'

'Bendy's ready with his story now.' Tommy danced her clown along the top of the wall, leaping him — gender definite, then — over the protruding stones. 'Bendy woke up and he thought he would learn a new trick but there wasn't nobody to teach him and all the other clowns ran away.'

'Why did they run away?' Cassie decided to help. 'Where did they go?'

'It's a secret. Bendy wants to go on the tight-rope but clowns don't go on tight-ropes only he's got bendy legs, see? And he can balance, he's so brave.'

They rounded the corner, saw a crowd ahead, and Cassie's stomach dropped. Two women and several children of different ages filled the road, coming towards them, loudly arguing. Paul and Lucy had stepped off the pavement to avoid them and were almost out of sight.

The big woman had dense black hair and the other made herself look taller, with multi-stranded blonde hair piled on top of her head. Cassie knew her at once, and knelt down, shaking her hair across her face, pretending to retie laces on her trainers. The twins knelt beside her, gleeful. This was another game.

'If I'd told you once, Taylor Lawson, I've told you a million times, you are not getting another tattoo so shut it.'

'You never should've let her get that piercing,' said the woman with blonde streaks. Her voice carried a shrill self-congratulation that made Cassie shrink against the wall. She had all the proof now, not that she had doubted it. Taylor's mum had a sister whose stepson was Kyle. He was a sort of cousin to Taylor.

Freddy said, 'I'm going to tell Lion's story to Daddy,'

and trotted back towards Paul.

Cassie drew a tight breath, still unknotting and retying her laces.

Tommy whispered into Cassie's ear, her warm breath a tickle that made Cassie shiver. 'I got to go on with my – no, I got to go on with Bendy's story.'

'Yes, but don't shout.'

Tommy's eyes widened. She clapped a hand across her mouth and spoke through her fingers. 'The man said Bendy was no good at tight-ropes. Bendy told the man to shut it.'

'Don't say shut it, don't let Mummy or Daddy hear you say it.' Cassie tried to make her whisper sound urgent, but now Tommy was dancing the clown along Cassie's bent back, giggling. Taking her time, Cassie stood up, rearranging her hair around her face, and held out a hand. 'Let's wait for Mummy and Daddy.'

The black-haired woman could not stop. 'I didn't let her get it, she went in on her own, told you before. I went into that place and I made them give me the money back. Shut it, Tara. I said I'd tell the police, interfering with minors, doing piercings without my say-so. Tara if you don't want to feel the back of my hand.'

The child burst into tears.

'Look what you done, Taylor, you keep shoving her. Hold her hand properly like I told you.'

There was a low mutter from Taylor. Would they never move on? Tommy's clown doll appeared under Cassie's nose.

'You can carry Bendy for a bit if you like.'

How did the child know Cassie was upset? 'Thank you very much.' Cassie kept her voice as low as she dared.

'Hurry up, kids,' said Paul, materialising beside them. He must have run back, with Lucy. Cassie's heart thundered so loudly it was hard to breathe. His tall figure was too thin to hide her, but with Lucy's arrival there was a kind of comfort. 'We've lots to do in that garden before lunch. You okay, Cassie?'

His voice was too loud.

She could not prevent herself from glancing behind. Taylor was staring. Her startled expression quickly changed to a scowl until the woman grabbed her shoulder. Cassie glimpsed a flicker of something on Taylor's face she had not seen before. Anger? Fear?

Taylor was being spun round. Her mother's voice was loud. 'Who'd have kids? I dunno why you do this fostering lark, Nancy. It's bad enough having Taylor and Tara. Who'd have girls?'

'You're right about that but they don't let you choose, those social workers. You got to take the ones they send. I'm getting shot of this lot when schools go back. Kyle's lost that job so he's back. Brian says he'll have to knock sense into him.'

Their voices echoed in the narrow street. Cassie knew Nancy's tones so well she could almost predict what she would say next, but if Brian had knocked sense into Kyle instead of believing him when he called Cassie a dick-sucker, things might have changed for other foster-children. Kyle would never change. She remembered standing in Nancy and Brian's green and pink bathroom, trying to wash Kyle's spunk out of her mouth. Her stomach heaved.

Lucy wound her arm around Cassie's shoulders and gently pressed her forwards. 'Come on. Fresh peas.' Cassie longed to lean against her but dared not, in case Lucy thought she was feeble. 'You know those people?'

'That girl.' Acid burned in her throat. Why didn't Taylor shout at her mother the way she yelled at other girls, at Cassie? She could be nice as pie to teachers. Maybe her mum was like Nancy and she didn't care about anyone else except herself. Sisters had so much in common ... If Lucy had a sister she'd be lovely.

Lucy said, 'She's at your school. Don't answer. That woman with black hair, she's a foster-carer. I've seen her before. She's always got about three or four children to foster and they always look a bit down. Does the other one foster too?'

'Giddy-up girls.' Paul hoisted Freddy on to his back and lifted Tommy into his arms. He neighed and pretended to gallop ahead.

'Mm.' Cassie couldn't breathe properly. 'You stayed with her?'

'Mm.'

'Poor kid.' Lucy took Cassie's hand and squeezed it.

Cassie stared at her trainers, concentrating on each step. She was not going to cry or throw up, not with Lucy holding her hand and Paul being a noisy horse a few paces in front of them. 'She didn't believe me. They never do. She just left me at the offices.' Cassie's heart sank. 'I don't mean – fuck. I don't mean you never believe me.'

'I know that.' Lucy gestured at Paul. He was swinging the girls wildly so that they shrieked and complained. 'I know I said one day I'd tell you why we wanted to foster you, Cassie. I couldn't think when would be the right time. I put it off. I'll tell you now.'

'Don't, not if you don't want to.' Cassie's skin tingled with an upwelling of panic.

'It's okay. I don't know how those women get the placements. I guess social services are desperate for carers. They're always advertising. I suppose I've no right to pass judgement.' She squeezed Cassie's hand again. 'It was different for us. I'm not getting into details, Cassie, but we always wanted children. We had IVF. You know about IVF?'

'A bit.' Cassie was afraid to say she had heard the term but didn't know what it meant.

'Well, it's hard.' Lucy rubbed her face. The freckles stood out clearly on her pale skin. 'Soon as we realised we weren't getting pregnant, we went for tests and were told we'd never have kids of our own without help. Well, we got twins. It was like winning the lottery, only better. You get that?'

'I don't know.' What was she supposed to say? She was the child handed from one set of adults to another and nobody wanted her to live with them.

'Well, we promised ourselves we'd give something back. We'd give a home to someone else. We'd been so lucky. We wanted some luck for you.'

Cassie writhed at the idea of being someone else's good deed. 'I see.'

Lucy was like a mind-reader. 'That came out all wrong. IVF, you can't imagine how humiliating it can feel, not producing the eggs without getting a course of injections, and there are women desperate because they keep getting pregnant and it kills them. Anyway, when the twins were two or three, we realised how much we wanted an older child, the one we could have had when we first started trying and realised I wasn't going to get pregnant. Sorry. Too much information. You don't need the details.'

'No,' said Cassie. A door in her mind slammed shut at the idea of Lucy, Paul, sex.

Lucy laughed and squeezed her shoulders. 'What I mean is, once it occurred to us we could ask to foster a teenager we got very excited.'

'You're crazy,' said Cassie, her eyes prickling.

'So are you, Cassie Fenton. We'd like – we'd really like

you to settle with us.'

Cassie rubbed her eyes. Her fingers were damp. 'How do we pick peas?'

She was wandering back through the village an hour or so later, still chewing a pea, and swinging a bag of newly-picked dwarf green beans, when Taylor leapt out of the pub garden and snatched the bag.

'You say a word at school and I'll kill you.'

Cassie lunged for the paper bag and it tore, scattering beans across the path and into the road. With a groan, she fell to her knees, trying to scoop the beans into the folds of her tee-shirt but Taylor delivered a kick to the ribs that made her gasp. 'I will, I'll kill you if you tell.' As Cassie groped towards another handful of beans, Taylor stamped on the back of her hand, before scattering the beans with sweeping kicks.

She stopped at a yell from the garden. 'Taylor? I told you to watch Tara.' Sobs broke out, a small girl's. 'You skiving off to buy fags again? You're for it when we get home.'

Gesturing furiously at Cassie, Taylor retreated through the gate and Cassie was left to scrape up the beans. She would not cry. She would tell Lucy she'd been daydreaming, dropped the bag – anything but the truth.

Staring across the lunch table, spread with bread and cheese, crisps and sweet-smelling baby tomatoes, Tommy said, 'Bendy saw a nasty girl kicking Cassie. Bendy didn't like it.'

'Are you sure?' Paul popped two tomatoes into his mouth, filling his cheeks. He winked at Cassie.

'Bendy don't tell lies.'

'Bendy doesn't tell lies,' said Lucy. 'Bendy can tell really good stories. What's Bendy's story?'

'He says the nasty girl kicked Cassie and Cassie kicked her back and they pulled each other's hair.'

'That's a horrible story.' Freddy stood up so fast that her chair fell over. 'Lion says Cassie never kicked her back, the nasty girl trod on Cassie's hand and Cassie picked up all the beans and she put them in her pocket and the fairy godmother said she could plant them in her garden and get lots and lots of new beans.'

Lucy said, 'Does Cassie have a story?'

Cassie's eyelids tightened. She shook her head.

'It was that girl, wasn't it? The one we saw earlier, the one who bullied you so badly at school.' She reached across the table to grasp Cassie's hand. 'Her mother was a piece of work. People say, like mother like daughter, but it doesn't have to be. If I'd been there to see it –.'

'Good thing you weren't or we'd have had a law suit on our hands.' Paul cut himself another slice of bread. 'We thought about a proper fell-walk before half-term finishes.' He looked at Lucy. 'You've got that prize-fighter expression on your face, Luce. Eat up, twins, sit down, Freddy. I'm putting Lion on the dresser till you finish your lunch. Cassie, did you know Plato wanted to keep storytellers out of his ideal country? He thought they were liars. It's a provocative idea. Some kids still get confused between telling stories and telling lies.'

Lucy rubbed her face. 'You've finished the lecture, have you? Anyway, I don't believe kids are always confused. It's the adults giving them disinformation.'

'Maybe.' Paul stared at his plate. 'I've just been reading about how scribes worked, copying out books in the Bible. I'm told it was probably the same for Shakespeare. The more intelligent the scribe, the more alterations from the original.

The scribe thinks something isn't right and tries to correct it, so more and more errors creep in.'

Lucy said, 'You may be on to something. Getting patients to explain exactly what's wrong can be a nightmare. They tell you right at the last minute.'

'My accountant brain is struggling, I must confess.'

'You would choose to do this.' Lucy got up, piling plates together. 'What are you doing this afternoon?'

Paul ran his hands through his hair. 'I've an online call at three. Sorry. Carlisle office. Better that than driving in. I can make supper.' Cassie watched them looking at one another, Lucy looping back her hair, Paul tugging an earlobe. They weren't talking to one another and yet they were. Was it something about Paul's new work, or the twins, or Lucy's job? She seemed to get a lot of texts.

Lucy said, 'That's helpful. I want to get under the girls' beds and sort out the clothes for Oxfam.'

'Not my flower dress.' Tommy set up a wail. 'Your flower dress doesn't fit any more.'

'I can wear it.' Tommy wriggled on her seat and Lucy caught Cassie's eye. She was trying to keep her face straight.

'Maybe they're getting into practice for being unreliable witnesses,' she said.

Tommy was already on her way out of the kitchen. 'I'm hiding my dresses in the wood. Catskin hid her dresses.'

'Oh Lord,' said Paul, getting up. 'Art giving birth to life or is it life imitates art?'

Cassie said, 'Lucy, can I help sort out clothes?'

'Don't you want to carry on writing?' Lucy paused, halfway through stacking the dishwasher.

'I've got a sort of idea but it won't come straight.'

Freddy snatched her Lion toy from the dresser and ran out of the room.

'There might be warfare over dresses,' said Lucy. 'I don't know why they are so keen on dresses. I wear uniform half the time. Paul goes to work in a decent suit.'

Later, after distracting the twins so Lucy could stuff old dresses, tee-shirts, shorts, socks and other clothing into a big black sack, Cassie went back to the laptop and notebook and sat by the window, thinking. The sight of the binbag had unsettled her for a while, reminding her of how often her own gear had been dumped outside social security offices. Then Lucy talked about Oxfam and buying preloved clothes – that was the name for them, rather than second-hand. She'd also seen a sign for Vintage Treasures and liked that too. So much could change with a name. Calling that other Cassie "Emerald" was starting to change the way she thought about staying with Nancy. Even the memory of Kyle was beginning to fade, as if she'd thrown a black veil over it. Hearing her mother shout at Taylor – would that change anything? Taylor would be a bully till somebody stopped her, and it probably wouldn't be Cassie but Taylor was being bullied, and Cassie was living with parents who took care to be kind as well as firm.

She opened the folder of photos on her phone to look at the poem again. Learning by heart was one thing, seeing the words was another, and seeing the words on the bench was different again. Her story would begin with a girl on the bench.

Stella

Forty: Thursday 09:00

Josie: Oh, Stella, glad to have caught you. This phone line's not very good. Can you hear me?

Stella: What?

Josie: I'd like you to make time for a chat. Teresa says it went okay this time, when you saw her. How are you getting on with a letter for your daughter?

Stella: This mobile's useless, I can't hardly hear you.

Josie: Hang on a minute – the office phone never stops. Okay, somebody's grabbed it. Something Teresa said made me think. I'd like to help you reach Cassie. If that's what you truly want.

Stella: That fucking woman should keep her mouth shut.

Josie: Don't be so offensive. Teresa Stainton is a total professional. She hasn't disclosed anything confidential. She merely says it would be helpful to you if you wrote a letter to your daughter, as we've discussed, instead of just talking about it. I promised I would help.

Stella: You want to write it for me now?

Josie: You need to sort out your attitude, Stella. You'd make a saint weep.

Stella: Why can't we meet in a café? Why's it always your office, his office, her office? Why can't I

	choose where? She says that therapist I got choices, well I never get to choose anything, not unless it's soap.
Josie:	For goodness' sake, Stella, stop complaining. Do you want to see your daughter or don't you?
Stella:	I'm fed up being put in the wrong when it's not my fault. You're all out to make me feel bad, that's what, you make me feel it's okay for you, you got proper jobs money coming in, nice places to live. You got no idea what it's like for me.
Josie:	Suppose you try writing the letter. Do something positive. Behave like a grown-up. Try presenting yourself to Cassie as an adult. Bring it into the office.

Stella rings off.

Forty-one: Letter

Dear Cassie

I am very sorry I was such a rotten mum. I did my best but they say I didn't try hard enough. I really want to meet you again. You must be getting very grown up now. Please will you change your mind and let me see you? I am your mum, after all. We could live in a nice flat together and I can get a job.

It's been horrible not seeing you. I bet you look really nice. You used to have such pretty eyes and nice soft hair.

I really miss you. Please tell your social worker you will come and see me. We could go out to tea. There's lots of nice cafes everywhere.

Lots of love

Mum

Forty-two: 10:39

> **We're waiting for your call.**
> Whatever you're going through, a Samaritan will face it with you.
> We're here 24 hours a day, 365 days a year. Call 116 123

H86: Hello, Samaritans
Caller: I know where she is, I'm going to get her.
H86: *I beg your pardon. This is Samaritans.*
Caller: She'll have to talk to me.
H86: *You sound rather excited. How can I help you?*
Caller: I'm wasting time. Goodbye. No, wait, I got to tell you I'm gonna wet myself I'm so excited I went to see that social worker supposed to be looking after me. She couldn't look after an earwig. She's always giving me an ear-bashing. Well she told me to go and see her and when I got there she'd fucked off. Some excuse about emergencies. There's always emergencies with those social workers. Same with you I bet. What would happen if I rang you lot and nobody answered?
H86: *Someone always answers. We are always here.*
Caller: Even if you want a piss?
H86: *We are always here. You seem very bothered about being able to get in touch with your social worker.*
Caller: There was this girl in the office. She looked like she only just got out of nappies. It was magic, like, I told her I wrote a letter to my daughter, I

brought the letter and the social worker'd fucked off. This girl, she said she was the duty person, could she help. I said I didn't have an envelope and that's the truth, I didn't, so could she give me one. So she had a rummage in a drawer and she gave me one and I stuffed the letter in it and stuck it down, and she said didn't my social worker have to read the letter first? They never give up, it's like being a prisoner. I said what about the address and she dabbled about on the computer and I told her, my girl's called Cassie Fenton, and she found it and she wrote the address on another envelope and took out my letter and put it in the new envelope. I read the address upside down. She got huge handwriting, all loopy. Cassie's in one of the snobby villages. There's never a bus to touristy places like that but I'll get a lift, there's always people driving out, day trippers. And I'll get there and I've got my knife and if I've got to stick my knife in those foster-carers I will. I'm getting my girl away from them no matter what. I'm not waiting for any social worker rabbiting on about her rights and doing the right thing when they know fuck all about us. Nobody knows the right thing for me and Cassie except us.

H86: *That's a lot for you to think about. Could you tell me why you want to take a knife with you?*

Caller: I'm not going to stick it under her nose, am I? Except, if one of those fucking foster-carers tries to hide her, that's when the knife's coming out.

H86: *If your daughter sees this, won't she be rather frightened?*

Caller: If I want to frighten her I can. She's mine. That cunt in the next room stole my stuff. Whatever I'm going to find Cassie and get her and we're going to catch a bus she'll come with me and we'll go to Carlisle. No, we'll go to Scotland. They got different laws there. We'll be safe there.

Caller rings off.

Cassie
Forty-three: Thursday mid-morning

Bendy and Lion were being trained to climb a mountain. They had to carry out some exercises to make them strong, like climbing over rocks, or up a rope. Cassie had already been asked to find the ball of string and some proper cutting scissors, not the bright red play scissors which only cut zigzaggy bits of paper. She had been commanded to tie a firm knot of rope at the top of the climbing frame. The training instructions were very loud.

She stood at the kitchen window for a couple of minutes, watching them scramble over the climbing frame, their long brown legs amazingly agile. *Agile* was a good word. It could mean a way of thinking as well as how to move. She wanted to be *agile* herself. Lucy had to rush into work to fill in for a sick colleague for a couple of hours, so it was just her and Paul looking after the twins. She was going to write a story just for them.

> Once upon a time there were two children called Bendy and Lion. They were very good at climbing and running and standing on their heads. Bendy could bend over backwards and touch the ground with her hand, and then she could flip herself over and do lots of somersaults. Lion wasn't bendy but he was strong. He could lift Bendy up in the air over his head.
>
> Bendy and Lion's dad was not very kind. He

wanted to make them go in a circus to get him money. He said their tricks were annoying but people might pay a lot to watch them and he started to make them practise and practise till Bendy's back hurt and Lion's arms ached. One night they decided to run away and find an aeroplane so they could fly to the other side of the world where he never would be able to find them. Only they worried about their mum. She kept having to go to bed. She said she felt poorly and their dad didn't seem to notice. They did not want to leave her behind and they knew they would never be able to steal an aeroplane.

One night when their dad was out, they were getting ready for bed when they heard their mum calling from her bedroom so they went to see what she wanted.

The door banged open and Paul appeared in the kitchen, carrying a jute bag. 'Would you be okay if I popped round to Sue's garden again? I thought I could get some fresh lettuce and see if the potatoes are ready. I'll water the carrots, anyway. You've got your mobile. I'll take mine. I'll be round the corner. You know where I'll be.'

'You don't mind me being in charge?'

'Not one bit.' He paused in the doorway, gave her a serious look.

'Your hair —.' Cassie gestured. His thin brown hair was plastered over his eyes. 'It's all in your eyes.'

'Accounts. They make me break out in a sweat these days. I'll be glad when all my hair falls out. I'd like a number one cut but Lucy won't let me.'

'She couldn't stop you if you just went and did it,' said Cassie, feeling bold.

'Could I cope with the telling-off afterwards?' Paul waved, stepped out into the garden and disappeared.

'You can say your hair's fallen out with worry.' This brought a laugh from Paul. The garden gate swung on its hinges, latched shut. He was right, Lucy wouldn't believe him.

She stretched and wobbled on the stool, almost losing her balance. They trusted her to look after the twins, for as much as an hour, even. Whatever Paul said, he would not be rushing back. She had already seen his eyes brighten when he stood beside the long rows of carrots, beans and peas. He would be unfurling the long hose, cursing when it got into a tangle. She shook her head. Lucy had been through horrible stuff to get these little girls. Cassie had already looked it up on the laptop. Lucy had to inject herself every day, then get a needle poked up her vagina, into her ovaries to get the eggs – Cassie stopped reading when it came to needles. The NHS website had too much information on it. Sex was meant to be nice, wasn't it? What was nice about going on and on, trying to get pregnant. Could people be making love if all they thought about was getting pregnant? Except Lucy and Paul wanted children of their own and then, then, they wanted to foster a teenager. They were saying a kind of thank-you.

If she went on thinking about it, her skin would burst open and her insides would overflow across the kitchen floor. The picture in her mind made her grin to herself – the sort of picture an artist might draw in a book for children, so they could screech and say it was scary and ask to see it again and again. Children liked being scared. Maybe it was practice for truly being scared.

Maybe she was able to bear writing about Kyle, now, because she had told scary fairy stories to the twins and a sort of 'fright' part in her brain had got stronger.

She tapped on the keyboard to bring the screen to life. She could give Bendy and Lion a fright, too, to make them stronger.

Bendy and Lion's mum lay flat on the bed with her eyes closed.

Bendy said, 'She shouted to come in.'

Lion said, 'She said, I got an idea.'

'She didn't say that.' Bendy pushed Lion.

Lion pushed back. 'You weren't listening.'

A sort of big sigh came from the bed and they turned to look at their mum. Bendy said, 'Why are her eyes closed?'

Lion said, 'Why isn't her chest going up and down?' Bendy went close up and looked at their mum's face.

'Where did all her breath go?' Then all of a sudden the window flew open and they heard the wind outside, making all the branches rustle. 'Did she float out of the window, Lion? Where did she go? I want to go too.'

'You got to come out and play.' Freddy banged open the kitchen door, making it shiver in its frame.

'Don't slam – the door. Oh Freddy. You know what your daddy said about banging.' Paul had asked them before to open and close the door gently, until he could replace the hinges.

Freddy was not interested. 'We got a good game. You got to come.'

'Do you actually need me to play with you or am I being

the donkey?'

Freddy stared, chewing a lock of hair. 'We haven't got a donkey in our game.'

The twins had dragged an old groundsheet out of the garden shed and were trying to drape it over the climbing frame. Bendy and Lion were going to camp on the mountain. The groundsheet was green and creased, with oily marks and a sprinkling of mould. 'Let me clean it first,' said Cassie. 'People have to take clean things when they go camping.'

'They don't,' said Freddy, waggling Lion. 'Mummy says a bit of dirt doesn't hurt.'

'I don't believe you,' said Cassie, yanking one end of the groundsheet. It smelt stale. Bits of grit dropped out of the creases. 'She makes you have a bath practically every night. Spread it out on the grass, all nice and smooth, and I'll get a cloth.'

She returned from the kitchen with clean blue cloths from under the sink, washing-up liquid and a small bowl of warm water. The twins thought the new game was wonderful. They sent soapy streams across the groundsheet and into the grass, soaking one another. Cassie stood back beyond the splatter range. Tommy's hair dripped across her face, and Freddy's bright hair was glued to her forehead. They gave up pretending to clean the groundsheet and swished water at one another, screaming when they scored a hit. Would they like her story about Lion and Bendy when she'd finished it? She hadn't worked out yet how to get the characters flying on the wind and out among the stars. There'd have to be a reason, a purpose. The poem was about not looking, but the most interesting stories were all about looking for treasure, or trying to rescue someone, or beating an enemy.

'It's not fair, Bendy's better than Lion at tents.'

Tommy's angry voice pulled Cassie back to the present.

Freddy had snatched the little clown doll.

'I got a sword, my Bendy's going to –.'

'No, he isn't.' Cassie snatched the bamboo pole from Tommy's hand. 'Where did you find this?'

'In the shed.' Tommy pouted.

Cassie had a long-ago memory of grabbing a ruler and pretending it was a sword and swishing it through the air, cutting off heads, and Rod snatching it out of her hand. Childe Rowland had to chop off the head of everyone he met in Elfland if he was ever to rescue his sister, Ellen, from the King of Elfland. Cassie hadn't told that story to the twins, yet. She wasn't sure about explaining what happens when heads are chopped off. Tommy's bottom lip was sticking out further than ever, and Freddy must be in the shed because she wasn't in the garden. 'If we're going to play duels or sword-fights we have to make rules.'

'Okay.' It was like magic, the way Tommy's mood changed. 'I'm going to fetch towels. You're soaked. Your daddy will be cross with me for letting you get all wet.'

'Can we have biscuits?'

'Tommy, it's not long since lunch. Don't make faces. I'll have a look.'

Forty-four: Thursday, midday

Back in the kitchen, she found the twins' mugs, filled them with orange juice and set them on a tray, together with cheese sandwiches she found ready-made in the fridge. The girls were always hungry. The laptop was still open on the table, the screensaver displaying one photo after another of mountains, lakes, streams, skies. She wondered if Lucy or Paul had taken them. Curious, she tapped the keyboard and was instantly presented with the lock screen. Had she remembered to save the story so far? It wasn't exactly perfect. With luck, Paul had set up an automatic save for her. If he hadn't, she'd have to write the story again but she might change it anyway. The kitchen door flew open with a bang and Freddy ran in. Her hair was flattened in dark red curls across her forehead and the soaked fabric of her tee-shirt lay close to her ribs. 'A man wants Daddy.'

'I'd better get dry clothes for you both, or you can. I'll come out and see what he wants. Do you know who it is?' Fresh clothes were stored in the small pine chests of drawers between their beds. 'What does he want? You shouldn't let a strange man talk to you.'

Freddy seized her wrist and dragged her towards the door. 'His car is all yellow.'

The only person Cassie knew with a yellow car was her new social worker, Samuel. If it was Samuel, something bad had happened. She had to let herself be pulled outside.

Samuel stood at the garden gate, chewing his lip. His face relaxed when he caught sight of Cassie. 'You're here, good. Can I have a few words with the Robinsons?'

'They're out for a bit,' said Cassie, wanting to smile, but

her face felt stiff. 'I'm in charge. Paul's in the village. He's not far, I can get him.' Her heart gave a painful bound. 'He's just round the corner. It's okay, isn't it? I mean, I haven't got to come with you?'

'No, no, nothing like that. No, I had a talk with him yesterday. They're really pleased, Cassie. Don't panic.' He must have seen her eyes flicker.

'Do you want me to fetch him?'

'Just tell me where he is. I came to alert them to a bit of a problem, that's all.'

'What's he saying, Cassie?' Tommy ran over to hang from Cassie's spare hand.

'I'm coming in a minute. I've got an idea for Bendy and Lion's adventure.'

'Tell us now, please, please please.'

'Go up to your bedroom and change, can you? Then daddy won't be cross with me when he comes, letting you get all soaked.'

To her relief they went back into the house.

'What's a bit of a problem?' Cassie took a deep breath. It must be something about school, or Taylor Lawson.

Samuel swung the gate on its hinges and adjusted his jacket. He would not catch her eye. 'We had an unfortunate incident at the office this morning. Your – your mother's social worker, Josie, she'd been trying to get hold of her, your mother I mean, but she'd gone out on an emergency call. Your mother turned up at the office asking for Josie and the duty social worker, she's new, she's only been with us a week, she shouldn't have been on her own but they're so short-staffed ...' He took a deep breath. 'I'm sorry, your mother's got hold of this address. Josie rang and I drove here as fast as I could. Holiday traffic's bad this year, isn't it? Don't panic. I'll sort it out.'

Cassie tried to listen to what Samuel was saying but a

picture roared in her head. The last time they took her to see her mother, meaning to leave her there, her mother was taking pills, talking non-stop. 'Does she want me to go back and live with her?' She was not going to stammer.

Samuel lightly patted her shoulder, snatched back his hand as if she had given him an electric shock. 'Sorry, not supposed to touch my clients. You don't have to do anything you don't want to. You're old enough to know your own mind.'

'Client?'

'Social worker jargon. Sorry.' His mouth twitched into half a smile. 'I am responsible for you. Calling you a client is meant to make you feel equal. Something like that. You're not a patient or a customer. You can choose what you want to do. Clients choose. That's what they tell us, anyway.' He lowered his gaze and looked straight into her eyes. His voice was firmer. 'You don't have to go back and live with her.'

'I'd die.'

'Well, no, you wouldn't, but it wouldn't be terribly good for you.' He slid his hands into his pockets. Today he wore a loose white linen sort of jacket, a bit creased. Cassie had thought from the first time she saw him that he was quite good-looking. His jaw was square and he was tall, broad-shouldered, like Paul, only not so bony, and his brown hair was thick, cut short at the back and sides, much longer on top. Today, though, he looked a bit grey.

'I won't go.'

'Where's Mr Robinson? Paul? Stop worrying about it.'

'He's round the corner. If you go to the end of the road and look across, you'll probably see him in a garden.' She felt herself sounding calm, in control, but her ears hurt from the pounding of her heart. Her back locked itself into a rigid upright.

Samuel walked quickly away, waving, saying he'd soon be back. He'd soon be back. Could he stop her mother from heading here like one of those homing rockets she'd seen on television, aiming for a target?

She ran into the kitchen, scattered some plain biscuits on to a plate and placed it on the tray between the mugs. Tears dripped into the corners of her mouth. She brushed them away with the back of her hand as the twins clattered down the stairs. 'Daddy's coming, he'll be back soon.'

They seized the biscuits, complaining, as she lurched into the garden and out into the street. She did not know what she meant to do. The gate clicked shut and a cry came from Tommy. 'Where are you going?' Tommy was trying to balance on one foot in the kitchen doorway.

An old woman walked past, red-and-white striped shopping bag banging against her leg, dragging her sideways. 'You okay? Those twins have got lungs. You're the new girl at the Robinsons. Cassie, isn't it? What's up with Freddy and Tommy?'

'I got to go – I got to go to find Paul. There's a problem, only I'm looking after the twins.' She was almost panting with stress.

'You get along. I'll stop on till you comes back. I saw him watering our Christine's beans. You know where that is, don't you?'

'Thank you.' The words did not say enough. 'Thank you Mrs Matthews.'

'They can help with my shopping, little monsters.'

Cassie barely heard as she backed away, turned the corner on to the main road and broke into a sprint, heading for the edge of the village. Everyone would say she couldn't be trusted, and she couldn't. Something wild and dark was sending her away, ignoring the voice in her heart. *You can't just leave them. Nobody's ever going to want you again, leaving little girls all on their own. You're as bad as your mother. It's in your genes.*

Forty-five: Thursday early afternoon

Minutes had passed before she registered that she was running along the road towards the Pass, and had to slow down, hug the verge. Drivers were as impatient to escape as she was. Even the cyclists were racers. Five in a row, all lycra and water bottles, swerved around her, the rush of air shoving her against the wall. Rough stone grazed her bare arm and blood dribbled on to her white blouse.

She would go to the river, to Doctor Bridge, and wash off the blood in clean, cold running water. She might even paddle — no, she'd wade into the middle of the river and lie down, letting the water carry her — except not like her mother, half-submerged in bathwater discoloured by blood, with the flesh on her wrists jaggedly cut open. Cassie had got soaked, trying to wind towels around the cuts.

Nobody had told her to do that. She'd written something wrong, made up a detail instead of trying to remember properly. Sudden tears pricked her eyes and she began to run again, frustrated by the drag of her jeans and the slack laces of her trainers. She ought to stop and tighten them except she had to get off the main road. Did the taxi driver have the same thought when he swerved into the narrow road leading to Doctor Bridge? She was there now, already feeling a bit safer because there was nobody here. Nobody would see her. She wasn't far from the bridge and the poem on the bench. She walked more slowly now, aware of leaves rustling overhead, and the sweet green smell of the River Esk bubbling in its channel nearby. She loved that it had a name. The taxi driver must have been panicking if he drove into a wall and a wheel came off his taxi. People said the wheels came off, when they meant things went wrong. He was Derrick Bird and he shot people whose names he knew really well, and then he shot people he didn't know. He must have been past caring, until something else happened and although he had his gun he didn't shoot anyone at Doctor Bridge. Maybe he was taken by surprise, meeting tourists who asked if they could help. Was he sort of coming back to himself?

People still remembered him well enough. All the reports she'd read on the internet gave his name, but it was harder to find the names of the people he'd killed and wounded.

Cassie stopped dead, had to prop herself against the wall. She'd lived in Boot long enough for Mrs Matthews to know her name, and she knew it was Mrs Matthews and Mrs Matthews knew the twins and had offered to help. People could be so unexpected. Lucy and Paul had their twins but they still wanted to foster somebody. They could have been given someone who'd be much less trouble than Cassie. She'd got this so wrong, made such a mess, just when she thought she'd got things straight.

Her phone rang.

She pulled it out, stared at the screen. Paul was calling. She waited for the call to go to voicemail and stuffed the phone back into her jeans pocket before walking fast towards the bridge. As she reached the arch in the middle, the phone vibrated. Someone was sending a message. She would not read it. Green light streamed down, like a dream of heaven. It would have been heaven but she'd spoiled it all, running off. Green trees arched over the river, and green-tinted boulders edged the water. Cassie rested her elbows on the stonework and gazed down into green, cool water, at the long strands of greenery rippling on its surface. The twins had waded right under the arch the last time they'd come.

Cool air floated up and she tipped back her head. The air dried her face but tears kept coming and her hair stuck to her neck. Lucy had promised her a haircut. Now it would never happen.

Lucy would be so disappointed in her.

From this viewpoint, the water was no longer green but clear, gurgling over grey and white stones, catching sunlight in its curves and whorls. Last time, the twins had started to build a harbour and the small wall had survived, forcing the flow of the current round it. They said they would bring boats from the bathroom next time.

The little red powerboats wouldn't last long in this flow.

How lovely it would be to step into the water, lie down and close her eyes.

Another tear trickled down her cheek and she slapped at it, tasting salt on her fingers. She could have looked up why tears were salty if she were back at the house, using the refurbished laptop. She pictured Paul opening the lid, resetting the password. Would he find the story she had started for twins?

She splashed into the river, doubled over and dunked her head until cold water ran into her nostrils and ears. She opened her mouth and swallowed, choked, swallowed again. The water tasted of mountains and greenery and slate and earth and something else, something old and distant, out of a story and she realised, with a jolt, that she couldn't let the water wash away all her feelings. There were too many stories to tell, too many feelings.

Scrambling up the bank she lost her footing, jarred her elbow on a rock. Someone once had lifted her up, stroked her hair and said, 'Never mind, I'll kiss it better.'

Only Rod or Sarah would have kissed it better when she was little. Blindly she stumbled along the path, lost her balance and banged her leg. The pain startled her. She was standing by the bench.

The dead person was somewhere else, somewhere far away, not dead – or dead in one way but alive in another.

Cassie would get far away, too, make the mother believe that she was dead, or whatever the poem meant. She would be dead to Paul and Lucy and the twins, too, but at least they would not be attacked by the mother whose name Cassie would not speak.

She sat down, leaning back against the plaque. Water dripped on to the bench. There was a story in her red book about a girl climbing a glass mountain, wearing glass shoes ...

How could she have run away without getting her book? And her journal, what about her journal? Her phone rang. She ignored it. Three buzzes vibrated, one after another. Paul, Lucy, Samuel, all demanding to know where she was?

Catskin ran into the woods to hide.

Cassie put Catskin out of her mind. Catskin was brave in a fairy story and Cassie was a coward in real life and that's how it was. She leapt up, hurried back to cross the bridge, take the path and find yet another route, zigzagging steeply up the fellside between the trees. It was not very clear, winding between boulders and uprooted trees, but Cassie pushed on, bracing herself when her feet slithered on loose stones, and found her way into a whispering, cool green shade. She squatted on her squelching shoes, wriggled to adjust the soaked jeans, dropped her forehead to her hands, and waited.

Stella

> **We're waiting for your call.**
> Whatever you're going through, a Samaritan will face it with you.
> We're here 24 hours a day, 365 days a year. Call 116 123

Forty-six: Thursday 12:47

W139: *Samaritans, how can I help you?*
Caller: I done it, I got here.
W139: *I'm sorry, could you please say that again? The line is not very clear.*
Caller: I got here, I found the place where they're keeping my baby.
W139: *Someone is keeping your baby? Could you be a little more explicit, please?*
Caller: It's sort of like birthday cards here, very pretty. There's a pub and cottages and people in the pub garden drinking pints and stuff in fancy glasses.
W139: *You are ringing from outside a pub garden?*
Caller: There's two little girls playing in the garden. They got water. They're throwing water at each other. It's so lovely. She ought to be here. I'm going to ask them.
W139: *Do you know these children?*
Caller: They got a huge climbing frame. They're spoiled.
W139: *Can I ask you again, do you know these children?*
You rang Samaritans. How can we help?

Caller: All my babies got taken away. You never stopped my babies getting stolen. I'm taking these babies, nobody's looking after them, I deserve to have them.

W139: What makes you feel you deserve these children?

Caller: You wouldn't understand. Nobody knows. You have your baby inside you and then it's outside and they take it, you don't get to hold it, nothing.

W139: You are with some children now? I can hear them.

Are their parents there?

Caller: They're playing on their own, they got water, throwing it. I'm taking them now. They'll come with me. They like me. They're smiling at me.

W139: You mean to take these children?

Caller rings off.

Cassie

Forty-seven: Thursday mid-afternoon

Cassie's waiting room was a hollowed-out space between a collapsed stone wall and an old tree trunk, half-rotted. The twins would have loved this place. They'd have imagined it for Catskin, hiding her glittering dresses. Dark brown soil crumbled around the exposed roots. She sucked her finger, where a splinter dug into the quick of the nail. She must have snagged it against the tree. There was nothing in the story about Catskin getting splinters. She made a mental note. Good stories had detail like that, for the reader to know how it felt to be Catskin, pushing her dresses into a hollow tree.

She chewed her chin against her knees, feeling the bones, wondering how to get back into the cottage without anyone seeing her, how to collect her stuff and leave a note – it wouldn't be right to skip off without leaving a note – only, what would she say? They'd bought new clothes. She would have to leave everything. Maybe her school bag would be okay for carrying her knickers and toothbrush and a jacket. And her favourite book. She would have to leave behind all the books Lucy had given her. Her nose ran.

A small wind scurried up the hill, lifting the edge of her blouse. It had been a pretty white cotton blouse with lacy bits, before she got blood on it. Lucy said she'd bought it without trying it on, it was too tight round the boobs, she'd love Cassie to take it off her, make her feel less guilty.

With a shake of her head, she looked around more carefully. Outside this hollow, the trees were straight and tall, with pale bark, like columns in a kind of temple, as if somebody had planted them, but hadn't bothered to check the broken branches. In biology they were told about leaving dead branches and twigs so little creatures could nestle into them. She was a little creature herself among the stones. Green moss smothered them. Nearby a tree trunk was covered in scales, like little discs or plates, the same colour as the tree, and between the roots of another tree lots of creamy toadstools made a kind of miniature forest. A long black slug slowly rippled over a twig. The breeze dropped and she heard the tinkle of a little gill, not far away. The Robinsons called all the streams gills. Everybody called them gills. She was like a foreigner, not realising what the proper names were, reaching out to discover the language she ought to have known.

It was like the time she stayed with foster-carers who sent her back to the primary school where she had started. She could almost smell it. She was so far behind in all the subjects nobody wanted to sit with her. She had cried every night. The foster-carers were kind and thought she ought to go to a different school, start again, so the social worker sent Cassie to Carlisle and it was so big, the school and the place, she felt nobody noticed her. At least they didn't ask her questions she couldn't answer.

A soft green leaf drifted from an overhanging branch, landing in her lap. She turned it between her fingers, feeling for the fine line of its midrib and the little veins shooting out towards its edge. They'd learned the parts of the leaf in science. She'd been more interested than she expected. Writers needed lots of words to describe. Writers who concentrated on choosing the best words did not have to spend time feeling sorry for themselves. Being sorry for oneself was a waste of energy. Where had she heard that?

She frowned, worrying away at the splinter with the tip of her tongue and her teeth. Her finger tasted of dirt.

Lucy said the taxi driver who shot people in the face was

probably sorry for himself. Cassie hadn't meant to read so many online articles, police reports, even what psychologists said. They used ideas she'd never heard of, like 'radical theory'. In the news, the prime minister said the killings were a one-off, the act of a truly evil man. He was wrong about it being a one-off. Lots of people did evil things. Being a murderer might not be the worst thing ever. There was Kyle. Having to live and remember what Kyle did, tried to do – she bit her tongue and swore. There was blood in her mouth. It tasted of iron. In the residential home they'd all had a go at pricking their fingers to get blood, tasted it and then licked an old penny the manager kept on a bookshelf.

Cassie shifted, moving a stone from under her bottom. Her phone vibrated again so she tugged it out of the pocket, set it on the ground beside her. She would not look at the screen. Her jeans were beginning to dry out, giving off a stale smell. How would she wash them?

One day, after she'd got the notebook back, she'd have to write about staying with Paul and Lucy and the twins, but it would be harder than anything she'd written so far. Her stomach knotted. This time it wouldn't be their fault. Maybe when she wrote it down it might not be her fault, but her mother's, not staying away. Why couldn't she accept Cassie never wanted to see her again?

One day she might turn her foster-placement story into a novel. If there was *How to Train Your Dragon,* there could be *How to Train Your Demon,* by Cassie Clearwater. Maybe not a *Demon* but *How to Train Your Ghost.* She might as well have been a ghost for all the times foster-carers made her invisible.

The ruined stone wall was gritty, sucking the warmth from Cassie's body. She imagined the taxi driver crouching here with his rifle across his knees, waiting for the police. The news reports said the police were very brave, entering the woods with their dogs and knowing a killer with a gun was hiding, ready to shoot them. Local people still remembered the shootings. Writing things down in the red and gold book was a bit the same. People loved stories.

He had definitely come into Oak Howe Woods. Did he smell the clean, fresh leaves or listen to the birds? Maybe all he could smell was gunshot and blood. He did everything not to be invisible. He shot strangers, people in the villages – someone delivering leaflets, cyclists, a man in a field – and then he ended up here in Boot. Why did he turn off towards Doctor Bridge? He must have known there was no way out if he knew all the routes, like people said. He must have been crazy when he crashed against the wall. People walking past stopped to ask if they could help. He got the gun out of his car and said no. Weren't they scared? They wouldn't have heard about all the people he'd already killed that day, or they wouldn't have stopped to talk to him.

If he sat in this hollow, with his gun, he could have been on the lookout for someone's head to appear, and then he'd have shot a policeman in the face. Maybe he got fed up with all the killings. Cassie felt sore in her heart from all the bullying and being pushed from place to place. She didn't want to shoot people, though. Lucy said, 'I could kill them,' but she didn't mean it. She loved the twins more than anything.

Cassie had been safe with this family.

Why had she run off?

Why did the woman who called herself a mother leave her little girl all alone in the flat after she'd cut her wrists? What did she think would happen to Cassie?

With no warning, she found herself clenching her fists, digging her nails into the palms of her hands, banging her head against the wall until her head hurt. The feelings would not go away. She'd been calm, sitting in the hollow with trees all around to protect her. One day she would write a book, she would describe foster-carers who said she couldn't be trusted, they couldn't be responsible if she kept running off.

Yeah. They were angry. She took a deep breath, held it, while the pounding in her head slowed down. Maybe they were just as furious with themselves. They'd got into something they weren't prepared to cope with.

Paul and Lucy didn't send her back even though she hit that visitor in the InfoTech class, Mr Collins. The head and Dr Hume, they were decent, they truly were. Lucy fetched her from the bus stop. Paul told Dr Hume he and Lucy wouldn't be chucking her out, whatever the school decided, and then he rang Samuel and told him the same. Cassie had stood beside him when he made the call on his mobile.

That taxi driver had got in a strop. The newspapers said he was certain everyone was out to get him. Cassie bet everyone wasn't really against him. It was the story he had told himself. She felt almost out of breath though she'd only been squatting in the hollow. Stories you told yourself could be helpful, but if you changed the story, lied or not remembered properly, you might end up in trouble. Trying to unremember didn't work.

Taylor's mother yelled unkind, bullying words. Cassie realised she would now always have to remember a sneaky feeling of sympathy with Taylor. Even if she was bullied by Taylor again, she would not be able to forget Taylor's mum being a bully. Taylor was an evil bitch, yes, but maybe she couldn't help copying her mother.

There was nothing much online about the taxi driver's parents. People said they thought he was okay, quite nice. He'd cooed over a baby the day before he killed his twin brother. He had children of his own.

What did it feel like to turn a gun upside down and stick the end in your mouth and know you would fire it? Did you imagine the bullet exploding in your head? Did bullets explode? Did he think about bits of his brain flying all over the place?

    The leaf was crushed. Her fingers were green, smelling of sap.

    She had not meant to spoil it. She picked up the phone.

> Where are you? pls ring paul x

> Cassie, call me at once. Samuel

> Twins not here where are you? Paul x

> Where are you? Lucy xx

> On way home pls pls ring Lucy xx

    She leapt up, crashed down the hillside, dodging between fallen trees and leaping over heaps of stones, thinking of nothing but the twins, and where they were, and cursing herself for leaving them with old Mrs Matthews.

Forty-eight: Thursday afternoon

When she heard the high, excited voices, her knees gave way and she fell against a tree, wrists clenched under her chin. She smelt dirt and sap and green stuff on her fingers and almost shouted with relief. The twins were by the river, playing. Maybe Paul had brought them and Lucy didn't know, or Lucy had returned early. Whatever, nobody'd stuffed them into a car and driven off with them.

She clambered to her feet, stomped downhill, and turned along the path towards the bridge. The twins were up to their knees in the river, struggling with a couple of large stones. For several seconds she stood still, watching them, in her imagination giving them both a hug. She remembered what Paul said so often, 'Thank you, God,' and found herself repeating it. A huge piece of good luck had kept the twins safe – an unexpected act of kindness in the universe, maybe? They must have walked along the road all on their own.

She should never have trusted that old woman, Mrs Matthews. Old people forgot stuff. Lucky them. She probably forgot watching the twins and wandered off with her shopping. Her bag was heavy. Cassie ought to be sorry for her, maybe, but that old woman didn't picture them walking along the road with all the cars and vans and coaches and cyclists not paying attention, going too fast.

No. That was Cassie's fault.

Paul trusted her. He didn't know she would fob it off on Mrs Matthews. They were only little girls. They were not dead, had not been smashed up by a lorry, they were heaving stones towards their harbour wall and their clothes were soaking wet. Lucy wouldn't mind how wet they were as long as they were safe.

Cassie would take a photo, send it, make Lucy and Paul relax, or at any rate, stop panicking.

As soon as she reached the bridge, she dragged the phone from her pocket and put them in the frame for a photo, pausing as the camera brought into focus a woman sitting on the bank, arms twisted around her knees. She must be a tourist, with a picnic.

Freddy turned towards the woman and her shout carried. 'I can't lift this stone.' She dropped it to make the point. Cassie recognised the ploy. Freddy would let her little thin arms dangle till anyone watching her would assume she had no strength. Cassie began to grin. Poor sod of a woman watching. 'You got to help us.'

Cassie thought the woman didn't look like the sort of person to go paddling. Where did she find that jacket? Cassie once saw one like it in a shop window, blue and green squares, red flowers and black stripes, expensively patched together. It was too thick for summer, and the ripped black jeans, bare white legs on show – a fashion statement? And flip-flops? Well, it was a nice day. Maybe she'd got a car or a bicycle nearby but most people on bikes wore fancy trainers or those cycling shoes with spikes on the bottom to fit into the pedals.

The woman turned her head to say something to Freddy.

The earlobes ... small earlobes, pierced all round so the lobes sagged. Nobody else tied her hair in such a tight ponytail.

Acid rushed into Cassie's throat. She bent double, her heart pounding so fast she could not swallow. She gripped the rough grey stonework of the bridge, snagging a nail, tore at it with her teeth, spat out the sliver, tasted blood.

The gash was red and raw and Cassie was five years old, her body aching from the sobs she could not stop, leaning over the hard cold edge of the white bath and Mummy's skin was all cut open, and the water was pinky-red and Mummy's eyes were fluttery –

Mummy?

This woman did not belong on a riverbank. She was struggling to stand up, stones slithering under her weight, throwing her sideways. One of her black flip-flops slid off.

Cassie would die if her ponytail looked so skanky. People mustn't be able to say, if they looked at Cassie, that she was just like her mother.

I am not like her. I am never going to be like her.

Cassie must have moved, for Freddy began to dance in the water, waving her arms. 'It's Cassie, we said you were here, Cassie, Cassie, you got to come. This stone won't move.'

Tommy threw water into the air. 'You splashed me, I got water in my eyes.'

For once, Freddy was not interested in a fight. 'Cassie, Cassie. You got to come and see your mummy. Your mummy's come. Cassie, Cassie, we said you'd be here.'

Great shudders ran through Cassie's body. The woman was trying to put on her flipflops, but she kept losing her balance. One of the patches on the jacket flapped down, and the black lining of the jacket showed through. She might have got it from a charity shop.

I am not sorry for that woman. She is not my mother.

The twins waded towards the bridge, still calling for her.

Cassie did not want to be the sort of person who left little girls with an old woman because she got in a panic. She did not want to become the person who thought it was okay to leave a small girl all alone in a locked flat with a dead body. What the fuck was the woman doing with the twins, anyway? How did they know the mother was her mother? What had she been telling them?

'I came to see you, Cassie.'

The voice was thin and hoarse, not as Cassie remembered it. 'We got to talk. You got to talk to me.' The wobble in the voice made Cassie's skin prickle. She swerved off the bridge and down to the bank where Tommy ran into her, the impact of the hard little skull under her chin making her teeth knock together. Tommy's cold, wet arms encircled her waist and river water from her soaked shorts and tee-shirt began to seep into Cassie's clothes. 'She's your mummy, she said she's your mummy. Is she going to live with us too?'

Cassie knotted her hands behind Tommy's back, and stared at the bright, metallic object in the woman's hand. She could not blink. Her phone was in her back pocket.

'You've grown,' said the woman.

Tommy's hair smelt of water weeds and lemony shampoo from last night's bath.

'Are you glad to see me?'

'What do you want?'

'You're my baby. You're my only baby. They brought me.'

'Cassie's a big girl.' Freddy was still in the river, clutching a stone to her tummy. Her red hair had darkened. 'Our mummy says she's a big girl. She's not a baby, she's going to be old. Are you coming in the water now? We can build the wall and your mummy can help too.'

Tommy's voice vibrated through Cassie's chest. 'She just sits down. We brought her to see you only you weren't here. She's not much use.'

Cassie tightened her grip. 'Freddy, do you want to bring me the stone?'

'It's too big,' said Freddy, letting the stone drop. Water splashed into her face and her lower lip trembled.

'Did you help Mrs Matthews carry her shopping?' Cassie tried to slow her breathing so that her voice would sound calm.

The woman lifted the knife.

'What?' Tommy tipped back her head to stare up at Cassie. 'You know.' Cassie stroked the wet hair from her wide white forehead. 'She had a huge bag of shopping.'

'Oh yes.' Freddy waded closer to the shore. 'She got all these tins in her bag and we took them out and we took them to her door and we made a tower on the doorstep.'

'She must have been very pleased. You were really helpful.' 'Yes and Mrs Matthews went in her house because your mummy came. I carried a tin of tomatoes.'

'Well done, Freddy.' Cassie felt as if she were turning into Lucy, dishing out *well done* and *good girls* to keep the peace, except now she was making the woman listen, turn her head to stare at Freddy, at Tommy, at Freddy again. She must tell them the woman wasn't really her mother. She didn't have a mother.

'I had twins, little boys, I had twins.' The voice was sing-song, and the knife swung from side to side, catching the light.

Freddy stared.' You got a knife. Have you got apples?'

The woman's eyebrows lifted. 'Apples?'

'Are you peeling apples for us?'

It was as if a switch had been pressed. The woman tugged the patchwork jacket tightly across her body. She really was thin. 'I wrote you a letter.' The face worked. Cassie scarcely recognised the features and yet they were horribly familiar. 'I shouldn't have to write a letter to my own daughter. You should have stayed with me. You should have let me know your number so I could phone you. Say something. You should say, hello Mum.'

Tommy unwound her arms and turned round. 'You're rude.' Cassie's knees wobbled but she stiffened her spine and laid a hand on Tommy's shoulder. Tommy's whole body shook. Cassie could not let herself picture what would happen if Tommy decided to run at the woman and collided with the knife.

'Twin boys?' For a second she saw her mother as a child getting ready to cry.

The hand holding the knife tightened its grip. Cassie was close enough to see the knuckles whiten. Her heart began to gallop, its beats uneven and painful behind her ribs.

'I want an apple, Tommy wants an apple.' Freddy jumped up and down, slapping the surface of the water and whipping herself into a frenzy. 'Are we doing our wall? I want to do our wall.' Tommy ran back to her sister, screaming, and Cassie felt her life being washed away – everything soiled and bloody and wrecked –

– but this was the twins' favourite place.

She breathed fast and unevenly through her nostrils. This was a favourite place.

Bubbles glinted on the river's surface, and green reeds were tugged flat by the current. Grey stones beneath the ripples caught the light, were green and sparkling, grey again. This was the River Esk, running clear and lively, and she was here to see it. She clenched her fists and said, 'I am not there.'

'What?' The woman lifted her chin and for a wild moment Cassie thought there were tears on her cheeks, only that wasn't possible.

'It's a poem. It's on the bench over there.' She had to distract the woman, anything to keep her away from the children. 'Do not stand at my grave and weep, I am not there. I do not sleep.'

'What? What about sleep?'

'It's along the path, that way.' Cassie waved vaguely. She felt unnaturally calm, carried on reciting.

'I am a thousand winds that blow.
I am the diamond glints on snow.
I am the sunlight on ripened grain.
I am the gentle autumn rain.'

The woman put her hands over her face and stood very still. She had dropped the knife. It glittered among the stones on the bank. Slowly, so as not to draw attention to herself, Cassie bent, covered the knife with her hand and, just as slowly, stood up. The blade was about as long as her forefinger, very bright, as if it had been sharpened, and the black handle had a slit where the blade should fit. She turned her back, attempted to fold the blade into place but the hinge was strong. She was about to give up when the knife snapped shut, catching the tip of her little finger. She stuffed the knife into a back pocket and sucked her finger. The cut was small but blood already oozed.

'Tommy, Freddy, this is Stella.' Her voice sounded oddly deep and throaty. 'Why don't you show her the poem?'

Her mother's shoulders heaved. She had given herself up to weeping. Cassie seized her chance, rummaged for her phone in the other back pocket and called the first number to register. Lucy.

'Lucy, sorry, we're at Doctor Bridge, it's not safe.'

She rang off before Lucy could answer, and saw Tommy tugging at her mother's sleeve, telling her not to cry. 'Grown-ups don't cry.'

'It's okay, I'm coming. Let's show her the poem.'

Freddy splashed out of the water and grabbed Cassie's wrist with a cold, tight grasp. 'She's not very nice.' Tommy was already leading her mother along the path towards the bench. 'I thought your mummy was nice till you came and she turned a bit funny. Why was she a bit funny?'

Both girls were soaked. Cassie's trainers squelched. The

thin body of her mother, in its bizarre patchwork jacket, was too close to Tommy for her to feel easy. 'We'll all need a hot bath when we get back,' she said, relieved when Tommy ran ahead, reached the bench and flopped down. The woman moved more slowly and awkwardly, as if her legs weren't following instructions.

Freddy overtook her and pushed Tommy sideways. 'You're sitting on the poem.'

'You can't sit on it, it's on the back.' Tommy pushed back.

If the twins were going to fight, what would her mother do? 'Stop pushing each other, for goodness' sake.' Cassie felt as if she were turning into Lucy. 'Get off the bench so we can read the poem.' She stood behind the bench, ready to spring to the twins' defence if it were needed.

Her mother began to read under her breath. She spoke the last two lines aloud in a puzzled voice. 'Do not stand at my grave and cry; I am not there, I did not die.' She turned on Cassie. 'Where's the body? Is it a joke? I never saw my baby get buried. They burned her.'

Cassie began to gabble – anything to stop the twins hearing the terrible things her mother might say.

'When you awaken in the morning's hush
I am the swift uplifting rush
Of quiet birds in circled flight.
I am the soft stars that shine at night.'

The woman tugged her patchwork jacket tight. Buttons were missing. She did not seem to notice, fingers fumbling as though trying to slip buttons into buttonholes. 'You know all the words. Why do you know all the words?'

'I learned it by heart,' said Cassie. Her heart still bumped in her chest. She was the same height as the woman with small earlobes, like her own, and a way of tilting her head …

'I don't know what it means. Will you cry when I die?'

'Thank God,' said Paul. 'You're here. Thank God.'

'You're treading on my foot,' said Tommy, shoving. Freddy pushed back.

Cassie's breath came unevenly. Paul wore a blank expression as he knelt on the path and grabbed the twins, pulling them so tightly that at first they wriggled, backs arched against his muscles. Freddy draped a strand of her father's hair over his nose. Paul gazed up at Cassie and still she could not interpret his expression.

'I'm so sorry.' She had to get it in before he blamed her for running off and not looking after the twins. He would send her back to social services.

'Good God, no. Come here.' He opened his right arm. 'Come on, group hug.' He smelt sour and hot. She had made him afraid.

'You're squishing me,' said Freddy.

Paul set them back and stood, dusting soil from the knees of his jeans and grabbing the girls' hands. 'You must be Cassie's mum. Stella, is it? We'd better get back to the cottage. Come along, petals. Samuel's waiting, Cassie. He's already rung your mother's social worker.'

He led the girls along the path, with Stella following. As soon as they reached the road, he turned to Cassie, letting her mother edge past. She leaned against the wall, clutching her jacket across her chest. Paul's voice was low. 'I don't know what happened here but it's not your fault. Got to keep an eye on her, though,' nodding towards her mother. He still held the twins by the hands, so tightly that they complained.

Cassie's eyes watered. Of course it was her fault. She hardly knew how she reached the road, and stumbled to a stop at the sight of Lucy, running.

Forty-nine: Thursday mid-afternoon

Lucy still wore her nurse's uniform, its skirt crumpled as she pounded along the road, left arm outstretched against the traffic, warning the cars to steer round her. 'Hey, twins, there you are!' Ignoring several loud hoots, she dropped to her knees and pulled the twins away from Paul. Her hair fell over her face in damp strands as she trapped them in a tight hug.

Paul seized Cassie's hand and tucked it into the crook of his elbow. She felt she should separate herself from the family, and when Lucy shook the hair away from her eyes and met Cassie's gaze, it was plain Lucy was furious. Cassie's stomach turned over. Lucy got to her feet and strode off, holding each twin firmly by the hand, throwing a comment over her shoulder. 'Rather a lot to discuss, Paul.' The twins skipped beside her, occasionally hanging back to kick each other.

'I want to finish the wall.' The complaint carried over the traffic noise. Paul turned to the woman.

'You go next. We'll follow,' but she stumbled, and Paul had to catch her elbow.

'These cars go too fast,' said her mother, pursing her lips, shaking herself free.

Why can't she say thank you? Cassie squelched along behind them, damp jeans rubbing against her inner thighs. Her skin would be so sore by the time they got to the cottage but there was nothing she could do, unless she stripped off her jeans. That would stop the traffic. Her vision filled with the imaginary picture of jeans in a heap on the road, and Cassie's bare, damp legs exposed. When a group of cyclists shot past, shouting to one another, their wheels humming, she started, stumbled, saved herself by grabbing the wall. Three walkers with bright backpacks sprinted across the road, dodging between the cyclists and a sporty orange car, roof down, revved up before swerving into the opposite lane. It seemed as if everyone else was in a hurry and they were the unimportant stragglers, being smothered by exhaust fumes and dust blown from the grey road. Cassie ducked under overhanging branches, brushed grit from her eyes, and tried not to think about what Lucy would say.

"Come here. We need to talk."

"Don't give me that insolent look. There are other children in this home. We have rules."

"Cassandra, I am expecting an answer. If you don't come when I ask you, there'll be trouble."

Of course, Lucy would find different words, different comments. Cassie had never before been trusted with looking after little children. She'd never get the chance again. She didn't know till now how important it had felt. She'd know soon enough what Lucy would say to her. They were almost at the cottage.

A stranger sat in a small green car parked by the low garden wall. Samuel, in a thin white shirt and knee-length black shorts, leaned on the roof, half-bending to talk to her through the open window. Stella stopped dead, spun round, and plainly meant to run back to the main road, but Paul barred her way. He said something Cassie did not hear and she threw up her arms, arguing, Cassie guessed.

Samuel stepped away from the door so the driver could get out. Cassie saw plain white trainers, bare ankles, cropped jeans, a tight red jacket with big pearly buttons, and short grey hair. She looked like someone in business, maybe a shop-owner, except the purple shadows under her blue eyes made Cassie suspect she had been tired for ages.

Lucy was already pushing the twins through the kitchen door. Cassie heard, 'You're soaking, again. Yes, you've dried off a bit, but I bet your feet are filthy. Yes, I'll ask her, but not till after a bath. Wash your hands. Teatime.'

'I need to go and help. It's going to be hard to explain,' said Paul.

'We've got this. Catch you later.' Samuel watched Paul walk quickly into the cottage, before saying to Cassie, 'You okay? I didn't mean to scare you. I mismanaged that. I'm very sorry. How are you now?'

'I don't know,' said Cassie. She longed to go inside and lie on the bed with a book over her face.

The stranger held out her hand to Cassie. 'I'm your mother's social worker. Josie Graham. I'm very sorry, too. I really didn't expect to be meeting you in these circumstances.' Cassie was not used to shaking hands. 'Call me Josie, won't you? Do you want to leave us to deal with this?'

'I'm not sure.' The voice in Cassie's head shouted *I don't want to see her.*

'Fair enough.' She folded her arms and the buttons gleamed in the sunlight. 'You shouldn't be here, Stella. I had to drive like the devil to get here. Fortunately, Samuel rang as soon as he discovered what you'd done. Look at me, Stella. It's no good pretending I'm not standing in front of you.'

Her mother stared at the climbing frame. Her face wasn't the same shape as Cassie's, was rounder – well, it would have been but for the hollow cheeks.

Shrugging, Stella said in a tight voice, as if she had a cold or couldn't breathe through her mouth, 'I got a right to see her. I wrote the letter.' Her fingers twitched, tangled themselves together, flexed so that Cassie had to look away, in case her own fingers started twitching too. She gazed instead at the big pearly buttons, bobbing up and down on the red jacket, at the layer of dust on the green car, the pattern of cracks on the pavement, at Samuel's tanned knees. He kept shifting his weight from one leg to the other.

The whine in her head was unbearable. 'She had a knife. She had a knife.' Everybody jerked, apart from Stella.

Josie put her elbows on her hips and shook her head. 'Stella, for God's sake! Where is it? What did you –? Give it to me at once.'

'I lost it.' The voice was tiny, a small child's.

'Cassie?' Samuel moved closer, laid a hand on Cassie's shoulder. His touch was light and it was possible to breathe again.

'The twins thought she would peel apples. We take picnics, sometimes. The riverbank's their best place. I didn't want them to be frightened.' Slowly, she reached into her jeans' pocket. 'I picked it up. It was difficult to fold.'

'I don't know how you did that. How very sensible. You've got your head screwed on. Samuel said you were a sensible girl. Let me have it now.'

Cassie glanced at Samuel, astonished at Josie's comment. He grinned, then grimaced. 'You're bleeding.'

Cassie grew hot and cold. 'I cut myself folding the knife.' She tugged it out of her pocket, glad to get rid of it. She had seen it before. She knew it, now.

Josie weighed it in her hand, frowned, put it in her pocket before nodding at Samuel. 'They can look so harmless, can't they? Short blade, sharp, plenty of damage potential.' She sighed. 'Something went badly wrong at our end. Trouble is, we're so short-staffed. I lost my temper with our office manager, she's too busy making coffee.'

Samuel leaned back against the garden wall and gazed up

at the sky. Cassie's toes cramped in her trainers.

'Where's my letter? Did you bring it? I wrote it for my baby.' The wail was so loud a passer-by hesitated, before moving on, scowling over her shoulder. Cassie shrank back till she perched against the low wall alongside Samuel. She hated strangers being around to hear and see her mother's state. How could this woman be her mother?

Josie said, 'Of course I didn't bring it.'

The woman had such thin legs. She looked ill. Her fingernails were dirty. Maybe she lived in a squat, or slept on a bench. Homeless people carried plastic bags with their stuff in and the bags looked ready to burst and their stuff would fall out and get dirtier. Cassie wondered if she could sidle past the adults, creep into the house without alerting Lucy or the twins, change her jeans and trainers, wash her face, hide.

Samuel said, 'It's a good thing I went into the office, actually. My supervisor asked me to pick up some papers, that's why I went. At least I could ring you, Josie, get you here.'

'My letter was okay.'

Samuel's voice was fierce. 'You took advantage of somebody new in the office. And you carried a knife? You really think anyone is letting you near Cassie after you took a knife to a meeting?'

'You stole her.'

'We've been through this.' Josie scratched at her scalp so that short grey hair stood on end. 'Your daughter is entitled to make her own decision about seeing you and you can't just barge in, not with your record.'

'You can just fuck off, telling lies about me.'

Samuel turned so sharply Cassie could feel the vibration of his anger. 'You watch your language in front of young people.'

'Stella, get into my car now. Before you undo all the good work you've tried to do.' Josie plucked at Stella's jacket, she twisted away and the fabric tore. 'Drat. Sorry.'

Samuel hesitated, and Stella doubled over with a long, low howl. Tears dripped from the end of her nose. She was trying to say something but Cassie could make no sense of it.

Samuel gestured with his hands. 'Do we report the knife incident to the police?'

Josie unbuttoned her jacket, eased her jeans and crouched beside Stella. 'Anyone got tissues? Left mine in the car.'

Cassie said, 'Don't tell the police.' She did not know where the words came from.

'Don't tell the police what?' Paul leaned over the wall, glanced at Cassie, ran back into the kitchen and reappeared with a roll of kitchen paper. 'She's not been sick, has she?' His face was bonier than usual.

'Is Lucy okay?' Cassie did her best to sound casual. He waggled his hand. 'So-so. She'll get over it.'

'I'll tell her it was my fault. You left me in charge and I – I really wanted to be in charge.' Her stomach churned.

Paul threw his arm round Cassie's shoulders. 'You're cold, sweetheart. Is this about the knife and reporting to the police?' He swung his legs over the wall and stood next to her.

'She's furious with me, not you. Let us deal with that on our own. Why do you say don't report it, Cassie?'
'I – don't think – she didn't mean to use it.'

'Really?' Josie's voice was muffled as she mopped Stella's face. 'Weren't your little girls frightened, Mr Robinson?'

Paul gave a sharp, barking laugh. 'Not them. It's turning

into a big adventure.'

Cassie wrapped her arms around herself. 'She saw them playing and she cried. She said, she said, she had twin boys, babies.' Her voice stopped working because her throat got in the way.

'She had twins?' Josie stood up, eyebrows raised in dark arches. 'I suppose – I haven't seen all her medical records.' The howling grew quieter. 'I know she had other babies removed.'

Cassie felt Paul become very still. When he spoke, the words seemed remote. 'Removed as babies?'

Josie nodded. 'It's a tough one. I think the term is "maternal outcasts".'

'Too much information.' Paul shook his head. 'Can we let Cassie made the decision? She's old enough, surely.'

'I understand Cassie has chosen for years not to meet her mother.'

'That's all I've been able to choose,' said Cassie, finding her voice again. She gritted her teeth. 'I've been writing down about my placements, a teacher at school, she said – and it helps. It does.' If she said anything else she would burst into tears.

'Samuel? What do you think? I'm not sure of our legal obligations.'

Samuel rubbed his chin. 'What would you like to happen, Cassie?' His skin rasped.

'Maybe I ought to go to a meeting.' She spoke so quietly Samuel had to lean down, ask her to say it again. Josie lifted Stella to her feet and began guiding her towards the car. The rest of the kitchen roll lay on the pavement.

'Well, let's see how we go,' said Samuel. Cassie sensed him exchanging glances with Paul. 'I'll take some advice from my supervisor.'

A car door slammed. Josie ran around the front of the car to the driver's side, got in, slammed her door too. Cassie saw her mother waving her arms but the engine revved and they drove away.

Stella

Fifty: 17:52

Josie: It's no use sighing and fiddling with the seatbelt, Stella.

Stella: I wrote a letter. You said I ought to write a letter.

Josie: I can't always be in the office. I have other clients, other people to see, whole families. Fridays are always difficult. Placements break down, people have crises. I need to sort out their weekends.

Stella: It's Thursday.

Josie: Towards the end of the week is always difficult. I try to stop problems from getting worse. What did you think you'd gain from this jaunt?

Stella: She never read my letter.
She didn't want to look at me.
She cuddled those children. It's not fair. I'm her mother.

Josie: Stella? Are you okay? I'm pulling over. Have you any tissues? Try the glove box? Excuse me while I reach. There you are.
I know it must have been very upsetting. She's a feisty girl. I'm glad I've met her.
She seems very happy with the Robinsons.
The little girls seem very attached to her.

Stella: I had twin baby boys and they took them away and I thought, I never got to see them playing together. The

	little girls played rough.
	I thought they weren't like little girls.
	I haven't seen little children playing.
Josie:	How old were your babies when they were – when they were taken into care?
Stella:	I held them. They let me hold them. I went in hospital because they were twins and there was an old midwife, and she was really kind. I never held the others, not till Cassie, but she said it wasn't kind. I ought to see my little babies before they were took. Taken. They were going straight to people. They never tell you. They take your babies right away, far away, so you don't see them by accident. First one came out and then the other and she put them on my chest and I put my arms around them and they went to sleep. And then a young one came in and told her off, the nice old one, and then I didn't see them again. I called them Andrew and Peter. They're posh names, aren't they?
Josie:	I've never heard you talk so much. Are you okay for me to start driving again? I don't want to be too late back.
Stella:	What about me?
Josie:	Well, I'd like you to go back to the hostel. Will you stay there? I can't deal with this now. I could call out the emergency team but I don't know – what will you do if I take you back to the hostel? Wait a minute, I've an idea. I'll just make a call. Stay in the car, will you? I shan't be long.
Stella:	I'm not a baby. I'm getting out.
Josie:	You are infuriating. I want to have a confidential conversation.
Stella:	Everyone does stuff behind my back.
Josie:	Be quiet then, please ... They're putting me through ...

Hello, yes, Dr Fleet... Yes, it's Josie Graham. I'm so glad I caught you... Ah, late night ... Well, that's helpful. Could you possibly do an emergency appointment tonight? ... It might make all the difference. I think you've seen Stella Fenton a couple of times... There's been an incident.... Yes ... I quite understand ... Well, tomorrow morning would be fine ... I'll bring her along. Thank you. Goodbye.

Stella: There you go again. Why've I got to see that doctor? He's only a kid himself. Why've you got to take me? You can't make me see him.

Josie: I want to be sure you go. Please fasten your seatbelt, I don't want to make bad worse. I'd like him to check you out. I know I'm seeing you fairly frequently but you looked so thin and miserable back there – and there's the knife. Teresa Stainton's on a course tomorrow, well, she's leading it, I think. I want you to see someone this weekend.

You're very quiet.

Stella: Those little girls aren't identical twins. That lovely red hair. One's a bit taller than the other. They got long legs. They scream a lot. My babies never screamed.

Josie: I didn't really pay them much attention. Their mother whisked them in. She has the same red hair, I noticed. Beautiful colour.

Stella: Bit of a temper, their mum.

Josie: You realise why I want you to see someone professional. You're quite observant –.

Stella: Just because I got nowhere to live doesn't make me stupid. You don't want me doing something stupid and you get blamed for it.

Josie: I know you've tried to kill yourself a couple of times. I finally got to read your notes properly. Where did you get the knife?

You can't have bought it. Flick knives like that are – are they legal? There are legal makes. It looked old. Stella?

Stella: Belonged to a bloke. One of my blokes. I took it off him. He never noticed.

Josie: How long have you had it?

Stella: These trees are nice. I could go in a wood. I wish I had a little garden with flowers. It was quite nice sleeping in the park till I got chased off. We never had a garden at home when I was little. Only a yard.

Josie: You obviously haven't taken a proper look round the hostel. There's a beautiful garden at the back and Gillian, the warden, you know, she's always wanting volunteers to help.

Stella: Don't know about flowers and plants and stuff.

Josie: When we get back, I'll ask her to show you the greenhouse. She'll probably want help this weekend. My garden needs a thorough going over.

Stella: She's not gonna let me anywhere near her precious greenhouse.

Josie: I think she might, if we can resolve the matter of that knife. You had trouble in the hostel but I don't think you brought out the knife then.

Stella: Stupid cunts. Don't care about them.

Josie: You were very agitated about the other women, Stella. You accused them of stealing, of walking in on private conversations. You were properly upset about being there. I don't think a shrug is an answer but I'll leave it to Dr Stainton. I'm satisfied that you didn't intend to hurt anyone in the hostel – well, apart from the usual pushing and shoving.

	You still don't want to tell me why you took the knife.
Stella:	Don't go on about it.
	Well, I thought, I thought, maybe, those foster-carers wouldn't let her go – I thought, like, I had a weapon. They got Cassie and I don't.
Josie:	A threat? You were going to threaten them?
Stella:	Don't get all snobby at me. I never would've done it. Anyway, soon as I saw them playing with the water in the garden, they were throwing it at each other, and dancing around and they'd got their little toys and I thought, I'll just ask them. Soon as I said I was Cassie's mum it was like they couldn't do enough for me. How long she been there? They love her already. When I saw her I thought, she's just ordinary, same as me, and then I saw her smile and the dimples and I remembered Shane.
	Her dad. He was a looker. Maybe she'll be a looker one day.
	She's dead skinny.
Josie:	She looks like you, Stella. From what I've heard, you should be proud of her.
Stella:	I never done much for her. I never got the chance after they took her.
Josie:	You looked after her well enough, Stella, till you couldn't deal with your life problems any more and our service had to step in.
Stella:	I said I could be a brilliant mum. I said that. Nobody gives you a chance. Only she's got those snobby people looking after her now and she won't want to come with me, not even if I got a proper nice little flat somewhere.
Josie:	Don't give up yet. You'll have to talk about carrying the knife, you know. We'll all have to be totally sure you won't ever use one.

That was a huge yawn. Close your eyes for a bit. We'll soon be back. You're exhausted.

Cassie

Fifty-one: Thursday evening

Bath-time tonight was bad-tempered. As soon as Cassie went into the bathroom she knew there was trouble. The twins didn't want to hear their mother's ticking-off.

'What did I say about not talking to strangers, not going off with people you don't know? Stop kicking Tommy.'

'She's Cassie's mummy, not a stranger. Tommy got my speedboat. Tommy, you're sitting on my boat.'

'You got my frog.'

'It's our frog, not your frog, I can have it. Auntie Jo gave it to both of us.'

'You got my boat.'

'Will you two stop it right now.' Lucy's face was red. 'Let's get this straight. Freddy, you don't know Cassie's mummy.'

'Yes I do I do I do. Why don't I? She said she was Cassie's mummy and she wanted to see Cassie and Cassie went off.'

'Cassie went to the river.' Tommy's lower lip trembled, she tugged a strand of wet brown hair across her eyes and began to hiccup. Cassie feared she would burst into tears herself if the little girl started to cry, even if it was pretend-crying. Lucy had asked her to help. It was like a truce. The green towel was draped across Cassie's left shoulder, bath-side, ready for Tommy. Her knees were so fiercely clenched she was not sure she would be able to stand when the moment came. Lucy had the yellow towel on her lap.

Cassie must have made a noise because Lucy grasped her wrist. 'Don't, Cassie. Later.' She leaned into the bath water and pulled out both the boat and the wind-up frog, tossing them into Cassie's lap. 'Enough. No more fighting or I'll send the toys to the charity shop.'

The twins turned their big brown eyes towards Cassie, lips trembling. 'Will you look after them for us?' said Freddy in her pathetic voice.

Earlier, there had been such an argument. Lucy was so angry with Paul. She was still so angry. Cassie would have hidden in the wardrobe or under the bed if the spaces had been big enough. Words spoken kept getting between Cassie and the now, this warm, steamy bathroom with twins pretending to be upset. The row wasn't over.

'We want a Cassie story.' Freddy stood up, hands on her hips. Her tummy was soft and rounded, but she was beginning to get a waistline. Cassie wanted to put her arms around her and say everything would be fine – but Freddy started to clamber out of the bath, expecting Lucy to catch her, and Tommy grabbed her leg, pulling her back into the bath. Elbows banged, real tears flowed and Lucy climbed into the bath to yank out the plug.

'Stop it, stop it, I've had enough. Stop it.' The window rattled in its frame.

Both girls cried more loudly than ever. They stood side by side, their wet, slithery bodies held apart by Lucy. The floor shook from someone running up the stairs and Paul stood in the doorway. His lips were pursed and his hair flopped into his eyes.

Cassie grasped the side of the bath and pulled herself upright. Her knees ached and her calves throbbed as the blood swirled back. The green towel flopped to the floor and it was like when Rod died and Sarah cried and cried and didn't want her any more.

Lucy said, 'Cassie, whatever is wrong? What now?' She hopped out of the bath and Cassie saw Lucy had rolled up her jeans, taken off her socks. The sob she had tried to swallow for so long burst out. She clenched her fists and beat against her chest, trying to hold her breath, so that no sound would come out, but the tears and the snot ran down out of her nose and into her mouth.

Lucy put her arms around her, laid Cassie's head on her shoulder. She picked up a dry flannel from the towel rack and pressed it to Cassie's nose. 'Don't bother, what's a washing machine for? It's all okay, let it out.'

'You and Paul, you got so angry –.' She couldn't get any further.

Paul was wrapping the twins in their towels. 'Freddy, stop fidgeting. Take your finger out of your ear, Tommy. Cassie needs a good cry. Everyone needs a good cry sometimes. Off with you. Maybe she'll come and say goodnight.'

'Is Cassie poorly, Daddy? Is she having a tummy-ache?'

Lucy stroked the back of Cassie's neck and spoke quietly into her ear. 'Idiot children. I expect you're having a heartache now, but it'll go.'

'Don't want to read that letter.' The words choked her.

'You absolutely don't have to read it. There, there.'

'It'll be all lies anyway.'

'There, there.'

'I found her in the bath and she cut her wrists and I was five, I was five, and she let me find her.'

Lucy's stroking hand stopped for a moment. 'Well. There will have been a story. And anyway, we've found you now. I know it's not the same.'

Cassie did not realise she had fallen asleep against Lucy's shoulder until she woke out of a dream, and was in bed, the landing light was on and the sun had gone down. The curtains were still open to a streaky green sky. Pictures from the dream were shredding like wet paper – Sarah with a palette and brushes, Cassie mixing yellow and blue paint and making

251

a magic green, Sarah's long yellow hair hanging in plaits –.

Cassie sat up in bed. Quite suddenly she recalled the sensation of holding Sarah's hair and learning to make a plait.

A glass of water stood on the white-painted chest. She swung her legs over the edge of the bed, drank.

The smell of toast drifted through the door and her stomach gaped.

Lucy and Paul sat either side of the kitchen table, a pile of rough-cut toast on a large white plate between them. Lucy held a glass of red wine and was flicking the rim with her forefinger. Paul turned as Cassie came barefoot into the room. He raised his eyebrows, reached behind to the dresser, hooked open a drawer and lifted out a wooden-handled knife. 'You didn't eat anything. Toast and butter. I should have laid for three. I've made enough toast for three. You need a plaster for that finger.'

Cassie pulled up a stool and sat down. Lucy must have taken off all her clothes and put her into her pyjamas, as if she were too small to do it for herself. Tomorrow she might be so embarrassed she wouldn't be able to look Lucy in the face, but tonight she was too tired for anything but eating toast. Her fingers fumbled with the strip of plaster and Paul had to help her. He said, 'We've finished the row, Cassie, if that makes you feel better.'

'For the moment,' said Lucy, but she took Paul's hand. 'If we don't speak truth to one another we're done for.'

'I thought, we thought, tomorrow we might walk up Harter Fell. We promised you a mountain walk. How do you feel?' Paul stuffed a whole piece of toast into his mouth, making his cheeks bulge.

'You make sure you don't do that when the girls are around,' said Lucy, wagging her finger at him. 'You've only done it to embarrass Cassie. We've taken the twins out into the fells before but not right up to a summit. With you, they might just do it. What do you think?'

'Is it a long way? I haven't got – have I got the right shoes? Will trainers do?'

'Boots. Your trainers are too soft. I've a spare pair of boots and you'll need at least two pairs of socks. We won't rush. We take a picnic. It's years since we were up Harter Fell. It's a beauty.'

Paul went into the sitting room and returned with a map which he unfolded and spread out at the end of the table. 'Compass, wet-weather gear just in case, sunscreen, hair ties for you women, whistle. Did we keep all the kit together in that big rucksack?'

Cassie sat back, eating, listening, only half-understanding what they were discussing. Lucy gave her a book with black and white pictures and what looked like handwriting only it was printed. 'Here. Wainwright's mountain guide. We've another couple of guidebooks too but the path is so clear we'll never get lost.'

'We got lost on Scafell,' said Paul, looking at Lucy with a particular smile that made Cassie's heart flip.

Lucy patted the end of his nose. 'We weren't concentrating. It was that year.'

Neither of them explained. They were having a private moment. Then Paul turned to Cassie. 'Early up, to prepare for a lot of complaints.' He was still smiling but Cassie felt he was still seeing Lucy, and not her. She found she didn't mind.

Later, lying in bed, drifting again, she mulled over what happiness could be like. She couldn't find words for it, but there had to be a look exchanged, and something shared. She was inside their family but outside Paul and Lucy. Did the twins feel like that? They didn't seem to mind either.

Stella

Fifty-two: Friday 08:17

Dr Fleet: Come in. I haven't long but I thought I'd better see you before the rest of my list.

Stella: I don't know why she thinks I got to see you again.

Dr Fleet: It was a serious episode.

Stella: I went to see my daughter. What's the fuss?

Dr Fleet: You're going to wear out my carpet pacing up and down. Please sit down.

Stella: I can't sit down. I can't sit still not with you fuckers planning about me, talking about me behind my back. I'm not going back in that locked ward, no way, not for no reason, I'll kick up such a stink –.

Dr Fleet: Sit down. Thank you. That's better. I'm going to take your blood pressure. Okay?

Uncross your legs, please. Don't talk. Were you drinking yesterday before you went? Don't talk. Nod or shake your head.

That's good. I hoped you would take my advice. You should be following my instructions for taking the medication.

Okay. Well, a bit on the high side.

Stella: So what.

Dr Fleet: I came in early to read your medical notes thoroughly. It's very alarming. You took a knife

	with you to see your daughter, and to all intents and purposes abducted the little girls belonging to her foster-carers. Don't pull faces at me. I have deliberately tried to keep you alert and not sedated, to help you cope with your addiction to alcohol. I read about the foetus you miscarried.
Stella:	It's not fair writing that down. It wasn't my fault. You don't understand. You're too young. You're fucking rude.
Dr Fleet:	Well, you're thirty-five and I'm thirty, so not that much younger than you. You look surprised. I accept I've had a much better life than you but you need straight talking and I don't have time for anything else this morning. The baby girl you were carrying five years ago had foetal alcohol syndrome. You never saw the foetus, I'm sure. I've no idea if it was deformed but many who survive have facial deformities, all sorts of other conditions that badly affect them. They're innocent. The mother who drinks so much isn't. Don't interrupt. You were, what, approaching third trimester? Twenty-eight weeks? She could have survived if she'd been healthy. Yes, I'm talking bluntly because you want custody of your daughter, but your previous behaviour probably brought about the pre-term death of one of your babies.
Stella:	I'm not staying –.
Dr Fleet:	I want to help you. I don't want to sound uncaring but this matters and you took a knife to see your own child. I'm going to modify your prescription, give you an anti-depressant for a

few weeks. These pills will, as you put it before, mess with your mind. When people get depressed it's because there's a chemical missing in your brain. These pills put it back till your brain sorts out the problem for itself. You'll feel calmer. You'll find it easier to think about what you are about to do before you actually do it.

Stella: I never meant my baby to die.

Dr Fleet: Of course you didn't. I've a couple of other youngish patients who've had several babies removed. It must have been appalling.

Stella: Why can't I have a baby?

Dr Fleet: Oh dear. Tissues.

Stella: I'm not crying. Fed up with crying.

Dr Fleet: Well, good. If you are finding other ways of managing yourself.

Stella: You don't come from round here. You sound posh.

You think you're posh.

Dr Fleet: I was born in Carlisle, Miss Fenton. I went away to boarding school because my dad was in the army, stationed overseas. I always wanted to come back. Here's your prescription. Don't take the benzodiazepine. You shouldn't have many left, anyway. And don't drink more than half a pint a day.

Stella: You got bossy at that school.

Dr Fleet: My mum's bossy, as a matter of fact. Strong woman. See you in a week, please. Please come back. I think I've probably lost all my tact this morning.

Stella: You're okay.

Dr Fleet: I'll be okay if you do what I tell you. Really. I

	mean it. You've had a very rough time. Let's see if we can get you established in a better time.

Stella: You married?
Dr Fleet: Go away. Goodbye now.

Fifty-three: Friday 09:01

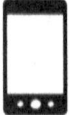

Phone recording

I got a funny feeling in my gut after talking to Dr Fleet. Thomas. I saw it on the list outside. He can't be queer, he was having me on when he said his husband was a doctor too. He's so lovely ... he's got these nice brown eyes and he's lots better looking than Shane.

Never thought I'd say his name again. Shane. He's the devil and Dr Thomas, he's like an angel. Angels don't get born in Carlisle. I don't believe he was born in Carlisle.

I'm on his list now. I can see him any time I want. Now I got to see Josie. Maybe I don't mind so much any more

Recording clicks off

Fifty-four: 09:30

Josie: So, good morning, Stella. Here you are. Gillian's making us some tea and I brought in croissants. It's kind of Gillian to give up her office. You saw Dr Fleet.

Stella: He's fit.

Josie: Well, that's not a reaction I expected.

Stella: He's rude. I really like him.

Josie: You're very lucky. I've now got the full story from the girl in the office. I realise you've traumatic memories to deal with but honestly, Stella, you know perfectly well you manipulated the girl on reception to get your daughter's address. We ought to have given her a formal reprimand. Did you have time for breakfast?

Stella: Not hungry.
I don't feel –.

Josie: Good heavens, are you all right? Let me help you sit down. You're trembling. Your hands are so cold. Look, here's a croissant. Hang on, use this old magazine for the crumbs. Hope that tea arrives soon. I don't take sugar. We have to talk about this knife, you know, but eat something first.

Stella: I'm not hungry.

Josie: When did you last eat?

Stella: Don't care.

Josie: Your daughter tilts her head like you.

Stella: She said don't tell the police. Why did she say that?

Josie: You tell me. Don't you like croissants? Take a bite.
Stella: It's quite nice, I suppose.
Now you gone all silent on me, like the Samaritans.
Josie: If you ring Samaritans, that's good to know. Really, that's good.
Stella: It was like a pain in my gut, wanting to see her. I got a lift from some tourists. And there were these little girls, little twin girls, playing in the garden all on their own. Then they took me to the river and they got in and they were playing so nicely and I never saw my baby boys playing like that. They could be playing somewhere right now and I can't see them and it's not right.
Josie: How old would they be now, these boys?
Stella: Older than Cassie. Couple of years.
Josie: Did you tell Dr Fleet about them? or Dr Stainton?
Stella: Don't know what I said.
Josie: Dr Fleet's got your full records now, of course. Maybe I should fix a meeting.
Stella: It's not right you talking about me behind my back.
Josie: Come in, Gillian. Thanks so much. Do you want sugar, Stella? Drink up. This is most welcome. I'll catch up with you soon, Gillian. We'll be out of here in a few minutes.
Stella: I can't stand you talking behind my back. Where's my knife?
Josie: I have it. However badly you wanted to meet Cassie, it wasn't fair, just springing on her like that.
Stella: Seeing them play, I kept thinking what my little boys would be like. They can ask to find me can't they? When they're eighteen. Soon as I told the little girls I was Cassie's mum they were sweet as pie. They thought I was going to tell them stories. They go on like little birds. Keeping them safe on the road was a proper

	nightmare. They kept hopping about. They were all excited going to this place by the river and the road's really narrow, and the cars don't seem to care if they smash you to bits. Croissant sticks between your teeth.
Josie:	Didn't it occur to you their parents would be frantic?
Stella:	They just left them. That's not right, is it? I looked after them properly. They knew where to go. They been lots of times to that river. There's a poem by that river, did you know? Can I have another?
Josie:	Croissant? Have this one. I don't need it. I had muesli for breakfast.
	You were saying about the parents?
Stella:	All I saw was some old woman waving at us. She had all these tins of food on her doorstep. She was crazy. Will I get my knife back?
Josie:	Why do you keep asking? Where did you get it?
Stella:	It was Shane's. Never told you about Shane, did I? Cassie's dad. He was fit.
	He was a bastard. Used to say he'd cut my boobs if I didn't let him ... anyway, when he tried belting Cassie I got in front of her. He banged my head against the wall and I went all dizzy and he was scared. That was the only time I saw him scared. He thought he'd done me in. Anyway, he was kneeling down and the knife fell out his pocket and I rolled over, pretended I couldn't breathe and I lay on it. Then I stuff it up my knickers and he can't find it but he's too bothered to make a fuss in case I'm dying.
Josie:	That's a dreadful story.
Stella:	You don't believe me.
Josie:	Oh, I do. What happened after?
Stella:	Oh. Well, he kicked me a bit and then he run off and

	left us, Cassie and me. He never came back. He had such a lovely bum but I didn't fancy him any more. I got marks on my back he gave me. Do you want to see?
Josie:	I don't think so but I do think you should tell Dr Fleet. And Dr Stainton. Your story keeps changing.
Stella:	I remember different bits, different times.
Josie:	I suppose so. I still don't know why you carried that knife when you went to Cassie's address. What had you in mind?
Stella:	Nothing. I got nothing in my mind. That poem. I wish I could remember it. It said Do not weep. I am not there. Can you get it for me?
Josie:	Where is it? I don't think –.
Stella:	Cassie knows. She remembers everything. Is she clever? I think she's clever. How did she get to be clever?
Josie:	If she is willing to meet you, you can ask her about herself. That would be good.
Stella:	She won't be interested in me.
Josie:	I suspect you're wrong there. Anyway –. Finish your tea.

Cassie

Fifty-five: Friday morning

Paul stood in the kitchen, making cheese and chutney sandwiches with hefty slices of sourdough bread and somebody's homemade chutney, explaining to Cassie why she needed two pairs of socks inside the walking boots she was borrowing. He had already dug out one of Lucy's old green waterproofs for her to carry in a rucksack. The rucksack was old, too, green and black, with straps to fasten across her chest and around her waist.

'Why've I got to carry this extra sweater? It's going to be hot, isn't it?'

Paul waved a fork. 'Down here it's hot, yes, but up on the tops, you never take a chance. You saw me packing extra sweatshirts for the girls.'

'Your backpack's huge. Why are you taking a whistle?'

'Whistle and compass, map, small torch, just in case. First aid kit.' He pointed at a black rectangular box with a red cross on the lid. 'You might slip, twist an ankle.'

'You said a walk, not an expedition.'

She was interrupted by Freddy, who pulled her into a corner to explain she wanted to take Bendy the Clown and a ball to play with at lunchtime. Bendy's green and white striped trousers and frilly white shirt were beginning to look dirty after spending so much time on a wet groundsheet. 'Mummy says she's going to wash him and hang him up and he don't want a wash.'

'Can't you take Peter Rabbit? You leave Peter at the end of your bed and you never give him a cuddle.'

'He's only a rabbit.'

'What's wrong with rabbits? Rabbits are clever. They dig burrows right down deep into the earth and they come out when there's nobody else around to eat grass.'

'How do you know about rabbits?' Freddy half-crouched, pretending to hop.

Cassie knew Paul was listening because his hands stopped moving, and his head tilted sideways. 'Haven't you read Peter Rabbit books? Paul?'

Paul shoved packets of sandwiches into a zipped section of his rucksack. 'You think Peter Rabbit books provide reliable information about the lives of rabbits.' He would not look at her but she could see his grin. His face looked oddly bonier than usual. Maybe it was because he hadn't shaved and the pale stubble made his jawline stand out.

'Have they read Peter Rabbit books?' Cassie knew there were Beatrix Potter books in the twins' bedroom.

Paul swung Freddy into his arms. 'Would you like stories about rabbits, my poppet?'

Freddy wriggled, dropped to the floor. 'I'm taking Bendy up a mountain. He never been up a mountain. Peter been up a mountain already. Anyway, Bendy's got to learn acrobatics.'

'I really have to wear these thick socks? They're so hot. I'll roast.'

Lucy said, 'Cassie, you choose between big fat watery blisters on your heels that rub off and leave red raw skin for days and days, and feeling a bit hot. Hurry up, everyone, we're late getting out.'

They drove along the road that Cassie was getting to know, past the turning to Doctor Bridge, past the Woolpack Inn – lots of cars parked outside – past walkers carrying huge bulging rucksacks, who had to sway into the verge when cars approached, past cyclists in bright lycra. The cyclists swerved from one side of the road to the other as if leaning so far forward over the handlebars made them not see the sharp bends in the road ahead.

'Mummy, you got to honk at them, they get in front of us, you might hurt them.'

'They're working a lot harder than you are, Tommy. Pipe down.

They've as much right as us to be on this road.'

Cassie heard their voices, but the chatter passed through her mind like automatic eating, like realising she had finished her toast without tasting it. She had never been on a route like this before, all zigzags and steep corners where cars jerked and grumbled, some of them stalling. On either side, the land swept up in swathes of green, gold and purple, splattered with huge greyish boulders, meeting a blue so intense she could not stop gazing up at it. The tingle seeping along her nerves made her hold her breath – but this "holding" was completely unlike *not breathing*. It was stillness, the very heart of stillness.

The moment snapped when Lucy began to manoeuvre the car into a parking place, squeezing between a huge black car with windows so dirty nobody could have seen out or in, and a little red Fiat. Paul said he couldn't imagine how a car with such small wheels handled the incline. Lucy said they used to manage it themselves in their Mini. The little girls, seated either side of Cassie, snapped open their seatbelts and hammered on the doors for the child locks to be released.

Cassie climbed out after Tommy and loosened her new green tee-shirt from the waistband of her shorts. It was "wicking", whatever that meant. The boot of the car was already open. Paul and Lucy heaved out rucksacks, boot bags, walking poles. Walking poles were another strangeness. Tommy showed Cassie how hers to adjust to suit her height, and Cassie wanted to say, *Walking sticks? Do we really need these?* Tommy was so proud of her own red poles that Cassie did not dare to voice her doubts. She didn't want to squash Tommy's excitement, or to look stupid herself, but it was more than that. The methodical, practised way in which all the preparations had been made, set her thinking. This family knew stuff she didn't – even the twins – and it wasn't horrible, like how to hide the drugs inside an old tv, or cover up the cuts on a girl's arms by making her wear a long-sleeved tee-shirt. They didn't pretend they were going to the shops after school on Friday when really they were taking Cassie to the social services office to abandon her there.

'Boots,' said Paul. 'You're daydreaming again, Cassie. Second pair of socks first, then I'll show you how to lace up so the boot doesn't slip.'

'These boots are much too heavy to slip,' said Cassie, grunting over the thick blue socks. Her feet felt constricted by the double layers.

'Your feet will slide inside the boots if they're not properly laced, and you could end up with a sprained ankle. Don't give me your best scowl. I'm used to it now.'

'I can lace up my own boots, thanks very much.' Cassie knew her face was reddening.

'Paul, shift yourself. You've got your own stuff to see to. I'll show you, my love. It's not the same, see?' Lucy crouched at Cassie's feet, demonstrating how to snick the laces through the eyelets and hooks in ways Cassie would never have used. Lucy was right, the boots did feel more secure, so much so that when she took a step, she felt weighted to the ground. Despite – because of? – the double layers of sock and thick, ridged soles, the earth beneath her feet became a solid, safe platform instead of an ordinary grassy path.

'Where are we?'

'Jubilee Bridge. Over we go. This is Hardknott Gill, Cassie.

Hardknott Pass. We'll go and look the fort afterwards. Bear right, Freddy, don't push, follow the path to the gates.' Paul shrugged into his rucksack, fastened the dangling straps around his waist and waved Cassie forward. 'The girls will get fed up in a bit. They always race ahead and then complain they're tired and that's when Lucy dishes out the raisins. Stops them moaning for a bit.'

A light wind brushed the hair from Cassie's forehead, and a robin hopped out from a hedge to perch on the ground beside her foot. It seemed entirely unflustered by her great brown boot but cocked its head, twittered, and fluttered back into the bush as if it had inspected her and decided she was no threat.

Paul lightly touched her shoulder. 'I love it when the birds aren't scared. Robins are belligerent, aren't they? Let's keep going or the twins will start trying to climb the gates instead of opening them.'

Lucy lifted her walking poles. 'If you use these correctly they help you to swing from your pelvis. It's much less tiring. Most of us never walk properly,' and she set off, looking back over her shoulder to see if Cassie understood.

'Or you can stuff them in the rucksack if they get in the way,' said Paul. 'There are loops on the back for walking poles, if you like. Do whatever feels easiest.' He followed Lucy, and Cassie was left to consider the walking poles dangling from her wrists.

Some distance ahead, Freddy shouted, and Paul speeded up. Lucy's laugh floated back and Cassie stood still for a moment, watching, listening, breathing deeply. They all seemed very happy today.

'I'm happy too.' Had she just spoken to a robin?

She felt as if she stood in the middle of a soap bubble, with rainbow colours painted over everything she saw – happiness, bursting out of her pores, transforming the world. She stabbed at the ground with one of the poles but the feeling did not change. Sarah would understand about colours and feelings. Cassie remembered playing with the paints, and Sarah showing her a colour wheel. Most of it she couldn't recall, except the shriek of pleasure when she mixed the colours and they changed.

She stepped on to the bridge, peered over the parapet and watched light bubbling on the surface of the gill as it cascaded downhill. Someone must have painted this bridge, this rush of water, this view.

'Come on Cassie, stop dreaming.' Paul's call set her moving. Her feet placed themselves on the ground, one after the other, leading her along the track as it wandered across the side of the fell. The walking poles tucked themselves under her left arm. Two sheep with black fleeces and broad white faces lifted their noses from grazing and watched her. Their eyes were tawny-coloured with black bands for pupils, not round like human eyes. Maybe it was how their eyelids worked. Maybe she might look it up, later. Did sheep stare at people and wonder how they were made?

Paul was waiting by the first gate, holding it open. He waved her through, clicked it shut. Lucy was well ahead. Cassie barely heard her calling to the twins to slow down. Her voice sounded thin in this huge, open space. Even the birdsong was distant.

Paul waded through the long grass beside the path, but he didn't say much. He pointed with his pole at little pink buds hanging heavily on heather stems, and deep green fronds of bracken, knee-high. Yellow flowers bobbed among the grasses. He told her the names of the flowers but she couldn't listen. She was part of the landscape, a figure passing through.

The ground dropped away on her right, into a long green

valley marked by dry stone walls, hedges, three or four grey buildings. Maybe they were farms, almost hidden among trees. A few grew on the steep slope but there was something about treelines, beyond which trees couldn't grow because the soil was too thin, though there was grass enough to keep the sheep fed. Did shepherds gathering their sheep create the paths up into the hills, before walkers came to follow?

'Paul, are there stories about all this?' Her voice broke and she coughed to clear her throat.

'About the fells? Novels? Poems? Lots. What had you in mind?'

She shook her head, unwilling to speak again in case she lost hold of the feeling.

Cassie

Fifty-six: Friday picnic

When they caught up with the twins, Cassie in the lead, it was obvious that there had been a quarrel. Both girls perched on small boulders, Freddy kicking her legs while Bendy the Clown lay on a bed of bracken. Tommy sat with her back turned and her arms tightly folded. Lion had apparently been told off for roaring at sheep and was in disgrace, in a side-pocket of Lucy's rucksack, until he apologised.

Paul ignored them, took Cassie's shoulders and turned her to look back at the view which lay behind her. 'See those hills? Scafell and Scafell Pike. Scafell Pike is the highest mountain in the Lake district. They were volcanoes, millions of years ago.'

'I'm never going up no other mountain, specially big ones.' Tommy was still complaining.

Cassie gazed at the mountains rearing up above the clouds, so high that their summits seemed unreachable. Her heart beat faster. 'Do people climb them?'

'We've walked up them both,' said Lucy, coming alongside and casting a warm arm across her shoulders. 'You only climb if you choose to get off the walking routes. But scrambling's fun. You'll like that.' Her hair tickled Cassie's ear.

'Will I ever –?' Again, her throat tightened. A huge emotion swelled in her chest.

'Climb the Scafells? Of course. You'll need to build up some stamina.'

'More time on lower ones like Harter Fell,' said Paul. 'We'd better get on. Tommy, if you want to get Lion from Mummy's rucksack you'd better sort yourself out.'

Cassie took a deep breath and walked on up the path. She

couldn't get lost when it was so clearly marked. She needed to clear her head, stop herself from bursting into tears. At a stream flowing over the path, she paused. It was deep and narrow, swirling quickly over the stones and threading its way downhill.

She rubbed her nose. There was nothing in stories about Catskin getting into streams. Maybe everyone travelling through woods or up mountains waded through streams or rivers and didn't bother to mention it.

It was time she did things for herself, not because Catskin did them first. It was time to feel and taste and smell and not just for stories in her head.

On the other hand, she could put into her story a scene about Lion and Bendy coming to the bank of a great river and having to decide how to reach the other side. They would argue, that was definite.

This stream was easy, anyway. She splashed across, deeply satisfied by the scrape of her heavy boots against the grit on the stream's bed. Sunlight glittered on another stream, further up the path and she ran towards it, almost falling over at a memory of jumping in puddles when she was little. *When I was little.* Did Stella ever let her jump in puddles?

She glanced around. Neither Lucy nor Paul was in sight. With a hiccupping laugh, she leapt into the middle of the stream, kicking at the shallow water and sending little stones flying. Maybe small creatures lived in the water. She crouched, letting her fingers dangle in the flow. Little-fishy, water-beetle-type creatures would be amazed at these long pink columns dropping out of their sky.

'That's what I like to see.' Lucy's voice made Cassie leap to the other side of the stream. 'Bet you've never played Poohsticks either. Paul's sorting the kids out. Let's go on.'

'I didn't hear you coming.'

'I should think not. You were having far too much fun.' With a neat jump, Lucy stood beside her. 'Look up, see that rocky summit. That's Kepple Crag. If we cross the stile we get on the Kepple Crag path but we're turning left. We've to watch out for a gate in a wall for our path.' She reached for Cassie's wrist. 'You've got a look in your eyes ... You really love this, don't you?'

Cassie bit her lips and plucked at the straps of her rucksack. Lucy said, 'The first time I went into Borrowdale – that's another valley, we'll take you – anyway, the first time I saw it I burst into tears. Let's carry on. I'll lead, shall I? I know what we're looking out for.' She swung down her rucksack. 'Give me your walking poles. You're not using them so I'll snap them into the loops on my rucksack. You might want them coming downhill. They can be handy.' Several red curls escaped from the band holding them back from her face and she brushed them aside, muttering to herself. The freckles stood out on her pale skin. 'Let's go.' She set off, swinging the walking poles in a regular, easy motion, almost as if they were extra legs for keeping balance. Cassie thought she might practise with hers where nobody could see her making a mess of it.

Lucy paused by the gate in the wall, gesturing at the rocky summit on the skyline up ahead. 'If we weren't bringing the twins we'd take the ridge route, over Kepple Crag. Ridge routes are wonderful. Today it's just up to the top and back the same way to cut out as much moaning as possible.'

'It looks quite big, that crag,' said Cassie, trying not to picture her feet losing their grip on rough grey rocks. No wonder there were Mountain Rescue signs dotted around in the valley, with warnings.

'You'll get used to it. This way.' The path wound left, narrowed, grew steeper, with bracken leaning thickly across the track.

Cassie soon was panting, and her hair had flattened itself to her scalp. Lucy seemed unbothered. She marched uphill, easily avoiding the stones that lay in wait for Cassie, who was beginning to work out why walking boots had to be so stiff and tight around her ankles. Even turning round to glimpse the others felt like a bad idea. Her thighs ached and she did not want to lose her balance.

When Paul caught up, carrying Tommy on his shoulders, balanced on top of his rucksack, Cassie shook her head. How was he so strong? He didn't look it. Tommy's face was screwed tight and Cassie's heart turned over. Was Tommy frightened, sitting up so high? She felt the urge to reach up and grasp one of Tommy's hands. 'Can I have a go with Lion, please?'

'What you going to do with my Lion?' Tommy shook her hair across her face so that her eyes peeped through, as suspicious as a stray cat.

'I thought I would brush his mane,' said Cassie, improvising. 'And then I thought I would show him how to jump over my back.' She bent double, slipping off the rucksack. Her boots skidded, and then settled. She muffled the sigh of relief.

There was a scuffle and small hands patted Cassie's head. 'Good dog, Cassie.' The soft toy was balanced between her shoulders, and Tommy's hand stroked her neck.

'You'll have to let Cassie stand up, Tommy, or she'll get a crick.'

'But she's my good dog.'

Cassie sneezed and the toy fell off.

Lucy had picked up Cassie's rucksack and dangled it casually. 'I wonder if you and I should go on a bit further. You twins and Daddy can stay and get the picnic ready and Cassie and I will go up to the top together.'

'I want to go to the top.' Freddy's cheeks flushed.

'Let's see how we get on,' said Lucy. 'You must stop fighting with Tommy. You need your energy in your legs and lungs. Legs and lungs, legs and lungs. When you're ready for the picnic, get Bendy and Lion to tell us.' She glanced at Cassie. 'Okay with you?'

'Okay,' said Cassie, inwardly reflecting that if she had truly been their daughter she might have picked a fight about being dragged up a mountain – not that she minded going on with Lucy. It was vaguely flattering, but she had learned over the years that most kids gave their parents a hard time. Foster-children were given different penalties.

They all set off again, Lucy pushing Freddy ahead of her, and Paul heaving Tommy by the hand. Cassie was glad to bring up the rear so that nobody would see her red face or hear her panting.

At last, the summit rocks of Harter Fell appeared. They looked far too steep for walking. Did Lucy expect her to be able to climb them? Her hair was damp, and the rucksack stuck to her back. Even Paul's red polo shirt was dark with sweat under the arms.

Lucy had tugged her shirt out of her trousers and flapped it. 'Stop here. We'll be – I don't know how long we'll be, an hour? Less than. Quicker coming down. Cassie, we'll leave our bags and just carry water.'

Water? Why hadn't she thought about water before? Paul pulled two bottles out of his pack, opened another and, leaning over, poured water over his head. He grinned at Cassie through the trickle. 'Try it. Glorious.'

'I thought I put in a bottle for you,' said Lucy, frowning as she mopped her forehead with her sleeve.

Wordless, Cassie felt about in a totally different section of the rucksack and found a small stainless-steel bottle. The water inside was still icy cold. She gestured her thanks to Lucy.

Lucy merely shrugged.

The path to the top veered right, and Lucy told Cassie to watch out for cairns. 'Little stone towers. When you pass a cairn you add a stone, so it gets a bit bigger every time. Cairns are life-savers.' They'd been right, too, about the route not being hard.

As they trudged up, Cassie was swamped by new sensations – hair wet from sweat – armpits damp but not disgusting – chafing around her ankles, thick socky material bunching between her toes, grit in a boot, tingling in her fingers, sweatshirt tied tight around her waist in case of blowiness on the summit – all these swallowed by an extraordinary feeling of lightness. It wasn't merely that she carried only a bottle of water.

No, the lightness was connected with light itself.

Everywhere the land spread itself below her, mountains and hills, little rippling streams, glistening lakes in the distance, farther off, even the shining surface of the sea. Light was everywhere. Light winked off a lake Lucy said was Devoke Water, light glinted in the rocks. They changed from grey slabs into precious stones criss-crossed with silvery seams or knobby whitenesses that glittered like jewels. Maybe the rock was precious. She would have to look it up. And the sheep, the black and white sheep – sheep drew the eye everywhere, in twos and threes, sometimes high on a crag where no living creature ought to go, sometimes sitting down beside the path, watching them pass. Their eyes caught and held the light, too.

Someone had built a small pillar on the summit. Lucy said it was the triangulation point but Cassie put off asking what that meant. The true summit was a set of jagged rocks close by, a bit higher. Cassie laid one hand on the flat top of the pillar, and felt she had placed herself at the spinning point of the earth.

Lucy leaned against the summit rocks.

'It's like the top of the world,' said Cassie, daring to raise her voice.

'Yes,' said Lucy, rubbing her upper arms.

'I wish I could see it all at once.'

'Just turn around, keep turning round.'

'Yeah, but I still only see one bit at a time.'

'You have to remember it. And come back, of course.'

A bird cawed harshly somewhere below. The wind passed by, lifting her hair. Deep in the valley a car hooted and a tremble began somewhere in Cassie's chest. She wanted to stop breathing, to stop her heart from pumping, to make this moment last for ever. She had never seen anything as beautiful, never been anywhere as wonderful and she belonged here. She had climbed all the way up on her own legs, and the world had opened itself around her, fold upon fold of mountain and valley, green and grey and purple and gold, overwhelming. *Awesome.* No, not that. *Awe-inspiring. Awe-struck. Awe.*

The stillness held until a hair strayed into her eye.

They half-ran, half-jogged back down the fellside to join Paul and the twins, who had finished their sandwiches, scattered crisps, and were learning how to blow across a blade of grass to make a whistling, screeching sound. Paul demonstrated and they complained, tried again.

Cassie thought she was too full of emotion to be hungry but cheese and chutney sandwiches were suddenly amazing on a mountainside. Lucy had wrapped sticky pieces of gingerbread in greaseproof paper, and Paul produced a flask of coffee for himself and Lucy. Cassie had a sip but preferred water.

As they were packing up, somebody said, 'I thought I recognised this family group. Hello, Mrs Robinson. Hello Cassie.'

It was Dr Hume, almost unrecognisable in knee-length pink shorts, a short-sleeved white shirt tied in a knot to show a tanned, muscled midriff, and a floppy yellow and blue sunhat. Her green rucksack looked exactly what Cassie would like. Instead of lying flat against her back it curved outwards as if on springs, and lots of webbing pockets were stitched outside. She caught Cassie's gaze, swung it off to show her the small stainless-steel flask, walking poles, map in a clear case, compass, all neatly stashed in the pockets but visible through the webbing.

Lucy invited her to sit down, and Dr Hume rummaged in her rucksack to produce a slab of something Cassie expected to be chocolate – although chocolate would have melted and Cassie reckoned Dr Hume wouldn't be eating melted chocolate. It turned out to be a solid, minty, crunchy sort of sweet, shaped like a bar of chocolate, called Kendal Mint Cake and it melted in her mouth.

Cassie couldn't concentrate on the conversation until Dr Hume said, 'Did you have a go at writing down your stories, Cassie, like I suggested?'

Paul said, 'Cassie's a tremendous teller of stories. She keeps our twins quiet, well, quietish, night after night.'

Cassie felt hot again. 'I've written lots. Paul gave me a notebook.'

'I thought that was for your stories,' said Paul.

Lucy shook her head at him but Cassie said, 'Dr Hume said why didn't I try writing down stuff about my – the foster-placements. She said sometimes you get to understand things better when you write them down.' She glanced sideways at Dr Hume. 'You were right, I think. It's a bit strange. Like, now it's turning into other stories, not about me.'

Dr Hume pulled off her hat and folded it, unfolded it,

shook it out. Her hair was dark with sweat too. 'That's good.' She pulled the hat firmly over her eyes and took it off again. 'Too hot to wear it, too hot not to wear it. I'd better get on.'

'You're a keen walker then,' said Paul.

'You can't live here and not. At least, not if you've lived thirty years in Manchester which I did before I moved north. I wouldn't go back.' She swept out an arm at the view. 'Look at it. Priceless. The people who've grown up here don't always see it the same way and I can't blame them for that. Not enough decent jobs. Unless you're a scientist or a teacher.' She sprang to her feet. 'That's another conversation, maybe. Maybe when we start thinking with Cassie what she's going to do.'

Lucy said, 'Well, she's going to be staying with us, we hope. That's what we'd like, isn't it Paul. And Cassie, Cassie wants to stay too.'

The twins were bored, ready to run around. 'Cassie's staying with us for ever and ever,' said Tommy, winding her arms tightly around Cassie's neck. Cassie stuck her nose into Tommy's hair, glad to hide her face.

'Until we all die,' said Freddy, turning Bendy the clown upside down.

Lucy knocked on Cassie's door at ten o'clock. 'You still up and going, my love?'

'Can I really stay till I die?'

Lucy crossed to the bed where Cassie had the laptop balanced on her knees. 'As long as you want. But you'll leave us, sweetheart. You'll be off to university, get a brilliant job.'

'I want to be a writer.'

'Then you will be a writer. Aren't you a writer already? You're a storyteller.'

'I'm going to be Cassie Clearwater.' Cassie shifted in bed. 'It wouldn't have happened – if I'd stayed with – she wouldn't have let me –.'

Lucy knelt beside the bed, pleating a handful of the creamy quilted bedspread with its design of bluebirds. 'You'd be Cassie Clearwater whatever happened. Don't doubt it.'

Stella

Fifty-seven: 18:33

Dr Fleet: Good evening, is that Miss Fenton? You asked for me to call you.
Stella: It's late, why did it take you so long?
Dr Fleet: Miss Fenton, I have here a note saying you are suffering from dizzy spells.
Stella: I don't feel right. Can I come and see you? They said you hadn't got appointments now till next week.
Dr Fleet: This is my last call, Miss Fenton. I've seen forty patients today. I saw you this morning at half-past eight and you weren't suffering from dizziness at the time.
Stella: I never told you I felt dizzy.
Dr Fleet: I took your blood pressure, if you remember. Your pulse was slightly elevated.
Stella: I took all those pills. I got panicky, I didn't like remembering. I kept remembering and it makes me feel – I told you. Why can't you see me? I can come now. The door's locked. Why's the door locked?
Dr Fleet: The surgery closes at six on Fridays. We have late nights on Tuesdays and Thursdays. If you're dizzy, you can ring 111 and get immediate help.
Stella: You don't care about me. I might die and it's all

	your fault.
Dr Fleet:	You're a patient I'm concerned for, Miss Fenton. If you ring 111 you'll get through to a nurse who will refer you to the emergency doctor, and she'll probably see you very quickly. If you really have taken all your benzodiazepines.
Stella:	You don't believe me.
Dr Fleet:	I believe you're supported by an excellent social worker and therapist.
Stella:	I haven't had nothing to eat all day.
Dr Fleet:	Before I go home I'll put through a call to your social worker. I have her number now.
Stella:	She's an interfering cow.
Dr Fleet:	Is that truly how you think of her?
Stella:	Why can't I see you now?
Dr Fleet:	What do you really want me to do for you? What can I do for you tonight that I didn't do this morning? Nothing is going to change. Don't drink alcohol. Take the anti-depressants. My prescription for you, this weekend, is – let's see – go for a walk along the sea-front. It's a beautiful evening. Go to bed early. Tomorrow, if it's fine, go to the marina and look round. The forecast is good. Some fantastic work is being done. Watch the boats sailing in and out. Sit at a café and buy a cup of tea. Treat yourself to an ice-cream. Miss Fenton? Are you still there? How does that sound?
Stella:	You never said if you were married.
Dr Fleet:	My husband's a doctor at another practice.
Stella:	You're never one of them.
Dr Fleet:	Human being? Doctor? Inhabitant of Cumbria? Goodnight, Miss Fenton. Come to see me on Monday.

Stella: You're making it up. You can't blame me for trying.
Why are you laughing?

Dr Fleet: Lay off the alcohol. There are several decent cafes near the marina. Good night.

Cassie

Fifty-eight: Saturday

'One of the schools I was in, we had a book to read I really enjoyed,' said Cassie, leaning her elbows on the table. 'There was a class, all the boys were given a big bag of flour dressed in rags and they had to look after it, like it was a baby. It was very funny. A boy got all emotional about his bag of flour.'

'That's silly,' said Tommy, spitting orange pips on to her plate. 'Mummy, have we got bags of flour? Peter Rabbit's coat got torn.' Lucy said, 'Have you finished your breakfast? You've been sitting there more than half an hour and you've only eaten half that orange.'

'I don't like oranges.'

Paul reached across for Tommy's plate, picked up the remaining slices and stuffed them into his mouth. Orange juice dribbled down his chin and Freddy jumped up from the corner of the kitchen where she had been feeding Lion small wooden bricks. She said they were bits of bread. Freddy did not accept that lions bit into animals they had chased and killed, even after Cassie had found a video online to show her.

Paul mopped his mouth with a napkin. 'Maybe we should have practised with flour babies before we had you kids. Who thought of flour babies anyway?'

'Famous psychological experiment, I think,' said Lucy. 'Twins, go and clean your teeth, yes, both of you, yes, you too Freddy. When you've done, please try out the climbing frame and give Daddy your report. Is it any good or not, he wants to know. Don't go, Cassie. I'm making a fresh pot of tea. There's stuff we ought to talk about.'

Cassie drew a deep breath. Her face felt stiff.

'It's okay. Nothing bad. Samuel asked us to discuss it.' Paul grasped her wrist. 'Relax. Shall we move into the sitting room? The kids won't look for us there for a while.'

The sitting room was not often used although it was, Cassie thought, a beautiful, calm place. Two deep sofas, covered in loose flowery fabric, faced each other on either side of the woodburning stove where she had discovered how bellows worked. Another chair, one Lucy had found in a charity shop, sat by one of the windows. The view of the fells kept changing, she said, depending on the weather and the time of year but it was always a place for sitting and looking. Bookshelves lined the alcoves. The books were stacked two deep so the ones in the back row sometimes got overlooked. Cassie had sat by the window on two or three occasions when Paul and Lucy argued over who had lent a book, lost it, only to find it hidden behind others. Paul had said he would use some of his study time to reorganise the books in alphabetical order of author. Lucy had told Cassie, later, she knew he'd be far too busy writing assignments.

Lucy set down the tray on the long, low wooden table between the sofas. 'Come and sit here, Cassie. Mind you don't snag yourself.' She handed Cassie a mug of tea.

The table was yellowy, with jagged edges.

'Why's it this shape?' Cassie ran her fingers over the surface.

'It's a chunk of yew. That's why it's this gorgeous yellowy colour. Paul went to woodworking classes for a bit and he made it.'

'I could have planed off the edges,' said Paul, coming to sit opposite. 'But I like the shape. It's much more original. We must stop the kids doing somersaults in here, though.'

Cassie wriggled back against a soft cushion. She wished they would get on with whatever it was they wanted to say.

She decided not to be afraid. 'You said Samuel –.'

'Yes.' Lucy sat beside her, cradling her own white mug. Cassie had the one with pictures of Keswick. Somehow it had turned into her mug. 'Samuel asked us to ask you what you really want to do next, about your mother.'

Very carefully Cassie put the mug down on the table. It was not what she had expected to hear. 'What about her?'

'You said you might be willing to meet her. She brought a knife, but you didn't want her reported to the police. Help us out. How do you feel about her now?' Lucy set down her own mug and took Cassie's hand. 'Gosh, darling, your hand's cold.'

'What do you think I feel?'

Paul leaned back and spread himself across the opposite sofa. 'I'm mansplaining. You two women can sort the world out.'

Cassie could not help laughing. With his long legs spread out wide, his long arms dangling, he looked like a puppet.

'I'm not a woman.'

He rubbed his face. 'I feel outnumbered.'

Lucy tugged at her hand. 'Come on. Tell us. Stop putting it off.'

'Why have I got to say?'

Paul jerked forward, and Cassie realised she could not escape the questions. 'If you truly are willing to meet her, you can't be alone with her. No, not just what happened before. Someone has to keep the balance, protect you. Protect both of you.'

'Protect my mother?' Cassie felt her face crumple into a scowl.

'As I understand it, you might both say things you don't really want the other to hear, or remember, anyway. I don't know exactly what therapists or mediators do, but I'm sure you will be asked if you understand what you're going into, if you agree to meet. I think she'll have to do the same. It has to be done right. What concerns us, both of us, is that she brought a knife.' He twisted his long fingers together. 'Someone who carries a knife – even if it's been taken away from her – well, we're both concerned, no, not concerned, worried about you. What if somehow she sneaks another knife in?'

'You're worried about me being safe?' Cassie's shoulders hunched.

Lucy threw an arm around her shoulders, rocked her from side to side. 'Of course, we worry about you being safe. We're awfully fond of you. Hadn't you noticed?'

For a moment Cassie couldn't see very clearly. She heard herself say, 'Can't you come with me?'

'I might slap her,' said Lucy. 'That wouldn't be very helpful. Well, I probably wouldn't but I'd feel like it. Why don't you want her reported?'

Cassie had never told anyone the whole story about the bath, the knife, the pale pink blood in the water, but the memory kept drifting to the surface, like a twig twirling along on a current, sometimes submerged, sometimes bobbing up. 'Something once – I don't want to talk about it now – except, I think she might have kept the knife to kill herself.' She noticed Paul's intent, bony face, his widening eyes. 'This time, she dropped the knife. She didn't have to. I saw her face. By the river, this time. I saw her face when she dropped it.'

Nobody spoke for a while.

Freddy's scream broke the silence. 'It's my turn, you got to get off, it's my go.'

Paul threw up his arms. 'I'll deal with them. Cassie, you never fail to surprise me.'

After he left the room, Cassie said, feeling awkward again, 'What did he mean?'

'You've been through a lot and yet you have this lovely,

generous impulse. How did that happen?'

Cassie was sure her face had turned red. 'Stories I read?'

Lucy crossed and uncrossed her legs, smoothing out the pale blue linen trousers. 'Possible. Probable? What you say is interesting. Reading stories by good writers somehow makes your world bigger, doesn't it? And you see more potential, you feel more. When we're treating patients we always remember that feelings affect judgements. I see a man regularly who gets panic attacks. There's nothing in his life to cause them, but he's got a vivid imagination. Feelings are real.'

'Like, my mother saying I was stolen?'

'Exactly like that. So whatever happens, I imagine your mother will need a lot of therapy to help her see things as they are. She's got a sensible social worker. I hope she can fix whatever your mum needs. You don't have to get involved with any of it, not if you don't want to. You're safe, with us. If you think being with us is safe.'

A loud lump on the ceiling, followed by screams, brought them both to their feet.

Lucy said, 'Whatever happens, you're not an au pair, not a nanny, not anything but the official storyteller. Okay? Maybe I should get you a badge. That's not a bad idea. It would keep the twins in order – might keep them in order.'

'She's not my real mum, Lucy. I don't have a real mum. You're like, acting, like stand-ins.'

Lucy said, 'Being a foster-parent isn't standing-in. Look up "foster", see what it says.'

Stella

Fifty-nine: Monday 4:30pm

Teresa: Come in, Stella. How are you?
Stella: I feel like somebody punched me in the gut.
Teresa: It's understandable. You've met Cassie, and she's willing to meet you. I'm very glad but there are several things we must sort out first. What's that you've brought?
Stella: That seahorse I took before. It makes me feel all funny, like, it's curvy only there's sticky-in bits. You could hurt someone, giving them a jab with it.
Teresa: Would you want to give someone a jab with it?
Stella: They'd think I was off my rocker, going round with a toy seahorse in my hand.
Teresa: Do you want to give someone a jab with it?
Stella: You don't give up, do you?
Teresa: I'll tell you how I feel, right now. I feel glad to see you, glad you accepted the seahorse, glad you've come back.
What are you thinking, Stella?
Stella: I don't know what to say.
Teresa: Can you explain to yourself why you are so determined to meet your daughter again?

Stella:	What sort of question is that?
Teresa:	You remember the little orang-utan with the baby in her arms? Here it is. What is the mother saying to the baby? Here, take it. You can put the fish on the table. I won't touch it. It's yours.
Stella:	I dunno. Ugly face. Suppose the baby's going to look the same when it grows up. She won't say that, though. She says, you're fucking heavy, know what? But I'm never putting you down. You can stop that crying. I got something lovely for you to eat. What do they eat? Don't you know? Well, this mum, she says, here you go, here's a nice bit of whatever they eat, and she watches the baby chew it up and she wants to make sure it gets everything it wants so it grows up big and has great long arms like me.
Teresa:	I've never heard you laugh before.
Stella:	Never had much to laugh about.
Teresa:	Well, that's what the mother says to the baby. What does the baby say?
Stella:	Don't be stupid, it can't talk.
Teresa:	Maybe it can. Maybe it's like a three-year-old child. Oh. Tissues on the table, here.
Stella:	I just thought, I thought, I never got to be with my babies when they were three. I only got Cassie and everything went wrong. Shane went off, I couldn't sleep, I don't remember what she was like when she was three, I can't remember...
Teresa:	I'm going to make a cup of tea.

Stella:	Why do you do this job? It's crap, people telling you to fuck off, being told to come and see you.
Teresa:	Well, my clients usually choose to see me. I want to help people understand themselves. When they understand themselves, they tend to feel calmer, more settled, even happier. That makes me feel good inside.
Stella:	What, even people telling you to fuck off?
Teresa:	When someone tells me to fuck off, I suspect lots of emotional turbulence and upset in their lives. Most of us want to have friends, to feel close to other people, to know that they look forward to being with us and we look forward to being with them. If I'm told to fuck off, I'm touching a raw nerve in that person.
Stella:	Anyone tells me to fuck off I want to give them a slap.
Teresa:	It's not personal. I'm lucky to have found a job I love. Why do you ask?
Stella:	Those people were there with Cassie. The foster-carers, a social worker, really young, he looks too young. Samuel something. He does stuff for Cassie. I heard his name before but I never met him.
Teresa:	You wonder why he is a social worker, why foster-carers choose to foster?
Stella:	I thought they'd be all do-gooders and I'd want to punch them.
Teresa:	How did you feel?
Stella:	Cassie's like another person, not the baby I had — she frightened me a bit. She like, took charge. I been imagining what it would be like to talk to

	her but I got it all wrong.
Teresa:	I suspect most parents are unnerved when they realise their babies aren't babies any more. It takes some getting used to.
Stella:	Those little girls, I could have stolen them. I wanted them so bad my heart hurt. They held my hands. They took me to this bridge place where they wanted to paddle. They said Cassie's their best friend. She tells them stories. They took off their shoes and got in the river and threw water and they wanted me to paddle too. They made me feel ... like there's something going on and I'm on the outside but they opened the door for me.
Teresa:	You told me before you felt as if you were scrabbling and scrabbling at something.
Stella:	T-Rex. That model you got in the box. I feel all big like I got huge thighs and a big bum and no proper arms. I couldn't hold a baby. Like those people born without their arms, you see them sometimes, they got little wiggly fingers, I always thought, gross, but it's not. I said horrible things about people in wheelchairs being lazy fatsos only I shouldn't. Should I? You're just nodding.
Teresa:	I'm listening.
Stella:	It's not like ringing the Samaritans. I've done that lots. They're good listeners only you don't see their faces. I don't want them to see me. It's different, you listening and me seeing you listen.

Teresa: We're talking. When you and Cassie finally get round to meeting properly, maybe you can do that with her. Listen. Talk.

Stella: She said something really got to me. I said I wanted her back and she said, she said she's not like a parcel, return to sender, like what people put on some letter. It's all very well telling me I can choose but I can't.

Teresa: Think about it. Think what you've been doing in the last few weeks.

Stella: You mean ringing up. You mean when I rang those Samaritans.
Every time I rang them I was choosing?

Teresa: Sometimes it's very hard to choose well. You chose well when you rang them.

Stella: What's the opposite? Choosing bad?

Teresa: What about choosing damage? It's a clumsy expression, I know, but did you ever mean to harm Cassie or anyone else?

Stella: I meant to hurt Shane, I can tell you.
He really hurt me, he hurt me even worse than my dad.
Maybe not. My dad started it, and his brother.
And the men over the road.
What am I supposed to say to Cassie?
I just said what I felt like to Samaritans, it's easy, they're kind. Teresa, I never thought that before. Being kind is hard.
I can't tell Cassie all the bad stuff's happened to me. I can't tell her.

Teresa: Have you thought why not?

Stella: I suppose bad stuff's happened to her. It must

	have. I can't make her think about what happened to me. I don't want to keep on and on about it. Not if she's going to listen to me. No, I got to listen to her. Haven't I? That's what you're saying, like the monkey and the baby, you try and try working out what they need but you can get it all wrong till they tell you.
Teresa:	Maybe one day you can tell her about your life, but if that's your instinct now, not to tell her, you should trust it. Oh, tissues again. I'm making that tea. I made a chocolate fudge cake to take round to my grandchildren later, but I think we'll cut into it this afternoon.
Stella:	What we got to sort out?
Teresa:	I'll explain once we've got the cake. It's about how to manage a meeting between you and Cassie. I've gone over it with Josie, and Samuel, Cassie's social worker. When the meeting takes place, I'll be there, to make sure you both feel safe, and nobody says anything they regret.

Sixty: Monday 23:06

> **We're waiting for your call.**
> Whatever you're going through, a Samaritan will face it with you.
> We're here 24 hours a day, 365 days a year. Call 116 123

J111: *Good evening, Samaritans. How can I help you?*

Caller: I don't know what to do.

J111: *Well, what's on your mind?*

Caller: I have to see her and now I'm scared. I won't know what to say.

J111: *You say you have to do something? Is this something you truly want to do?*

Caller: I do want to see her. I do. It's been like a fire inside me so many years only now it's happening maybe I don't want to see her at all.

J111: *You said you are scared. What is it that scares you? You want something so badly that you aren't sure how you will react now that the moment has come?*

Caller: She scares me. I saw her and she said a poem. I don't know about poems.

J111: *Are you scared you won't know what to say, or because you are afraid of your own response to something you have longed for?*

Caller: This counsellor woman, she says she won't let me say what I don't want to say. How can she shut me up? How can she know what I don't want to say?

J111: *You are working with a counsellor? I think you*

	can trust a counsellor.
Caller:	Oh. Maybe that's it. I don't trust nobody. Anybody. You don't know who I am and I don't know who you are.
J111:	*How do you feel about that?*
Caller:	You always ask that. It's kind of funny but maybe I do trust Samaritans.
C111:	*Could you try to trust the counsellor?*

Caller rings off.

Cassie and Stella

Sixty-one: Tuesday 15:30

Teresa: Come in, Cassie. Well, you haven't changed your mind.

Cassie: I feel nervous.

Teresa: That's okay. You remember what we said yesterday?

Cassie: I've got to be careful what I say in case I don't want Stella to know it.

Teresa: I'll tell her again when she comes that you prefer to call her Stella rather than Mum, yes?

Cassie: Yes please.

Teresa: And the same thing goes for you both. Don't repeat outside of this room what you hear or say inside it.

Cassie: Would she tell anyone else? Do you think she might?

Teresa: I hope I can so manage the meeting for you both that she won't want to share anything outside of it. Cassie, you're very brave to do this.

Cassie: I don't want her to say stuff about me to anybody else.

Teresa: Of course not. In the same way, I will not tell you anything Stella has told me in confidence.

Cassie: I suppose that's good.

Teresa: There she is now.

	Come in, Stella. I've made tea for us and there's orange juice for you, Cassie, if you prefer.
Cassie:	I'm okay with tea, thanks.
Teresa:	Stella, do sit down, don't hover. You know this room. Would you like tea? There are biscuits in the tin behind you, on the bookcase, if you don't mind picking it up. I meant to put them out. Oh, and Stella, could you reach a couple of plates from that cupboard, yes, that's the one. Thank you. It's okay. Come and sit down.. That's good. Oh, what's that in your hand?
Stella:	I brought something.
Cassie:	I haven't anything – I don't want anything from Stella.
Teresa:	It wasn't in the agreement. What is it, Stella?
Stella:	I got something for those little girls. It's not much.
Teresa:	Cassie? How do you feel?
Cassie:	She's brought two little lambs. I don't know …
Teresa:	We'll leave them on the table till you've both decided this meeting has ended. Why did you bring them?
Stella:	They're cute. The lambs are so cute. I can't give them to anyone else.
Teresa:	I believe it won't be for Cassie to decide whether to give them to the little girls. Their parents must decide, but Cassie will be able to tell them what she thinks. Is that fair?
Cassie:	They do like little models.
Teresa:	I have a model of my own, it's on my desk.

	Cassie, would you mind bringing it?
Stella:	It's a funny little man. Why's he dressed like that?
Cassie:	Isn't that – I think it's that Indian man. Isn't that Ghandi?
Teresa:	A reminder of one of the wisest people ever. How did you recognise him?
Cassie:	There ought to be a wise woman too. There's a photo at our school in the library. Those little glasses and his clothes. He looks poor.
Teresa:	You're right about a wise woman. We'll investigate later. Let's get going. Cassie, you would prefer to call your mother Stella. Is that right?
Cassie:	Yes.
Teresa:	Stella, although we've spent a lot of time together, I'm not here as your therapist but as the facilitator – as someone to help this meeting go well. I've explained to Cassie that I won't take your side or hers.
Stella:	Why've you got to call me Stella?
Teresa:	Cassie? Do you want me to explain?
Cassie:	It's okay. I can say it. You haven't been my mother for a long time. I don't feel you were ever my mother. I know you gave birth to me but that's not the same. It's easier to talk to you as Stella. Like I call Lucy, Lucy. Or Teresa. You said I could call you Teresa.
Teresa:	I did. Cassie, in agreeing to meet like this we recognise that you're taking a huge step. You choose to do it. You want this to work. Stella, can you confirm that you want this to work, too?

Stella: Why isn't it the same? You don't know what it's like having a baby inside you. You wouldn't be alive without me. I'm your mother whatever you say.

Cassie: Being a proper mother is bringing up your child, loving them, telling them off when they deserve it, giving them hugs, being there, like Lucy and the twins.

Teresa: Are you okay, Cassie? That was a very emotional statement, very truthful.

Stella: She's only a kid. What's she knows about anything?

Teresa: Cassie is worth as much in the world as you are.

Stella: All right. All right. You make it sound like legal or something.

Teresa: Cassie? You want to carry on?

Cassie: Yes. Give me a moment.

Teresa: Don't interrupt, Stella. You will get your chance in a moment.

Cassie: It's hard. It's harder than I thought.

Do you remember – it's the knife. You had a knife with the twins. I keep getting asked. I remember everything about it. You cut your wrists in the bath. You drank a lot of vodka first. The woman who came in, she said it was vodka only the bottle was empty. The bottle was by the bath. I saw it. It rolled under the towel rail. The water was dyed pink from your blood. I know now you'd tried to cut your wrists and it isn't easy, not like people think, cutting your wrists. I looked it up. The knife went under the bath. We

		didn't have a panel on the bath. I suppose it was not a very good flat. I never thought about the knife after. Maybe you found it when you came back. We did go back to that flat.
Teresa:	Do you want to stop for a bit? Have some water.
Cassie:	I don't like talking about it.
Teresa:	Deep breath.
Cassie:	I'm okay.
		When I saw the knife you brought to the river, it made me remember when you tried cutting your wrists. It was a bad, bad memory. I wanted to get the twins away from you. Then you dropped the knife and I thought, maybe, you were so miserable you might try again, on yourself. You had that jacket on, sort of expensive only it was all ripped. You looked kind of crumpled. Part of me wished you'd just do it, cut your wrists properly this time. Why do you want to meet me when you tried to kill yourself? It wasn't the first time, I remember. I would have been left all on my own in the flat. I'd have been locked in a flat with a dead body in the bath. Who would have found me? What do you want me to say? I can't make it different.
Stella:	I didn't think —.
Cassie:	What did you think would happen to me?
		What do you want now? You say you had me inside you but that's all. You stopped being my mother — you gave up —. That man who came in after he touched you up —.
		You were never my mother, not really.
		Lucy, she's like my mum. I know she's not but

	being like a mum is…
	I feel like I don't have a mum.
	I don't want to say any more.
Teresa:	Thank you, Cassie. It's fine. Stella, wait, please, don't interrupt.
	Cassie, are you all right staying in the meeting? I can see how upset you are. It's okay for you to go. If you are willing to stay, nod. Thank you.
	Stella, what would you like to say?
Stella:	Why does she say that woman is like her mum?
Teresa:	Cassie began this session by explaining what she thinks a true mother will do.
Stella:	I wasn't listening. She's just a kid.
Teresa:	You've been thinking of Cassie as a baby?
Stella:	I had her in my tummy.
Teresa:	Talk to Cassie directly. She talked directly to you.
Stella:	I didn't think it would be like this.
Teresa:	What did you think?
Stella:	I had her in my tummy.
Teresa:	You've already said that.
Stella:	She got no idea, all the others, I lost so many of them. They got taken away, they all got taken away – my little twin boys – was it all my fault? I can't –.
Teresa:	It's all right. It's fine to cry.
	Use my bathroom. It's the first door on the left.
	Yes, that's the way. I'll come and find you in a minute.
Cassie:	Is she coming back?
Teresa:	I think we must stop for the moment.
Cassie:	I don't want her to cry.

Teresa: You seem to think of yourself as responsible for her.

Cassie: I don't like her crying so much. It's all wrong.

Teresa: She has wanted to see you for so long. Cassie. You've surprised her in the best of ways.

Cassie: What do you mean?

Teresa: In Stella's mind you are still a very small child. Maybe when she saw you at the river she didn't fully understand. She sees you now as almost a young woman.

Cassie: I don't feel like a young woman.
Do I just go away now and she's crying and crying?

Teresa: I'm not sure how much sense she'll make.

Cassie: She hasn't said anything much yet. Is it right for me to go?

Teresa: Of course it is. Those little girls are very lucky to have you in their family.

Cassie: It's me that's lucky. I'll take the little lambs. What happens now?

Teresa: You can meet Stella again or not, whatever you would like.
Wait — get Lucy to give me a ring. She has my card.

Cassie: I don't know what I thought this would be like. Not like this.

Teresa: Give yourself time to work out what you want.

Cassie: I suppose I wanted to know the truth but there's not just one side, is there? Did she really have lots of other babies? What's happened to them?

Teresa: That's for another time if Stella wants to tell you. I must go and find her. You can be proud of

	yourself, Cassie. You handled that so well.
Cassie:	Um, I'm writing stories for the twins. Do you think she would like to read one?
Teresa:	I don't know but it's a wonderful idea. I had no idea you were an author.
Cassie:	I'm not really. Not yet. I want to be.

Stella

> **We're waiting for your call.**
> Whatever you're going through, a Samaritan will face it with you.
> We're here 24 hours a day, 365 days a year. Call 116 123

Sixty-two: Wednesday 17:09

G211: *Hello, Samaritans*
Caller: This counsellor, she's helping and my baby says we can see each other, long as somebody else is there.
G211: *Your baby?*
Caller: Yeah, well, she's my baby but she's fifteen. She'll always be my baby.
G211: *Is that what you would like to talk about, how you feel about your child?*
Caller: Can you say thank you to all the people I rang?
G211: *That's very kind. I can't, but you could write a letter.*
Caller: What do you do it for?
G211: *Why are we Samaritans?*
Caller: That's the one. Must get dead boring sometimes.
G211: *Never boring. Never. How do you feel today?*
Caller: Okay. I feel good. She's asked me to her birthday party.
G211: *This would be your child? You sound excited.*
Caller: She's a bit frightening. I didn't expect her to be all, like, grown-up.

G211: *Frightening?*
Caller: She's my baby.
G211: *You say you see a therapist now?*
Caller: I got a doctor, he's dead strict, he makes out he's a queer boy but he's fit. He's saying that to put me off. He's got these eyes. Like a film star, dark brown.
G211: *Can I help you with anything else? There are a few calls coming in.*
Caller: Okay then. Bye. Might ring again. Suppose I might.
G211: *We'll always be here.*

Caller rings off.

Cassie

Sixty-three: Wednesday early evening

'Come out and play. Cassie, what you doing? Come on, it's not our bedtime yet. We worked out a new game with the climber.'

Cassie heard the heavy tread of twins clambering up the stairs, but her door was firmly closed. She had wedged a chair under the handle. The story of Bendy and Lion's adventure had taken another twist.

"Emerald and the Lost Twins."
Emerald opened the emails and read them again.

> Urgent: come as soon as you can. Twins went missing last night, in the storm. Think they were snatched by my wicked brother. He wants the manor house. Emerald, I'm depending on you. Jo x

> Jo, where are you? I thought your brother was still in prison. How am I supposed to help you? Em x

Emerald picked up the photo of Bendy and Lion (their real names were Tommy and Freddy) and felt very worried. She was extremely fond of them. The storm last night had blown down all the trees along the lane outside her house and she did not know how she would get out unless she climbed around them. She went to the door into the garden and opened it. Twigs blew straight into her face. The wind was still high.

She stopped writing, read over the story so far and wondered if she could give it to Mr Hetherington to read once she'd finished it. He liked her writing. Maybe Dr Hume would read it, give her some advice. Authors often had editors. Scott Fitzgerald had someone called Maxwell Perkins to help him when he was writing *The Great Gatsby*. Cassie had looked it up on Wikipedia and Maxwell Perkins had made such detailed criticisms Fitzgerald changed his novel to make it better.

Somebody kicked the door, making it vibrate on its hinges. 'Please will you let us in? Why won't the door open?'

'Stop that at once.' The voice was Lucy's. 'If Cassie is busy you must leave her alone. She has lots of school work.'

Cassie swung round on the new stool Lucy had bought and smiled at her reflection. Her hair looked so cool, so sleek and shiny, close to her head like a hand curved round it. The hairdresser had known exactly how to cut it.

'It's okay,' she said, jerking to her feet and dragging the chair away from the door. 'You can come on in. I need some new ideas for my story. You're both good at this.'

The twins stumbled into the room. Freddy threw herself on the bed and bounced. Tommy ran to the window. 'You got to come out. We got a new game.'

'In a minute,' said Cassie, feeling excited. 'First, though, Freddy, if somebody kidnapped you, how would they do it?'

Freddy lay back and stared at the ceiling. 'They'd climb through the window.'

'You're in an upstairs room.'

'They would have a creepy ladder and nobody would hear it and they would climb in and give me some sleepy stuff up my nose and they would put me over their shoulder and climb down and the rungs would be all squeaky and Daddy would come. '

'That's no use,' said Cassie, rubbing her nose. 'Nobody has to hear.'

'I got magic ears,' said Tommy, dancing Peter Rabbit along the windowsill.

'That's no use either,' said Cassie. 'You've got to be kidnapped too.'

Freddy sat up and swung her legs over the edge of the bed, pulling the bedspread around her shoulders like a cloak. 'They get some magic stuff and they blow it in the room and we both stay asleep and they take us down the ladder.'

'Aha,' said Cassie. 'What sort of magic stuff? Stuff you breathe?

Stuff you hear when you're asleep?'

Lucy appeared in the door. 'You are not to give them bad dreams, Cassie.'

Cassie pinched her lips between her fingers and looked at Freddy, at Tommy. Ideas raced through her head. 'They're the heroes. They let themselves get kidnapped so they can find out what the wicked uncle wants and then Emerald finds them and they win in the end.'

'Yes,' said Lucy, sitting on the bed beside Freddy and running her fingers through Freddy's red hair. 'In the end is fine. In the middle is what bothers me.'

Freddy pulled away, smacking Lucy's hand. 'I don't like it.'

'In the middle is the most exciting bit,' said Cassie, watching Freddy as she sleeked down her hair. Freddy did not want to be the same as Lucy. Already she wanted to be different even if her hair looked the same.

Tommy said, 'Peter Rabbit, he got left outside last night and the wicked uncle, he put something in Peter Rabbit's tummy.'

'That's a very clever idea.' Cassie's fingers twitched. She longed to carry on writing.

'Come out and play. It's boring in here.' Tommy positioned Peter Rabbit between Cassie's legs.

'You won't win,' said Lucy. 'What happened to Bendy?'

'He's got a bad head,' said Tommy.

Lucy rolled her eyes at Cassie. 'Bendy came a cropper. His neck has a gap in it. I'll stitch his head back on when I've time.'

'Really?' Cassie bit back a smile at the vision of Bendy the clown losing all his memories of clowning. That could be a good story. How would Bendy the clown feel once his head was back on? Would his life be different?

Cassie Clearwater had a lot of ideas.

Cassie Clearwater might play games with six-year-old girls, but she loved their imaginations, and the way they infected hers. Could they be her editors?

Emerald was going to have a lot of adventures with the twins. Maybe Emerald and the twins would discover how to help Bendy be a clown again and get him – her? – performing in the circus. First, though, they had to find the wicked brother, whose name she had not yet thought of.

Maybe Bendy the clown would want a different life, after having his head stitched back on.

When you're Cassie Clearwater, writing stories, you can change everything.

Maybe Cassie Clearwater would send a book of her stories to Stella Fenton.

Acknowledgments

Thank you to Marilyn Molloy, trauma counsellor and wise friend, who read an early draft, advised me on what resources to consult and told me what worked and what might offend the ethics of counsellors. She taught me a lot.

Thank you to my fellow writers in the Writers' Rump – novelists, poets, playwrights, award-winners – for frank and unvarnished feedback, copious encouragement, tough questions and willingness to reread: Anne Banks, Anne Cleasby, Adrian Horn, Caroline Moir, Des O'Halloran.

Thank you to my typesetter, Debbie Aitchison, for her wonderful creativity and brilliant eye for detail, and thank you to my publisher, Matthew Connolly, for endless patient help.